WEDDING MINTS AND WITNESSES

A SEASONED SOUTHERN SLEUTHS MYSTERY

NANCY NAIGLE

KELSEY BROWNING

KICKSASS CREATIONS

WEDDING MINTS AND WITNESSES

ISBN: 978-1-944898-23-6
Print ISBN: 978-1-944898-34-2
Large Print ISBN: 978-1-944898-35-9

Cover Art Design by Elizabeth McKay

Digital release, May 2017
Trade Paperback release, May 2017
Second Edition release, March 2020

Kicksass Creations
P.O. Box 49662
Athens, GA 30604

BOOKS IN THE SERIES

IN FOR A PENNY

COLLARD GREENS AND CATFISHING

DEVILED EGGS AND DECEPTION

FRIED PICKLES AND A FUNERAL

WEDDING MINTS AND WITNESSES

Jenny & Teague Novellas

CHRISTMAS COOKIES AND A CONFESSION

SWEET TEA AND SECOND CHANCES

This book is dedicated to Eva Brown,
Kelsey's grandmother, who turned 100 years old this year.

Grandmom, thank you for keeping me when I was a little girl and for letting me snuggle close when you read to me, despite your "muffins."

And thank you for giving me plenty of inspiration for these spunky grannies. I think you might just recognize the ice water treatment Lil threatens Abby Ruth with. Sure glad you used that on my brother and not me.

CHAPTER 1

The sound of brass horns blasted through Summer Haven's first floor, and Lil jumped so high she almost lost her grip on the cookie sheet she'd been pulling from the oven. Before she could figure out what the jarring noise was, the horns were joined by the beat of drums.

Wait a minute. She knew that song. Abby Ruth often marched through the house to it, bellowing something about sawing Varsity's horns off.

Abby Ruth Cady had replaced Lil's beautiful doorbell chimes with "The Aggie War Hymn."

That woman...

Lil rushed from the kitchen to the foyer, her shoes tapping on the heart pine floors. Before she could answer the door, the person outside must've pressed the doorbell again, because the song started over.

Taking a calming breath, Lil opened the front door to find a smiling woman standing on the porch. Her trim, teal-colored pantsuit matched the late-May morning sky. With a slim leather bag in one hand and her blond hair neatly brushed into an updo, she appeared to be in her thirties.

"Good morning," she said, holding out a business card. "I'm Sharon Duncan."

Instinctively, Lil reached for the card and glanced down at it.

Sharon Dooley Duncan
Attorney-at-Law

The welcoming smile on Lil's lips froze in an attempt to control the tremble matching the hummingbird-pace of her heart.

A lawyer at Summer Haven? Lord, please no.

Dread filled Lil, and suddenly the sweet aroma of the sand tarts that she'd just taken out of the oven made her feel as lightheaded as a diabetic after slurping down a snow cone. The last time she'd talked with attorneys, she'd ended up sleeping on a dreadful prison camp cot for more months than she cared to remember. She should've known better than to sign her late husband's Social Security checks just to give him an expensive burial, but she'd paid her debt to society for it.

Her brain scrambling, she swallowed hard. Why would an attorney show up on her doorstep?

"The paperwork I have—" the woman's words dragged Lil back to the situation at hand, "—indicated I would be able to find the person I'm looking for here at Summer Haven."

Breathe. Smile. Breathe.

"Would you happen to be Abby Ruth Cady?" Ms. Duncan asked.

Hallelujah. Relief flew through Lil, but she hadn't meant for that joyous yelp to escape. She cleared her throat, hoping the lawyer lady hadn't noticed.

"Me, Abby Ruth Cady?" Lil could never be confused with Abby Ruth, not even on a day when popsicles were being served down below. Although she and the brassy Texan had learned to tolerate and sometimes almost like each other, they were still nothing alike. "I'm afraid not, dear," she said. "I'm Lillian Summer Fairview, Summer Haven's owner."

Her eyebrows drawn together, Ms. Duncan said, "My apologies. I must have received the wrong information. So sorry to have bothered you." She turned to head down the front steps, and Lil thought she heard something that sounded like, "Thanks, Uncle H."

Before Lil could tell the woman she was at the right place, Abby Ruth clomped down the stairs in those cowboy boots of hers, stepping right up behind Lil in the foyer and pointing a rude finger toward the lawyer. "Who's that?"

"Someone looking for you."

"Young lady," Abby Ruth called, "I'm Abby Ruth Cady."

Ms. Duncan stopped mid-step. This time, as she turned to face them, Ms. Duncan's words were clearly understandable. "Thank God and all the angels with him."

Lil held the door so Ms. Duncan could come inside.

"Is there a place where we could sit?" she asked. "I'm here to represent Hollis Dooley's estate."

"His estate?" Abby Ruth folded her arms, creating creases in her starched white shirt that matched the ones around her narrowed eyes.

"Sharon *Dooley* Duncan," Lil muttered to herself. "You're Hollis's family?" Lil's heart squeezed. It hadn't been but ten days since Hollis had passed away peacefully in his sleep, and the town of Summer Shoals was still grieving over the loss of their local curmudgeon.

"His great-niece."

"Didn't see you at the funeral." Abby Ruth straightened to her full height, towering over the young attorney.

"I was out of the country, but my uncle had his affairs in order. In fact, we updated his will a few months ago. Which

—" she leveled a stare in Abby Ruth's direction, "—is why I am here to see you."

Abby Ruth tapped her toe the way she did when she was antsy. She eyed the attorney suspiciously, sending Lil's Southern sensibilities into a twirl. She nudged Abby Ruth and gave her a warning glance.

"Are you saying Hollis left us something in his will?" Abby Ruth said. "Sure hope it's something good."

"Abby Ruth!" That woman had absolutely no filter. "We're so sorry for your loss, Ms. Duncan," Lil said, hoping to overshadow Abby Ruth's crude comment.

"Thank you." Ms. Duncan turned her attention back to Abby Ruth. "And yes, he did, Ms. Cady—"

"Call me Abby Ruth."

"Abby Ruth, this pertains to his most prized possession."

"We weren't that close." Abby Ruth shot Lil an arched-brow look.

Lil's hopes soared at the mention of a prized possession. Maybe Hollis had been one of those old guys who appeared to barely make ends meet but actually slept on a mattress full of cash every night. "Abby Ruth, why don't you show our guest to the parlor? I have a fresh pot of coffee brewed and cookies still warm from the oven."

Ms. Dooley Duncan tugged at the collar of her blouse. "I don't want to be a bother—"

"Be a bother. Otherwise, she'll ration me to two cookies." Abby Ruth pointed toward the front room that held a velvet divan, antique turned-leg ottoman, and a big-screen TV that still gave Lil heart palpitations when she saw it hanging on the wall. Never would she admit how much she enjoyed watching MMA fights on it when the other gals weren't home.

Lil rolled her eyes at her overly dramatic friend. "I'll only be a second."

As Ms. Duncan followed Abby Ruth into the parlor, she asked, "Was that 'The Aggie War Hymn' I heard when I rang the doorbell? I'm actually class of '01."

Although there was no rush, since Abby Ruth and the attorney apparently shared an alma mater, it took Lil less than five minutes in the kitchen to fix a tray—complete with silver coffee service and china plates along with the cookies. She carried it into the parlor and set it on her favorite piecrust-edged table.

"Now then," she said as she handed Ms. Duncan a cup and plate, trying to pause the tide of Texas A&M stories. "You said you had news for us?"

Hollis's great-niece set aside the refreshments to reach for her bag. "Yes, my uncle included Abby Ruth in his last will and testament."

"Abby Ruth and..." Lil urged.

"Just Abby Ruth Cady."

Abby Ruth jerked her head up. "Nothing for Sera? Are you sure?"

"Seeing as I'm the attorney who drew up the paperwork, I'm quite sure." She pulled out a thin sheaf of papers.

"Now that doesn't make a lick of sense," Abby Ruth muttered. "Hollis had a real soft spot for Sera."

"I'm sure he had his reasons. I'd be happy to read the entire document to you, or we can cut to the chase."

"A woman after my own heart," Abby Ruth declared. "Finally, someone who doesn't have to talk a body to death." She rubbed her hands together. "So, tell me what good ol' Hollis left me. It's been a hard year. I hope he had a gun collection. Wouldn't that beat all?"

Lil stared at Abby Ruth in disbelief. She could certainly understand someone hoping for money, even jewelry, but guns? Only Abby Ruth.

"He left in your care one of his most precious possessions."

"Well, don't keep me guessing then. What is it?"

"He left you Ritter," Ms. Duncan said, a light of what looked like relief and giddiness sparking in her eyes. "His bloodhound."

A chuckle bubbled up inside Lil, but she kept it down. Barely. Hollis had chosen Abby Ruth as the legal guardian for his dog, and it was the first time she'd ever seen the woman look as if she'd been bopped over the head with a piece of scrap wood. *Thanks for the humor, Hollis.*

Ms. Duncan turned the paper toward Abby Ruth, pointing a well-manicured nail to a blank line at the bottom. "I'll need you to sign right here, and we can make this official. There are only a few stipulations." She pushed a pen toward Abby Ruth.

Abby Ruth pulled her hands back. "What kind of stip—"

"Sign the paper, Abby Ruth," Lil urged.

"You, of all people, should know better than to sign something without reading it first." Abby Ruth shifted the papers closer and scanned them. "The document is pretty straightforward. Hollis left the care of Ritter to me. In return, I'll receive a small stipend." Lifting a page closer to her face, she muttered, "You gotta be kidding me."

"What?"

"That lawyer said I'd be compensated to take care of Ritter, but this stipulates I'll get a stipend of twenty-five bucks a month. That's barely enough to cover dog food these days. And Ritter remains in my care until the day of his natural departure. That could be a long time."

"You have to do it," Lil told her. "Hollis was a friend."

Abby Ruth glanced in Lil's direction, and she gave her a nod. Did a person really have a choice in this kind of matter?

"It was his final wish," Ms. Duncan added.

"There's been some kind of mistake. Why would Hollis Dooley leave me anything in his will?" Abby Ruth paled. "He should know I can't have a dog."

"As the document outlines, you'll be compensated for Ritter's care. Notice the clause at the end. As long as Ritter dies of natural causes, you'll receive whatever is left of the monies set aside. I might add that Uncle Hollis seemed to have an optimistic opinion of this dog's lifespan."

Was she saying it could be a tidy sum at the end? Lil's heart danced.

"How old is he?" Abby Ruth asked. Lil nudged her with a glare.

"Nine. Tell you what," Ms. Duncan said. "You sign that while I run out and get him."

"Ritter? He's here? Now?"

"Of course." She was out the front door and halfway to her car before the screen door slammed behind her.

Abby Ruth lifted her phone and asked Siri, "How long do bloodhounds live?"

Siri responded with a monotoned, "The answer is about 11 years."

Abby Ruth sagged. "Lil, please tell Hollis's niece we can't have that dog in your house."

"We can make it work." Lil patted Abby Ruth's leg. "And you'll be compensated."

"That stipend is barely break even. We aren't about to get rich, Lil. My luck that dog will outlive us both." She closed her eyes and swallowed. "Why on earth would he leave Ritter to me anyway?"

"He's a sweet dog."

"If you love him so much, then you take him."

"Believe me, I do *not* want that ancient, stinky dog in my house. But you can't deny Hollis's last wishes. Ritter can sleep in the garage." She eyed Abby Ruth, enjoying her predicament. "Everyone knows how much Hollis loved that old hound dog. You two must have been *much* closer than I realized."

Abby Ruth sat back, her lips curved down. "No, we were not!"

"Why didn't I see it before? He was using Sera to get closer to you. Of course. Clear as daylight." She pursed her lips, trying to hide the shifty smile threatening to reveal that she was giving Abby Ruth a hard time.

"No way." Abby Ruth's eyes widened, but she leaned forward and scribbled her signature on the paper.

Lil took pleasure in seeing the normally unflappable Abby Ruth tongue-tied and frazzled. "Actions speak louder than words." With glee in her heart, she headed for the parlor door. "I have to get the rest of these cookies off the tray before they stick."

She giggled all the way back to the kitchen. The last thing she wanted was a dog at Summer Haven, but if it riled up Abby Ruth, it might not be all that bad. And the cherry on the top was that the lawyer hadn't come to see her.

Thank goodness she wasn't in trouble again. She gave a silent thank-you-Lord. Was this His way of reminding her to be grateful each day?

She'd paid her dues for her wrongdoings, but it was easy to forget now that she was back home. Never again should she take for granted sleeping in her own bed or cooking in her own kitchen.

She reached for the coffeepot. Her brew tasted much better than the chicory swill that Sera—their natural food and yoga-loving friend—insisted on making when she was in residence here in Georgia.

With Sera in California for a few months with her famous husband, Lil was reminded how lucky she was to have these ladies in her life, even Abby Ruth. If Lil had never fallen into trouble, she and Maggie would've never made friends with Sera and Abby Ruth. Everything happened for a reason.

The screen door squeaked, and Lil cringed at the tippity-tap of dog toenails on her high-shine foyer floors.

"Get your slobbery lips off me," Abby Ruth called out.

Lil scooped the last of the sand tarts onto the cooling rack then hightailed it back to the parlor. "Where's Ms. Duncan?"

"She just did a dump and run with ol' Ritter here." Abby Ruth waved toward Hollis's beloved hound. The dog had drooping eyelids and enough extra skin and fur to outfit a Labrador retriever. "She didn't even say goodbye."

"Well, now," Lil said. "That's really not the type of manners I'd expect from kinfolk of Hollis Dooley."

Truth was it was a little hard to resist the hound's dignified look amidst all the flopping folds of skin. She reached a tentative hand toward Ritter, who lifted his nose in the air and sniffed loudly toward Lil. "I think he smells those cookies," she said with a laugh.

Ritter lifted a hind leg and scratched at his massive right ear until it was flapping back and forth against his nose and shoulder. The scent of old socks and Roquefort cheese wafted from him. "Oh, my. Speaking of smells, Ritter's hygiene could use some refining."

"He smells like that trash heap Hollis used to watch over out at the landfill," Abby Ruth grumbled, stepping back as if in search of fresh air. "Our taxpayer money at work."

Lil pinched her nose. "You'll have to do something about Ritter."

Ritter sniffed Abby Ruth's palm then jumped up, placing his paws on her shoulders, and gave her a slurp right on the cheek.

"Stop. Down!" Abby Ruth wiped her face in disgust. "None of that, you heavy beast. He must weigh a hundred pounds."

As Ritter landed back on the ground, Lil noticed the big shiny slobber trail on Abby Ruth's perfectly ironed jeans and on her once-pristine white blouse. "Oh, he's just giving you some sugar. He likes you."

Abby Ruth brushed at her pants with the paper Ms. Dooley had asked her to sign. "What did I ever do to deserve this?"

Lil wanted so badly to start running down a list of the things Abby Ruth had done since she moved into Summer Haven, but her manners wouldn't allow it. So rather than rub it in, she simply said, "Bless your heart."

CHAPTER 2

After taking Ritter outside for a potty break, Abby Ruth tiptoed through Summer Haven's front door with him at her heels. That dog hadn't left her side since the minute Hollis's grand-niece hightailed it out of the driveway.

With the coast clear, she nudged Ritter into the center of the foyer. He looked up at her, then snuffled the floor with jiggling jowls until he was once again at her side. Ritter thumped his tail, sweeping the leg of the end table cattywampus with a screech against the hardwood floor.

Poised for a hasty exit, Abby Ruth yelled toward the kitchen at the back of the house. "I need you to watch Ritter for a little while. I'll be right back." She beat a hasty retreat toward the front door, hoping to get to her truck before her words and their meaning registered with Lil.

She'd barely made a complete step before Lil was in the foyer. "Wait a minute. You're not dumping that dog on me."

Dang, Lil was a lot faster than she looked.

When Lil shook her head, her recently blued curls moved along with it. "Hollis left him to *you* to take care of."

"I have an important errand to run. It won't be long." The lie tasted bitter on Abby Ruth's tongue. "A few hours tops."

"No, ma'am." Lil stabbed a finger into the air, looking like a seventy-something-year-old female Napoleon. Abby Ruth didn't doubt this woman could take over the world if she put her mind to it. "I know how you feel about that dog," Lil said. "Next thing I know you'll have pawned him off on us completely."

Maggie strolled into the house, dressed in khakis and a Holloway Hardware T-shirt that stretched across her generous bosom. The screen door slapped closed behind her. "What's all the fuss about?"

Abby Ruth did a two-step around her to get closer to the exit. "I have somewhere to be. I was just leaving."

"Abby Ruth was in Hollis Dooley's will," Lil said. "He left Ritter to her."

"He willed his dog to *you*?" Maggie's lips made a circle of surprise, highlighting her round face and the dark bangs cut straight across her forehead. A streak of what looked like motor oil was smudged along her cheek. "That doesn't make a lick of sense."

"See? That was my reaction too," Abby Ruth admitted. She and Lil had always had a tenuous relationship, maybe because Maggie had welcomed her into Summer Haven while Lil was in prison camp. Lil was all pomp and circumstance. Well, she'd lightened up lately, but still Abby Ruth and Maggie had way more in common with their get-it-done attitudes.

Ritter plodded across the room to Abby Ruth's side. His tail swished back and forth in a tired way that reminded her of Eeyore.

Maggie gently patted the dog on the head. "He's a good ol' boy, and if it was Hollis's last wish, we have to do it. Guess we could build a fence easy enough."

We. She said we! "Thanks, Maggie. That would be great." And if anyone could put up a fence in a hurry, it was her. That woman could build or fix just about anything.

"Until then," Lil said, "that dog stays outside. And he goes wherever you go, Abby Ruth."

"I didn't know he would be dumped on me. Can't you give me a break here? I didn't get any notice, and I have some important things to take care of this morning. Please help me this once."

"Maggie and I made a commitment to help out at the church bake sale." Lil's lips set in a firm line, and her blue eyes lasered in on Abby Ruth, challenging her. "Unless what you have going on is more important?"

Abby Ruth knew that look. There was no point in arguing with Lil on this. She'd have to find another solution for Ritter, because she would *not* tell the girls where she was really headed this morning.

Rest in peace, Hollis, but darn you and your last wishes.

"Okay, okay." Abby Ruth picked up the dingy faded red leash the lady lawyer had left and snapped it onto Ritter's camo collar. Both had probably been scavenged from the local garbage dump. "We're out of here."

She shoved open the front door and waited for Ritter to pad his way outside. It took them a solid three minutes to make it from the porch to her truck, with Ritter lumbering behind her. Every three or four steps, he nudged the back of her knee with his big wet snoot. She opened the back door to her white Ford dually and pointed inside. "Get in."

The bloodhound stared at her with those drooping eyes. His jowls flopped with each huff and puff from the short walk.

"Look here, Ritter. Nine is equivalent to sixty-three in people years. You're acting like you're ninety. Let's do this."

He sat there like a speed bump. Patting her thigh, she tried using a singsongy voice. "Let's go for a ri-ide."

But her enthusiasm was lost on Ritter. He sniffed the air, then flopped to the ground and let out a groan.

"Really?" She left the door open and moved around behind him. She squatted and lifted him up onto all fours. Dang, what had Hollis been feeding this dog, steak and lobster? She gently pushed at his butt, urging him toward the truck. "Upsy-daisy there, Ritter."

He didn't seem to have any intention of jumping up into her truck. She picked up his front feet and walked him closer to the truck like they were dancing some kind of strange tango. All Ritter needed was a rose in his teeth. With a huff, she placed his paws on the running boards. "There you go, boy. Giddy on up."

A long low howl that could be heard two counties over filled the air.

"Great. I don't have time for this, Ritter. You really are trying my patience."

Maggie strode out of the house heading in her direction.

Please say you'll take care of this dog today.

"Need help getting him into the truck?"

Not exactly what she was hoping for. "Yes. He weighs a ton, and he doesn't look too motivated to help me out."

"I'd watch him if I were going to be around. I wonder..." Maggie scanned the yard, then snapped her fingers. "I know just the thing." She hurried over to the carriage house, then came out carrying one of the corn hole boards she'd built for a cookout last summer.

Abby Ruth smiled. That Maggie Rawls was one heckuva problem solver. When the G Team was in a fix, she always came up with an idea or two. "That should work."

Maggie pulled a bandana out of her pants pocket to lay

over the shiny aluminum running board, then gently steadied the corn hole platform on top of it.

"Grab hold of that side, I'll get this one." Together they lifted Ritter by the haunches and gave him a big heave-ho to slide him into the truck's back seat.

Abby Ruth tucked his tail under his butt, then slammed the truck door behind him. "Thanks, Maggie."

With a smile, Maggie scooped up the corn hole board by the handle on its side and headed back to the carriage house.

Abby Ruth jumped behind the wheel and fired up the engine. "You stink to high heaven," she said with a glance in the rearview mirror at Ritter. Trying to hold her breath, she pressed the window button. The way he smelled, no one in their right mind would babysit him right now.

Then again, Red Jensen had always been a little bit crazy.

She popped open the glove compartment in search of relief but found nothing. Spying the Yankee Candle Midsummer's Night air freshener hanging on the radio knob, she grabbed it and snickered. "Right now you smell more like midsummer night run-in with a skunk," she said to Ritter. "Let's see if this can sweeten things up." She twisted in her seat and wiped the fragrance-infused paperboard across the bloodhound's body.

She leaned closer. The woodsy scent peppered with patchouli and sage had Ritter smelling like a new-age Thanksgiving turkey. "Not great, but better."

Men liked Thanksgiving, didn't they? With the food and football, it was a pretty likable holiday all the way around. Maybe the smell would intoxicate Red into agreeing to take Ritter for a while.

A few minutes later she pulled up in front of Red's house. Technically it still belonged to her future son-in-law, Bartell County Sheriff Teague Castro, who'd lived there until he moved in with her daughter last year. Teague rented it to Red now. Still didn't make sense that a man who owned a ranch in Texas, a house in Aspen, and a condo in Hawaii would want to rent a little ol' house in Georgia, but who was she to judge?

Abby Ruth climbed out of the truck, and before she could turn to close the door, somehow Ritter had managed to make it from the back seat to the driver's seat and to the ground right behind her. Interesting how the old dog could move like a greyhound when he felt like it. "Great. Red will *have* to babysit you because I doubt I could get your butt back in my truck without his help." She tugged on the leash. "Come on."

Ritter's overgrown toenails sank deeper into the dirt with each of her tugs.

"Come on." She slapped her thigh, and finally Ritter set to what could only be called a galumph. Once she was on Red's porch, she hesitated. She needed Red to take Ritter without asking too many questions.

Ritter nudged her butt.

"Don't push me." She glared at the old dog. Hollis knew damn well she wasn't Ritter's biggest fan. Come to think of it, that was probably why he'd left the mutt with her. Hollis had a mean streak like that. Then again, his wry sense of humor was one of the reasons she'd liked him.

She slipped her fingers under Ritter's collar and held tight to keep him on all fours as she pressed the doorbell.

Red pulled open the door, standing taller than her by several inches. His lady-killer smile and the graying hair at his temples set her insides to the spin cycle, not that she was willing to admit that to him. The past year, with her fighting breast cancer, had been tough and had left little room for the romance Red kept hinting at. She'd barely gotten used to their renewed friendship.

Still, the man had some strange power over her. Probably always would.

"Hey there! I need a favor," she said before he could get a word in and stepped inside with Ritter in tow. Red turned, and she shoved the leash toward him, but he gazed at it with a bland expression. "I need you to watch Ritter. Least you could do for your old buddy Hollis."

"What are you doing with Hollis's dog?"

"It seems that Ritter is now *my* dog."

"Huh?"

"Yeah. Hollis left this mutt to me. His lawyer dropped him off this morning."

"You?" Red busted out laughing.

"I swear I have the worst luck lately." Ritter huffed as if insulted, and she couldn't stand being judged by a darned dog. She turned her back on him.

Red's laughter continued, with his face turning redder with every hee-haw.

"Quit laughing."

"Loved that Hollis. Boy, did he have a sense of humor."

"You're treading on thin ice here, Red."

"Ritter smells like two-day-old roadkill splashed with cheap cologne." Red took the leash reluctantly, and Abby Ruth whisked by him and into the kitchen.

"Best I could do in the time I had." She yanked open the refrigerator door and poured herself a glass of orange juice.

"Want some vodka for that?"

"No, I'm driving."

"Where are you off to that you can't take Ritter with you?"

She couldn't leave him in the truck because she had no idea how long her errand would take today. When her friend Stella Robino had called her asking her to come to Atlanta, she couldn't say no because she and Stella had been through so much during their chemo sessions together. Despite Abby Ruth's plans to keep herself isolated during her treatments, she'd met Stella the first day, and they'd become friends instantly.

When you were facing something like cancer, you got to know others struggling with the same challenge. Going through treatments had brought Stella and her closer than most people would be after years and years of friendship.

Since the day they met, Stella had looked forward to ringing the end-of-radiation bell. Rituals weren't Abby Ruth's thing, but she'd agreed to attend to help Stella celebrate. "I'm meeting a friend in Atlanta."

"What *kind* of friend?" His words were slow and precise.

"Red Jensen, are you jealous?"

"Should I be?" He leaned on the counter, putting himself within kissing distance, but she wasn't quite ready to go there yet. Soon? Maybe.

"No, silly. I'm meeting Stella." And the minute she said her friend's name, she regretted it.

"Really?" His eyebrows knitted together. "Is she okay?"

What might look like anger on another man was Red's way of showing fear. He'd worn that expression a lot while she'd been undergoing treatment. He'd been so good to her, but it had been the first time she'd ever seen him out of control of a situation, and he hadn't liked it. His worry had aged him ten years, and it had saddened her heart to be the cause of that worry.

"Stella's fine. It's bell-ringing day at the cancer clinic."

"Wait a minute," he said, straightening to his full six-foot-four. "You're going to Atlanta to ring the bell and you weren't planning to tell me?"

"I said Stella is ringing the bell." She avoided eye contact with him.

"Why aren't you ringing it with her?" He reached out to touch her, but she danced away. "Ru, what's going on here? You should ring that bell too."

"The cancer fight is behind me, and the less said about it the better."

This time, he didn't let her get away from him, pulling her into the strong arms that had been honed by years of major league pitching. "You're still scared."

Damn this man for knowing her so well. "I don't want to give cancer any more power. Not a minute more of my time. What if ringing that bell jinxes something?" she whispered into his shoulder.

"It won't." He pressed a kiss to her hair. "But if you ever have to fight it again, you know Jenny and I will both be right by your side."

A ping of alarm went through her at his mention of Jenny and himself in the same sentence. "Please, Red, just do me this favor."

"Fine. I'll take Ritter."

"Thank you."

"But he's coming with us to Atlanta to ring that blasted bell."

"Us? No, sir. You're not coming."

"I am. Maggie, Lil, and Jenny too. Think of all they did for you while you were going through treatment. We fought the fight together. We should all celebrate together. Admit it."

"I hate you."

"No, you don't."

"I would if you weren't so darned handsome." Flirting with him was way easier than talking serious, but his speculative eyebrow raise reminded her that he was more than willing to take their relationship out of the friend zone anytime she was ready. "Besides, we can't fit everyone and a giant mutt in my truck. In any of our vehicles for that matter."

Red released her, and that glint in his eye worried her. "But we *can* fit everyone into the church van. I happen to have it parked out back for baseball camp tomorrow night." He pulled his phone out of his pocket and made a call. "Lil, I need you and Maggie to be ready in five minutes. We're all going to Atlanta so Abby Ruth can ring the bell."

Abby Ruth gritted her teeth.

He gave her a crooked grin as he talked on the phone. "I'm sure you're right. The church ladies won't mind if you miss the bake sale this one time. Tell 'em it's Abby Ruth's fault. They'll believe that with no problems."

"I don't want anyone else to know about the bell ringing," she told him.

"But apparently she doesn't want you to let her secret outside this circle. You know how she is."

Abby Ruth wanted to grab the phone from his hand and end the call, but part of her was touched by the things Red did for her.

"Can you be ready?" Red said into the phone, nodding the whole time. "Yes. I thought you'd feel that way, and can you call Jenny and tell her we'll be by to pick her up shortly too?" With a smile, he ended the call and shoved his phone into his pocket.

Abby Ruth didn't have words for what he'd just done.

"Don't look at me like that." He picked up the keys from the hall table. "Your chariot awaits."

She stomped over in her red Lucchese boots and snagged the keys from him. "You may have gotten your way about this, but I'm driving."

"Never expected anything less," he said with a chuckle that somehow warmed her heart.

CHAPTER 3

Jenny and Grayson waited on the porch of the renovated church-house she and Teague had purchased not long after she moved to Summer Shoals. She loved everything about their home, from the white picket fence to the well-trimmed yard to the weathered tombstones lined up like gray soldiers in the distance.

Gravel crunched under the church van's tires as it pulled into the driveway. With the speed it was going and the sound of the radio blasting out a Florida Georgia Line song, the long white vehicle looked as if it was carting a bunch of rabble-rousers to a hard rock concert.

At this decibel level, it wasn't hard for Jenny to make out the words to "Dayum, Baby."

Dayum, Baby indeed. She turned to her son, who was standing beside her with Bowzer, their rowdy yellow Labrador. "You ready for this, Grayson?"

"Yeah." But his dark hair flopped into his eyes as he pressed his lips together, moving his mouth in a chewing movement like he was eating his own words, something he'd done from the time he learned to talk when he wasn't being completely honest with her. It would probably come in very handy when he was a teenager. "But I don't understand why we have to go all the way to Atlanta to see Mimi ring some stupid bell. There's a perfectly good bell at my school."

Jenny's lips quirked up. She knew her mother well enough to know that she'd rather yank that school bell from its moorings and toss it in the creek behind Summer Haven to celebrate rather than ring it in front of a bunch of strangers.

"Can we tell them our news?" Grayson's green eyes sparked, and his slim body vibrated with excitement.

"We'll see." Jenny prayed that somehow ringing the bell today would truly mean no more treatments for her mom. Because Jenny didn't know what she would do without Abby Ruth Cady at her side. She took Grayson by the hand, and they jogged down the steps toward the van. When she reached to slide back the side door, Red opened the passenger door and hopped out. "Jenny, why don't you ride up here with your mom?"

She gave him the once-over, noticing a few new gray hairs and a harried look around his eyes. "She's on a tear, isn't she?"

"Like a mongoose that's been backed into a corner."

That about summed up Mom in a mood. Jenny felt so much affection for Red, a man her mom had met when she was a sports journalist in Houston and he was playing for the Astros. He'd been a blessing over the past year, helping shuttle Abby Ruth to and from Atlanta for treatments and generally being a rock they could all depend on. Not to mention that Grayson's four-seam fastball had become almost unhittable. She gave Red's arm a quick squeeze. "Why don't you sit in the back and keep an eye on my out-of-control kid and my laid-back dog?"

"Really, Mom?" Grayson playfully grumped.

"Just joking," she said. "You're in charge of keeping Red in line."

While the guys clambered into the back, Jenny climbed in to ride shotgun and carefully fastened her seatbelt before giving her mom a sunny smile. "Thanks for letting us come along."

"Where's Teague? Isn't he coming, or is he planning to direct traffic while we pick up the rest of the population of Summer Shoals for this field trip?"

Jenny laughed. Her mom's case of the grumps wouldn't get to her today because it was a wonderful, glorious day. "He's on duty, and I know full well that Grayson and I are your last passengers."

Her mom glared into the rearview mirror at the passengers in the back, but Jenny didn't miss the small smile that said it all. Abby Ruth Cady might act like a hardass most of the time, but she had an ooey-gooey center.

"Then let's get this show on the road." Her mom punched the accelerator.

Jenny tried to suppress the nervous flutter in her stomach. This was such a monumental day, so she couldn't be upset with her mom for not telling anyone about the bell ringing. Over the past year, Jenny had come to terms with the fact that she couldn't change her mom's basic nature and had learned to be grateful for who she was.

Because in all honesty, her mom was the best.

For the first few miles out of town, Jenny bopped along to the upbeat country music on the radio and listened to the chatter and light bickering from the back seats.

Family.

She loved them all—her mom, Red, Lil, Maggie, Grayson, Bowzer, and...something that smelled of Thanksgiving dressing and gym socks left under the bed hit her nose. "What *is* that?" she asked her mom.

"What is what?"

"That awful smell."

"Don't look at me. I asked Red to keep him, but did he? No. He decided we needed to take this circus on the road. Everybody's gotta come watch me ring a bell, one I hadn't planned to ring, I might add."

"What does that roadkill scent have to do with you ringing the bell?"

"Every-damn-thing, apparently."

"You're not rotting from the inside out, are you?"

Her mom shot her a quick, sharp look. "If and when I become a zombie, you'll be the first to know." Her sigh was full of disgust. "That smell is Ritter."

Jenny pivoted in her seat as well as she could while staying strapped in. Sure enough, the hound dog was sprawled out in the seat at the very back, and she was pretty sure a string of drool had just landed on Red's nice plaid shirt. She turned back to her mom. "What in the world?"

"You know how some people fantasize about winning the lottery or being left a million dollars by some long-lost relative?"

"Yeah."

"Well, Hollis wasn't related, and Ritter isn't a million bucks."

Even though her mom was shooting her a look that spelled disaster, she couldn't stop herself from exploding into laughter. "You're not telling me that Hollis left you—"

"Yep. Now I'm wondering what the hell the inheritance tax on a four-hundred-year-old dog is. A forty-pound bag of stale dog food?"

"Wow, that's some surprise." Kind of like the one Jenny was about to lay on her mom. She blew out a breath, suddenly nervous to share her news. Maybe she could blame the nerves on hormones. She'd promised Teague they would get married within the month, so she had to let everyone in the van know the plan. When she turned down the radio volume, the chatter in the van muted as well. "Do y'all mind if I call Sera on speakerphone? I have something to share, but I want her to be a part of this too."

Her mom snorted. "Why don't I take a left on Interstate 20? Might as well drive on out to California and pick up her and Marcus, since everyone else is here."

Jenny patted her mom on the leg and hit Sera's phone number in her favorites. A ring and a half later, Sera answered. "Hello, Jenny! I'm so glad you called. You've been on my mind all morning."

Sera was one of the sweetest, sunniest people Jenny had ever met. And that woman could wrap herself into the most complex yoga pretzel she'd ever seen. "Hey, Sera. I've got you on speaker, and the crew is all here. Say hi!"

From the other end, Sera squealed. "Hi, girls. I miss y'all—did you hear what I said? Y'all!"

"You sound like a real Southern girl now," Maggie teased.

"Marcus has a little more work out here, then we're on our way back."

Jenny'd been hoping everything would work out so Sera and her husband would be back for the wedding.

"So what are y'all up to today?" Sera asked. "No, don't tell me. You took on another case." Excitement was clear in her voice. "Darn it. I wish I could be there now."

"Actually," Jenny said, "we're on our way to Atlanta."

"Oh." Sera's voice frittered from buoyant to flat. "What's wrong? Abby Ruth, what's going on?"

"Red's the one who started this," Abby Ruth said. "I'll let him explain."

Red leaned over the seat where Lil and Maggie were

sitting to get closer to Jenny's phone. "We're heading to the city because Abby Ruth is ringing the bell today."

"That's the best news I've heard in a long time," Sera said. "I'm there in spirit. You know that."

Knowing her, that could be true. It wouldn't surprise Jenny to discover that Sera had been able to feel their enthusiasm all the way out in California before she'd ever dialed the phone. Sera had meditation, intuition, and chakras out the ying-yang.

Jenny cleared her throat. "And...well...I called for another reason. I have some news for everyone."

Her mom glanced over sharply, and the van swerved right slightly before she expertly controlled it again. "Good news?"

"Well, I think so." She paused only for a moment. "Teague and I have set a date for the wedding."

"Finally!" Her mom gave a fist pump.

"In three weeks. Saturday, June fifteenth."

Lil gasped. "But that's not long enough to plan a proper wedding. You have to think of the dress, the cake, the attendants. So much to take care of."

"Teague and I have decided to make it official at City Hall. A quick appointment with the justice of the peace."

"You cannot be serious."

"It's the second marriage for both of us."

Her mom reached over and covered her hand. "Not really, Jenny. This is the first time either of you are marrying for true love."

A lump formed in Jenny's chest. Her mom was right, but time was of the essence. "That's not all. There will be an addition to the Cady-Castro family come December."

Laughter and whoops sounded from Lil and Maggie, and Sera squealed on the other end of the phone. The dogs barked, and Grayson clapped.

Jenny caught her mom staring into the rearview mirror

looking straight at Red. Then she turned and saw Red's strangely sad yet determined expression. What in the world? Maybe they'd been planning an announcement themselves. Of the marital type, not the baby type. "Mom, did you...were you..." Jenny could barely translate that thought into words. How weird would it be to plan her second wedding while her mom was planning her first?

Abby Ruth cut eye contact with Red and gave Jenny a big grin. "So, you've knocked Teague up and are finally gonna make an honest man of him."

Grayson piped up, "What's knocked up mean? Is that like when someone robs a convenience store?"

"Mom..." Jenny said. "Sera, I better let you go. Love you."

"Can't wait to see you all at the wedding. I'll be there with bells on! Congratulations, Jenny. And you too, Abby Ruth."

"I'm gonna be the big brother," Grayson boasted. "But, Mom, you never told me exactly where babies come from."

"Does parenting ever get easier?" Jenny asked her mom.

"Honestly? Not really."

Jenny gazed down at the beautiful sapphire-and-diamond engagement ring she'd been wearing for more than a year now. She was marrying the man she'd loved for more than half her life, and they were going to build a family together here in Summer Shoals. To say she couldn't wait was an understatement. *There's nothing too tough for me to handle when I'm with Teague Castro.*

THEIR ROLLICKING VAN OF PEOPLE AND ANIMALS MADE IT TO Atlanta. Now Abby Ruth watched as her buddy Stella marched up to the cancer treatment center's shiny brass bell. Her skin held a healthier glow than Abby Ruth had ever seen, and her dark hair had grown, allowing her to cut it in a sleek bob.

Over the months that Abby Ruth had come and gone from this medical facility for her own treatment, she'd seen dozens of people ring the bell signifying the end of radiation, but never had she felt so full of hope and happiness as she did right now watching Stella.

Bell ringing had seemed like a bunch of hooey, but now, with a broad smile on her face and tears glistening in her eyes, she understood the power it held.

With a quivering smile, Stella grabbed the long, braided rope that hung from the bell.

Everyone in the room recited the short poem:

Ring this bell

Three times well,

Its toll to clearly say

My treatment's done,

This course is run,

And I'm on my way.

Stella tugged on the rope, tentatively at first. Then with a burst of energy she followed up with two hard pulls that made that bell clang as loudly as one at a railroad crossing.

Everyone cheered, and Abby Ruth stepped closer to Stella. Taking her hand, she hugged her, less to comfort Stella's tears than to hide the fact that she too was crying. She turned her head and brushed away her tears, trying desperately to pull herself together.

"I can't believe it's over," Stella said.

Abby Ruth smiled gently at her friend. She looked so much better now. She'd been so sick—so frail—when they'd met. "We deserve to celebrate every day, and every little win along the way."

"I'm trying," Stella said. "It'll be wonderful to be a hundred percent again. I'm finally feeling stronger physically, but sometimes my memory and thoughts still get jumbled.

Believe me, my family is ready for me to stop forgetting things."

"I hated the memory problems." Abby Ruth glanced toward her family and friends, then pulled Stella off to the side. "I swear I thought I was getting Alzheimer's there for a while. I tried to downplay it, but I'm sure they noticed."

"Chemo brain is the pits. No one warned me about that either." Stella leaned in and whispered into Abby Ruth's ear, "I thought I was having another chemo fog last weekend. Scared me to death."

"What happened?"

"I was at a wedding with some friends, and would you believe it, I thought I'd left my purse behind?"

Abby Ruth had to laugh. The first thing she'd learned about Stella was that the woman was almost surgically attached to her handbag. She even carried a hanger gizmo to put on the table to keep her bag nearby and off the floor. "What happened?"

"I went to leave and discovered it was missing. I checked the bathroom, but it wasn't there either. I hadn't been anywhere else except on the dance floor, and I had it with me there. That's the whole reason I carried a teensy clutch."

"Did you ever find it?"

"I did. It was off to the side near the empty chafing dishes from the buffet."

"Maybe you dropped it while you were going through the food line."

"No, one of my friends was watching it at our table. I think someone may've picked it up."

"Was anything missing from it?"

Stella mumbled a few words that Abby Ruth couldn't catch.

"What was that?"

"Just some money and a credit card."

Oooh, a purse snatcher! Stella's words teased Abby Ruth like a bread spitball on a fishing line would a catfish. It had been a good long year since the G Team had solved a case. A *real* case. They'd investigated what one paranoid woman believed was a plot against her. Turned out, her friends had been sneaking around behind her back because they were planning a surprise party for her.

Abby Ruth missed the good old days of chasing down scammers and gun runners. Maybe the case of Stella's stolen purse was exactly what she needed to take control of her post-cancer life.

But before she could grill Stella for the rest of the details, the nurse announced, "Abby Ruth Cady."

Lil, Maggie, Grayson, and Red all clapped, and Jenny let out a whistle. They couldn't leave the dogs in the van, so Red had sweet-talked the clinic staff into allowing them inside for the ceremony, claiming they were as much family as any of the humans here. At the ruckus, Bowzer barked and chased his tail, but Ritter yawned and dropped down to rest his jowls on his paws. Obviously, he wasn't all that impressed with this circus either.

Red stood next to Jenny with a protective arm around her.

Abby Ruth's insides churned, both from those two standing together and the pressure to ring the darned bell. She'd much rather stay here and talk to Stella about her missing purse, but all eyes were on her.

The group recited the poem again. Emotion swept over Abby Ruth, so she tried to focus her mind on other things, like why Stella's purse might've gone missing at a wedding. Dang, she sure hoped a bad guy had snatched it. Then she and the girls could help track down the creep and get justice for Stella.

Abby Ruth stepped up and rang the bell like the end of

round eight when Mohammed Ali knocked out George Foreman at The Rumble in the Jungle.

For a moment, she almost allowed herself to believe that this part of her life was done. No more cancer. No more treatments.

She was thankful she was the last one to ring the bell. Her emotions were bouncing around, and she wasn't sure how much longer she could contain them.

Trying to regain her control, Abby Ruth tried to ease her way back to Stella's side, but Maggie and Lil had gathered around Stella as they walked down the long corridor to the exit. She couldn't shake the thought of someone stealing from Stella. And if someone had done her friend wrong, she wouldn't let the no-good person get away with it. Maggie and Lil had been so reluctant to take on cases while Abby Ruth was sick, but maybe could she change their minds this time.

As they strolled toward the door to the parking garage, Jenny caught up with her. "You're being awfully quiet. Are you okay, Mom?"

"Yes, I'm fine."

"I parked down at that end of the lot," Stella said.

"I'll get the van," Red said. "Stella, I can drive you to your car."

"Don't be silly," she said. "After ringing that bell, I feel like I could run to my car."

Abby Ruth wished she'd gotten that type of exhilaration out of the act of ringing the bell, but she was glad Stella had. She pulled her friend off to the side before she could skip away. "Before you go, I wanted to ask you how much money was missing from your purse when you found it."

Stella's face reddened, and she averted her gaze to the ground. "About a thousand dollars, but that's my own fault for carrying around so much cash. It's a terrible habit. My kids fuss at me about it all the time."

"Did you report the incident? You said you found it near the food stuff. Do you think the caterer or waitstaff could've been up to no good?"

"I'm not sure it matters. I'll be more careful next time."

Uh-uh. Abby Ruth wasn't ready to give this up yet. Stella's purse fiasco was the most interesting thing she'd heard about in a long while. "You wouldn't want someone else to fall victim to something like that, now would you?"

Stella's smile faded. "I hadn't really thought about it like that."

"I need every detail," Abby Ruth pressed.

She clung to every tidbit Stella shared. Unfortunately, instead of cluing in to a potential case, Maggie and Lil jabbered on about the plans for Jenny's wedding ceremony while they waited for Red.

"I have to run," Stella finally said. "I'm meeting my daughter to celebrate as soon as she gets off work."

"Let's talk about the purse thing again soon. Take care."

Stella waved and headed to her car, but Abby Ruth's mind was already clicking away at ideas about checking into the case of the missing purse.

A moment later, Red pulled the van to the curb in front of them. "Did you want to drive, Abby Ruth?"

She climbed into the passenger seat. "No, you can drive."

His forehead scrunched in surprise, and Jenny's expression matched his. Abby Ruth pretended to dig for something in her pocket. Anything to avoid the stares from Red and Jenny.

"You're sure you're okay?"

"I'm fine. I guess it was all the excitement." Abby Ruth took in a deep breath, pulling in the scent of rotten eggs and…taco seasoning? She sputtered. "Did that dog just fart? How can this be my life?"

Lord, between Jenny's announcement, Red's romantic overtures, and Ritter's digestive issues, things were getting complicated.

CHAPTER 4

Once she'd waved away Ritter's eau de stink, Abby Ruth's gut was twisting like it had the time her dad had caught her skipping school when she was fourteen and had decided she wanted to learn to smoke cigarettes. Only this time Red was the one making her dread what would come next. He glanced at her as he weaved through Atlanta's afternoon traffic back toward Summer Shoals. He'd been so comforting and reassuring through her treatments, but with Jenny's announcement earlier, his knowing gaze terrified Abby Ruth.

She knew what he'd been saying when he met her eyes in the mirror after Jenny told them about the baby. It was as clear as if he'd spoken it aloud.

"It's time to tell her, Abby Ruth."

She'd thought she had the past safely under control, that Red had come to terms with the way things had turned out. But the news of a wedding and a baby had shifted everything dramatically.

Right now, she felt like a stranger in her own life. She didn't want to disappoint the only man she'd ever loved, the man she might be falling in love with again. But she refused to hurt her baby girl, who was about to have a baby of her own.

Later. Abby Ruth would figure out her personal stuff later. For now, she would concentrate on what Stella had told her.

It only took a minute to push real life aside. Chemo brain, her butt. If Stella said someone had nabbed her purse and taken money from it, Abby Ruth believed her. Stella was a sweet lady, and anyone who took advantage of her deserved to be brought to justice. That was something Abby Ruth could control.

Abby Ruth was picturing herself running through the city streets chasing down a skinny little turd wearing plaid golfer pants and a bad toupee when she drifted off to sleep. Three dreams later, she'd caught a bank robber, a peeping Tom, and an art forger.

Someone shook her awake. "Ru, we're back home."

"Hmm?"

"I dropped off Jenny and Grayson, and Maggie and Lil are already inside Summer Haven. Want me to carry you in?"

That woke her up right quick. She did not need anyone—Red or otherwise—to carry her anywhere, so she shot straight up in her seat. It was bad enough all her friends and family had seen her when she was sick, sometimes so sick and tired she couldn't lift her head off the pillow. "I'm awake, and I don't want you to carry me." She shook her head to clear the cobwebs and orient herself to the fact that they were parked in Summer Haven's drive. The big white house and the expanse of gently rolling land around it had been a haven for her over the past few months.

"About Jenny," Red began. "We need to—"

"I've gotta pee." She reached for the door handle.

"Shouldn't have stopped for that gigantic cherry limeade. You know that stuff goes right through me."

Before she could jump out, Red grabbed her by the wrist. "You can't avoid this forever. You know that, right?"

She pulled her hand free. "I just need a little time."

"I've given you all the time in the world."

"But once you found out I had cancer, we agreed—"

"When I said we would leave everything be, you had your head in a toilet and my daughter wasn't pregnant. Dammit, Abby Ruth, it's time. She's getting married. I want to walk her down the aisle."

So far, Abby Ruth had managed to keep Red from divulging their secret, that he was Jenny's biological father. He wouldn't keep quiet now that they had a wedding and a grandchild in their future.

He was right. She knew he was right. But sometimes when you'd waited this long to tell the truth, it became worse than a bogeyman living under the bed. Because the secret about Jenny's father wasn't just something that could jump out and hurt her. It could drive her daughter away. Forever.

She turned back and lay her palm on Red's cheek. "I *will* tell her."

"When?" Suspicion threaded his words.

"Before the baby is born?"

"No way. That's months away. She's getting married in three weeks. You tell her by this time next week, or I'll do it."

Gratitude for the short reprieve overwhelming her, she leaned in to place a quick kiss on his cheek, but Red was still fast. Still sly. He turned his head so their lips met. And oh, didn't he smell good—like leather and ocean-scented shower gel. And his mouth was as knowing and nimble as ever. He'd always had the cleverest mouth she'd ever kissed.

They stayed like that—lips touching, his hand finding its

way to her hip, hers on his face—for long sweet minutes. It felt like heaven.

Like contentment. Real happiness.

Until something cold and wet jammed itself into Abby Ruth's armpit. She yelped, and laughter rumbled up in Red's chest, and the rich, warm sound of his amusement spilled out into the van. Although she'd been holding him at arm's distance over the past year, insisting they keep their relationship friends only, it occurred to her that she wouldn't mind listening to the sound of Red's laughter every day for the rest of her life.

But for now, she had a hound dog that apparently had no concept of appropriate personal space.

Abby Ruth gave Red another peck on the lips. "I'll pick up my truck tomorrow." She hopped out of the van and was about to close the door when Red said, "Not happening, Ru."

"What?" she asked innocently, as innocently as a woman who'd once shot the privates off a marble statue could.

"You're not leaving this dog with me."

"Fine," she sighed. "Night, Red." She grabbed Ritter's leash, and to her delight he didn't give her a bit of trouble.

"Goodnight, and don't forget what I said about Jenny."

Like she'd ever be able to do that.

Ritter stretched his long legs, and in two bounds he was out of the van and following her up the walk to Summer Haven's front porch.

Lil and Maggie were there, sitting in two of the half-dozen rocking chairs spread across the white-columned expanse.

"That was some kiss," Maggie teased.

Abby Ruth had hoped they hadn't seen her and Red.

Lil waved in front of her face as though cooling her cheeks. "You think Red has any buddies he could import from Texas? I never went for jocks before, but I do believe your young man has changed my mind, Abby Ruth."

Young man, that would give Red a good ego boost. She'd use that next time she needed to wheedle something out of him.

But for now, she needed to wheedle something out of Lil and Maggie. "So..." she drawled as Ritter flopped to his side on the porch and she reached to draw a chair close to her friends. She plopped down in it, narrowly missing catching Ritter's tail under the rocker. "Something's come up."

"I knew it!" Maggie crowed. "You and Red are getting hitched too."

A ping went through Abby Ruth's chest. She'd never been married, and although she'd once dreamed of a future like that with Red, it hadn't come to pass. That it could now was an exciting and scary notion. "Not unless he proposed while I was conked out, and I sleep-accepted."

Maggie's head dropped back against the rocking chair. "Darn."

"Don't look so disappointed. It's possibly something better."

Lil sat up straight in her chair. "Tell me Jenny has changed her mind about a full wedding here at Summer Haven."

Good Lord, didn't these two think about anything besides love and marriage? Then again, it made sense, seeing as they'd both been married for decades before their husbands passed away. "Stella told me something interesting today. Apparently, she had her purse snatched not too long ago. At the time, she thought she was foggy from all the chemo. I can understand that, but losing her purse isn't like her."

Lil's lips puckered. "That's terrible. I'd die if I lost my purse and everything in it."

"She found it."

"Why doesn't it sound like that was good news?" Maggie asked. "I hear a 'but' coming."

"But…all her cash was missing and someone had taken her credit card." Abby Ruth spoke slowly, hoping to draw them in more.

"Did she report it to the police?"

"No. Like I said, at the time she was doubting herself. But apparently, the more she thought about it later, the more it bothered her. By that time, she felt like too much time had passed to tell anyone. Honestly, I think she was embarrassed that she hadn't noticed right away."

"Was it a lot of money?"

"Close to a thousand dollars."

Lil's jaw dropped. Abby Ruth could just imagine Lil checking off a list of things she'd have done with an extra grand in her pocket.

"But the trail is weeks old," Abby Ruth said casually. *Take the bait, gals.* "Probably completely dead."

Maggie and Lil both nodded, but slowly, thoughtfully.

"I didn't say anything to Stella because I didn't want to get her hopes up, but what would the two of you say to poking around a little?"

The chairs rocked faster, which was an excellent sign.

"I know my being sick has slowed us down some. Lil had all those great G Team business cards made over a year ago, and we've barely used them."

Maggie's eyes softened. "You didn't slow us down. You gave us a reason to stay close to home, and I choose to believe Summer Haven and you are better off for it."

So true. Abby Ruth wouldn't have survived if these women hadn't been around to help her through the treatments and lethargy.

"What did Stella say when you mentioned that we could investigate?" Lil asked.

"I didn't get a chance to officially offer our services."

"We can't take a case without the person's consent," Lil said.

Abby Ruth's earlier excitement shriveled up. The girls would shut down this investigation before it even started.

But Lil held up a finger. "How about you call Stella and ask her to meet us at the diner tomorrow?"

"We're out of practice," Maggie said. "And without Sera? It won't be the same."

Lil glanced over at Maggie. "If we don't take action we'll be more out of practice."

Abby Ruth grinned so hard it strained her cheek muscles. Damn, she loved these gals.

She sent Stella a text message.

ABBY RUTH: Meet me @ Atlanta Highway Diner in Summer Shoals 2moro? Cake 4 brkfast. 10am.

She and Stella had talked about those five-layer cakes when they were both too sick to keep anything down, much less a piece of cake. They'd vowed then that one day they'd get together for cake. For breakfast, because apparently that felt totally wild and reckless to Stella.

Abby Ruth's text alert sounded like a pistol at the start of a race, and seeing Stella's enthusiastic yes made her feel as if she was back on the track and ready to run for the blue ribbon.

CHAPTER 5

The morning after Abby Ruth's bell-ringing ceremony, Lil pulled back the heavy parlor drapes to watch Maggie wield a hammer like a twenty-something-year-old construction worker as she pounded one of the loose rails surrounding the gazebo in front of Summer Haven. Lil's great-granddaddy Jessup Lee Summer had built the quaint structure for his crazy bride in 1867 when they'd gotten married here on the estate.

Maggie's gentleman friend, Bruce Shellenberger, was beside her and handing over a new nail each time she'd pounded in the one before it.

Ladylike or not, Maggie had skills, and they'd sure come in handy since she'd moved to Summer Shoals a few years ago. The past year they'd actually gotten the old house in pretty good shape with help from Sera's financial contributions, but the gazebo hadn't been high on the priority list. Not since the Cocklebur Cloggers had stomped a hole in the gazebo floor and moved their practices to the big room at Gypsy Cotton Art Gallery. Since Sera hadn't yet decided what she was going to do with the gallery building

Marcus had bought for her, she'd let the townspeople use the space.

But that gazebo was the perfect spot for a wedding, and Lil and Maggie had decided they would try to talk Jenny into getting married at Summer Haven, which meant the gazebo needed to be repaired in a hurry.

The phone jangled. She rushed to the kitchen and picked up on the third ring. "Helloooo."

"Lil? It's Sera."

"You must be missing us as much as we miss you. I was just thinking of you."

Sera was such a big part of Summer Haven now. The community had fallen in love with her, and half the town had taken at least one yoga class on the front lawn with her.

"I'm so sad I wasn't there for Abby Ruth's bell ringing."

"You know how she is about that stuff. She'd never let on that it meant anything to her. You can hand it to Red that we found out about it at all. Abby Ruth planned to sneak off and watch Stella ring the bell."

"She's one tough cookie, but she'd do anything for a friend. Maybe I'm sorry I missed it more for me than for her. I feel so out of touch."

Lil chuckled. "That bell was the least of Abby Ruth's concerns. She was way more interested in something that happened to Stella than ringing the bell."

"Is Stella okay?"

"Physically, she's fine, but she ran into some G Team type trouble recently."

"Trouble? What happened? You mean like a case?" The words tumbled out, each one higher pitched than the last.

"We're looking into something as a favor to Abby Ruth," Lil said. "Might turn out to be nothing. You know how it is, dear."

"I miss those cases." Sera's voice softened. "Maybe I could fly home earlier."

"It might not be anything. You should just sit tight for now." Lil felt a teensy pang of guilt for saying that, but the truth was this Stella thing didn't seem like a real case. She'd only gone along with it because Abby Ruth seemed like her old sassy self again, which was way overdue.

"Okay, but let me know if you need my help."

"Of course," Lil said, picking up a pad and pen from the desk tucked near the back door. She doodled a few hearts and floral arrangements.

"Meanwhile, I'll start thinking about how I can help from here. Three weeks sure is fast." Sera chattered on. "I still can't believe they're getting married and having a baby. It's so exciting. Are Maggie and Abby Ruth there with you?"

"No. Abby Ruth is at Jenny's house, and Maggie is out—"

"I'm out what?" Maggie said.

She lifted her chin from the phone toward Maggie. "I was going to say you were out working on the gazebo with that sweet man Bruce." Speaking into the phone, she said, "Maggie just walked in." Lil put her hand over the phone. "Maggie, go pick up the extension in my bedroom. It's Sera!"

Maggie hustled past Lil, her hammer thumping against the thigh of her khakis with each step. She came back, stretching the cord of the harvest-gold princess phone as far as it would reach into the kitchen. "Hey, Sera. I thought you'd be on set with Marcus today."

"I was so excited about Jenny's news that I stayed home to look for baby shower ideas. But before we get into all that, I want to ask how things are going with Bruce?"

"Good, but you know no one will ever replace my George." Maggie's eyes glassed a little like they always did when she mentioned her late husband. "Unlike George,

Bruce isn't very handy, but he's so sweet. He's been right by my side fetching tools and nails as I repair the gazebo."

"He's crazy about you. You know that, right?" Sera said.

"We're just friends. The male companionship is nice, but that's all there is to it. On a more important note, we're all excited about Jenny and Teague having a baby. I was thinking we could work on a grandmother's quilt. You know, with squares of fabric from you, me, Lil, Abby Ruth, and Teague's mom too. Do you think you could bring a couple old shirts or skirts when you come?"

"Absolutely. That's a great idea. I know just the things I'll donate."

"Lil and I can put it together," Maggie said. "It's been too long since she's done any quilting. It's perfect timing for this project."

"I hope they have a girl. Can you imagine how beautiful she'd be?" Sera said.

"Let's get her married first," Lil said.

Maggie laughed. "Folks don't always do things in that order these days."

"She's right," Sera echoed.

Maggie said, "I'm hoping if I can get the gazebo back in tiptop shape we can talk Jenny and Teague into having the wedding, or at least a reception here at Summer Haven. Can't you picture Jenny and Teague's first dance together there under twinkle lights? That would be so romantic."

The screen door slammed, and Abby Ruth strode into the kitchen, with Ritter plodding along behind her. Lil could swear he was casing the fridge and cabinets every time he snuck his way into this room. "There won't be any first dance," Abby Ruth announced. "Didn't you hear her yesterday? Jenny said that they'll be going to the courthouse."

"That's ridiculous," Lil said. "That's almost like eloping. The town's sheriff cannot elope."

"There's no time for a big brouhaha," Abby Ruth said, but her downturned mouth said she was a little sad about that.

Maggie pushed her dark bangs back. "Lil's right. He's an elected official. The town deserves to be a part of the celebration. We'll help plan the wedding. Won't we, Lil?"

Sera chimed in. "Me too. You'd be surprised how fast movie set people can get things done."

Maggie shouted to Abby Ruth from the doorway, "Sera said she has people who can help pull things together fast."

Abby Ruth stooped in next to Maggie to talk into the phone. "Hi, Sera. Jenny said she wants to keep it low key."

"No bride really means that," Sera replied. "Now about the gazebo. I can send out some people—"

"It's half fixed," Maggie said. "I've loosened the boards. If I don't finish now, someone might get hurt."

"Wait. Listen to me." Sera's voice rose across the line. "No matter what Jenny decides, I'm sending someone over to fix the gazebo. That's the least I can do. Maggie, you can focus on something else. I'll do this for Jenny, and if we don't use it for the wedding, we'll use it for the baby shower, which I plan to host. Deal?"

"Fine by me," Lil said.

"I can fix the gazebo," Maggie said. "Why pay someone to do what I can do myself?"

"It's my gift to Jenny. Please. I feel bad enough that I'm so far away. I want to be a part of things. Having the gazebo repaired is something I can arrange from here. Please?"

"Can't hardly blame Sera for wanting to help, Mags." Lil hoped Maggie would go along with Sera's offer, because the extent of repairs the gazebo needed had her worried. It was heavy work with all the boards that should be replaced. There were plenty of other projects Maggie could work on.

. . .

AFTER THEY'D TOLD SERA GOODBYE, ABBY RUTH HAD SECURED a very sad Ritter in the garage, and Maggie had shooed away Bruce so the gals could hustle on down to the Atlanta Highway Diner to meet with Stella. Now, the morning sun streamed through the diner's front window, reflecting off the mirror lining one wall and brightening the space filled with tables, booths, and an old-fashioned counter. But Abby Ruth hadn't taken her attention off the front door since they'd settled into the back booth, the one they considered their G Team spot since it was here they'd celebrated solving their very first case with a multi-colored five-layer cake.

At least here they could talk without worry of nosy neighbors listening in. All they needed was for someone to tell Teague they were doing a little investigating again.

Dottie, the diner's longtime waitress, dropped off a tray of waters and a carafe of coffee for them. "Heard your girl is getting married to the sheriff," she said to Abby Ruth.

Pride welled up inside Abby Ruth. "Yep."

"So exciting. Someone has been spreading rumors that they're gonna elope." Dottie snickered. "Like that would ever happen. A wedding at Summer Haven would be the event of the year."

"Wouldn't it, though?" Lil said, glaring in Abby Ruth's direction.

"Oops, there's our friend." Abby Ruth dodged the discussion and waved frantically at Stella. The diner was still humming from the late breakfast crowd, so Abby Ruth hopped up and rushed over to meet her at the door. "Welcome to Summer Shoals."

"The town is smaller than I imagined," Stella said. "But it's cute."

Abby Ruth slid into the booth first, and Stella scooted in next to her.

Lil poured a cup of coffee for Stella from the white thermal carafe. "I'm so glad you could come."

"Abby Ruth told me about the homemade cake they serve here. How could I say no to that?"

Lil and Maggie exchanged a glance.

"Well, that's not the only reason I invited you," Abby Ruth admitted.

"You didn't tell her already?" Maggie said.

"Tell me what?"

Abby Ruth sat up taller in the booth, glancing around. No one was paying them any attention, but she lowered her voice anyway. "I think we can help you."

"With what?" Stella's head swiveled like an owl's as she looked at each of them.

"We want to find out exactly what happened with your purse. I don't like that someone ripped you off." Abby Ruth pushed her mug away. "Whoever took it should pay."

Stella waved a hand, dismissing the comment. "Don't be silly. It's over and done with. I already got a new credit card."

"But he or she took advantage of you," Abby Ruth said.

"All they charged was birdseed at a Tractor Supply just outside Atlanta, and I'm disputing the charges with the bank. As far as the cash, I shouldn't have been carrying that much anyway."

"You can't just let him get away with it."

"I have to take some responsibility for it," Stella said. "I've learned my lesson, and that's good enough for me. Believe me, I won't be toting around cash like that again."

"But..." Maggie's shoulders drooped.

Lil was slumped so low she looked as if she might slip right under the table.

Surprisingly, Abby Ruth wasn't the only one who'd been looking forward to the chance to work on a new case. "Tell us more about what happened. Where were you? Did anyone look suspicious?"

"Really, there's no reason to—"

"I rang the bell for you," Abby Ruth said. "Please do this for me." Okay, so that was probably unfair, but desperate times called for creativity, and it was all she could think of.

Stella frowned, not surprising since she wasn't privy to any of the takedowns Abby Ruth and her gals had set up in the past. After taking a sip of her coffee, Stella finally said, "I was at a wedding and had left the table to get one last nibble before they closed down the buffet. I just can't say no to those pigs in a blanket. They throw all those extra hors d'oeuvres out, you know."

Lil visibly swallowed, probably sickened at the thought of eating tiny hot dogs wrapped in biscuits at a wedding.

"I thought you said your friends were at the table watching it."

"Only Virginia, and she's not always the most reliable. When I returned, Virginia was out on the dance floor, and my purse wasn't hanging on the table anymore. You know I always hang my bag by my purse clip on my left side." She gestured toward Lil and Maggie. "I'm right handed. That way I don't knock it while I'm eating or talking. I'm Italian after all. We like to do a lot of both—eating and talking with our hands."

Abby Ruth wanted to slap the table to keep Stella focused but tapped her fingers in an impatient rhythm instead. "You said you found it close to the catering supplies, right?"

"Yes." Stella blinked. "It may have been my imagination, but it seemed like a man kept trying to herd me away from the area where I found my purse."

Abby Ruth made a gimme motion with her fingers, encouraging Stella to spill everything.

"It could have been anyone. There were so many people

there. Thank goodness my purse was bright magenta or I may never have seen it tucked behind a stack of chafing dishes near the door."

"Chafing dishes?" Abby Ruth mused, turning that tidbit over in her head. "Had to be someone with the caterer."

"Not many people were still there when I came back looking for my purse. I do remember a tall, thin redheaded man with a mustache. I was in his way when he was clearing things off tables. But by the time I found my purse and turned around to explain, he was long gone."

"Interesting. He may have been trying to keep you from spotting your bag." Maggie rubbed her hands together. "Any idea who mustache man was?"

"Why are y'all so interested in my missing purse?" Stella asked.

Lil scooted herself back up on the bench seat and sat up straight. "We have experience dealing with criminals, and it does sound like you might've been the victim of a crime, dear."

Abby Ruth held back the snarky remark lying on the tip of her tongue about Lil having lived with criminals, which was how she knew how to deal with them. "We can track that snake down and get your money back."

"I won't lie to you. Having my money back would be nice, but I don't want people to see me as a victim. It's bad enough that some folks still think of me as weak and sick despite the fact I'm well now."

"We understand completely," Lil said. "But you don't want anyone to think they can take advantage of you either, do you?"

"No, of course not." She brushed at invisible crumbs on the table. "I suppose it wouldn't hurt for you to look into it."

Excitement coursed through Abby Ruth. Things might be a little rocky in her personal life right now, but this purse snatching was something she could grab on to and fix. "We'll take care of everything. Don't you worry."

"Do you remember anything else about the man?" Maggie took diligent notes on a sketch artist app for the iPad that Sera had left behind. Thank goodness Sera had found that app because Maggie had once tried to use a crazy Mr. Potato Head to pin down facial features of a bad guy they were chasing. Not exactly twenty-first century technology. "Red hair and a mustache, right? Did he have a receding hairline? Eyes? Full lips?"

"Gosh. Let me think." Stella's face contorted as she tried to remember. "Red hair, cut short. He had beady eyes. Kind of reminded me of a giant possum with his pale skin and dark dot eyes. A pinched nose. Oh, and he had this swirly tattoo on the side of his neck." She leaned forward with a smirk. "Chemo brain, my ass. I bet no one could remember that many details."

She and Abby Ruth high-fived.

Dottie, her striking, ash-blond hair pulled back in a twist and secured with a pen, returned to the table and ran down the specials. "Maggie, I have some of those cheese grits made with half and half just the way you like them. How 'bout I spoon you up a bowl? Or are y'all thinking lunch?"

"We're all having the same thing. A slice of your famous Summer Shoals Five-Layer Cake." Abby Ruth lived for the brown, white, pink, yellow and green layers. It might just be almond-flavored cake, but those colors seemed to trick the brain into believing it was something extra special. Something worth celebrating with. So what if this was before instead of after a case.

"And I'll stick with the coffee," Lil added. "Y'all too?"

Everyone nodded except for Stella. "Decaf tea for me, please."

Dottie jotted the order on her pad. "Got it. It'll be right out."

"I'm going to zip back to the ladies' room," Stella announced.

Lil, Maggie and Abby Ruth sat quietly as Stella rose from the table. As soon as the bathroom door closed, they all leaned toward the center of the table. "This will be a cakewalk," Abby Ruth announced.

"Still fun," Maggie said.

"The G Team is back in business."

"Abby Ruth," Lil said, "there were times during your treatment that you were, shall we say…"

"Squirrelly-brained?"

"I was going to say forgetful, and sometimes you remembered things incorrectly. You don't think Stella could be…"

"She blamed all this stolen purse mess on the residual effects from the chemo at first, but she changed her mind. I believe she knows exactly what she's talking about. Please don't say that in front of her. She's very sensitive about it."

"She's coming," Lil said in a hushed voice. "Then I added cumin to the sauce to give it a smoky flavor. It really was quite good."

"I love cumin in my recipes." Stella slid back into the booth.

"Speaking of recipes, Stella, do you think you could ask the bride at the wedding where your purse was taken who did her catering?"

Stella blushed and fiddled with her napkin, her discomfort obvious.

Abby Ruth hitched a breath. Was she still having some fuzzy memories? Maybe Lil was right to question Stella. "You don't remember whose wedding it was?"

"No. Yes. I mean, not exactly. But don't misunderstand.

This isn't a chemo fog. I remember the event just fine. It's just that...well...I'm not *really* friends of the bride."

Maggie nodded. "Don't feel bad. I get it. I've gone to plenty of weddings where I didn't see why in the world an acquaintance would invite me to their child's wedding. Always felt obliged to go though."

"Not quite like that either." Fidgeting with her napkin, she finally gave in with a big sigh. "I guess there's no harm in confiding in you, but please don't let this get around. You see, my girlfriends and I like to drop in on weddings on the weekends."

"Drop in?" Lil patted her chest directly over her heart. "You don't mean you crash weddings?"

Abby Ruth thought it sounded fun, but Stella's cheeks grew even redder, and she was squirming like a kid caught stealing cookies.

"We always put ten dollars each in the wedding fund box to cover the cake and champagne. We do love a good party, and at our age there's not much going on. That's also part of why I didn't tell anyone my purse was stolen. I wasn't an invited guest. We go to a lot of weddings at the Remington Club because it's one of the nicest venues in Atlanta." Stella rested her head on the back of the booth, avoiding all their gazes. "I'm so embarrassed."

Lil shook her head, her dismay clear.

"Oh, don't be embarrassed, Stella. Trust me, we all have our secrets," Abby Ruth said with a sharp glance in Lil's direction. Who was Lil to judge?

"You girls ready?" Dottie approached carrying a lineup of small white plates up her arm piled with slices of cake and scoops of ice cream. "Cake all around."

Stella picked up her fork before the plate hit the table.

"Anything else for you gals?" Dottie asked.

"Not a thing." Abby Ruth was already mentally planning

how she could find out who had catered at the Remington Club the day Stella crashed that wedding. Right now she felt as if her world was coming together again. Finally, she could begin to push aside that whole cancer mess, and she and the girls could once again make progress as the G Team. More than anything, she wanted to feel that excitement in her life again.

She turned to Stella and grinned. "How would you feel about coming on a field trip with the G Team?"

"What's the G Team?"

"Sugar—" Abby Ruth pointed at Lil, Maggie, and herself, "—that's us. And the G Team is about to show you some real fun."

CHAPTER 6

To Lil's relief, all it took was a couple of quick phone calls from the restaurant for Stella and Abby Ruth to track down the information on the suspicious caterer's whereabouts today. Chances were good that this was a solid lead. Maybe they weren't as out of practice as she'd thought.

The caterer was back at the Remington Club, setting up for a wedding reception this afternoon. On a Tuesday of all days.

Back in her day, people were married on a Saturday, period. Now, young folks were going all willy-nilly, tying the knot on a Tuesday afternoon.

Lil suggested they call ahead to the reception venue, but Abby Ruth put the kibosh on that idea, saying they didn't want to give the caterer any reason to think they were on to him.

The cake plates had barely been cleared from the diner table before the gals piled into Abby Ruth's dually headed for Atlanta. It seemed no time at all before they pulled up in front of one of the swankiest places Lil had ever been.

Why on earth hadn't she ever heard of the Remington Club?

This was the type of place she would've been invited to PP—pre-prison—but now she was barging her way in. Goodness gracious, she still didn't care for this part of the investigation business. Sometimes they were forced to be so pushy, downright rude and uncouth. And that was what this was, swaggering into a reception venue ten minutes before the bride and groom were due to arrive.

She and the others hurried toward the double mahogany doors leading into a redbrick building that sprawled for what looked like a mile. Lil was eager to get inside, but Stella was walking so slowly that even Lil, short as she was, could lap her. "Dear, is there something wrong?"

"I'm not sure about all this investigation stuff. It's been weeks since my purse went missing. I didn't think the police could track down the culprit. Why would the three of you believe you could—"

Lil gave her a haughty look.

"—find the guilty party?"

She allowed her indignation at Stella's lack of faith in the G Team to fade into a smile. "I forget that you haven't seen Abby Ruth at the top of her game. But once that woman gets the bit between her teeth, she's impossible to control. She goes into a wild gallop that an experienced bronc rider couldn't survive."

Outside the ballroom, Lil straightened her shoulders and the collar on her blouse, trying to project all the elegance her mother had taught her.

Look as if you belong and as if you're the one who should be directing the entire show, Lillian dear. Confidence with just a touch of arrogance will never fail you.

Thanks, Momma.

Lil sped up, as fast as her short legs would carry her. She

weaved around Abby Ruth and Maggie into a big room where people were scurrying here and there, setting up centerpieces and straightening tablecloths. "Ladies," she said, "we're going to play this my way."

"But—" Abby Ruth protested.

"Have you ever handled a catering staff?"

"No, but I ate plenty of catered food in the press boxes," she said.

"If you can tell me you've planned and pulled off a charity dinner for three hundred people, then I will certainly let you be the one to sweet-talk this caterer into giving us information."

For once, Abby Ruth remained quiet.

You give excellent advice, Momma. It even works on overconfident Texans.

"Wow," Stella said in a low voice to Abby Ruth, "you're friend here is a real firecracker."

Firecracker. Oh, Lil loved the sound of that. If she weren't in her seventies, she might chant that old "Firecracker, firecracker" cheer and give a high kick to go along with it. *Boom boom boom.* Unfortunately, at her age, that could put her in traction.

Lil pointed across the ballroom to a tall gentleman with both a slight spare tire and an apron around his waist. He was in front of a wall of windows overlooking a lush garden. "He's the caterer."

"You sure?"

"See the way he's watching everyone do all the hard work and adjusting small things?" Lil took a tiny gold compact mirror out of her purse and pretended to fix her makeup, trying to look inconspicuous.

"Yep."

"That means he's the boss."

"Does he look familiar?" Abby Ruth asked Stella.

"I don't think so."

And he definitely didn't match Stella's description of a red-headed possum boy. "Why don't we stroll around the perimeter on our way to talk with the caterer? Stella might recognize someone."

Abby Ruth was staring at the catering staff with an intensity that said she wouldn't be beyond yanking them to the side and giving them a good frisk.

"Stop," Lil said in a low voice. "You're scaring people. They probably think you're the Health Department or something."

"She's right," Maggie said. "You catch more flies with honey than vinegar."

"Never understood that saying," Abby Ruth muttered. "Why would anyone want to catch flies in the first place? A fly ball maybe."

"I'm sorry." Stella lifted her hands palms up. "But I haven't seen a single person I recognize."

Lil slid a quick look toward Abby Ruth, who gave her a sharp head shake. She still didn't want to think her friend could be mistaken. So be it.

When they made it to the other side of the room, the caterer was fussing with the placement of parsley on a fruit plate. "Your melons look lovely," Lil said.

The caterer's head jerked up, and Abby Ruth made a choking sound.

"Although I much prefer the fatter, juicier Jubilee grapes, those smaller ones are sweet."

"Is there a reason you're critiquing my fruit?" The man frowned and took a step away from the table.

"Forgive me." Lil extended her hand and gave him a gracious smile. "I'm Lillian Summer Fairview, from over Summer Shoals way."

"Summer what?"

Oh. Well, that was embarrassing. But rather than lose her starch, Lil simply rolled her shoulders back. "Could you be so kind as to help us with something?"

He looked over her head, not particularly difficult to do, toward the door Lil assumed the bridal party would be coming through. When his attention returned to her, his eyes went squinty. "Oh, I know what you're doing. You're trying to hit the buffet before the rest of the guests arrive. You probably skipped out on the wedding before the vows were finished."

As if Lil would ever do something so incredibly rude. Then again, it might not be the smartest thing to admit they'd just strolled in off the street. "Actually, I'm one of the great-aunts on the bride's side. Before the wedding, she was panicked there wouldn't be enough staff to handle all the guests. Would you mind letting me look over your list of company servers?"

"Good one," Abby Ruth whispered behind her, and Lil's chest warmed with pride. She was starting to really get this thinking-on-her-feet thing. Prison did that for a woman.

"Company servers?" He snorted. "No such thing. Most of these kids are college students from Tech or Emory, trying to make money to supplement their tuition."

"So they're temps?" Maggie asked. "No benefits?"

"If I paid benefits, I wouldn't be able to afford to import a single grape from Chile."

Oh, dear. They would have to come clean. Sort of. Lil sidled closer to the table. "Let me explain what's really going on. Apparently, there's been a rash of petty thefts at these weddings." She nodded toward Stella. "In fact, my sister was a victim recently. Right here in this very venue."

The caterer stiffened as if she'd just grabbed hold of the slightly askew tablecloth and pulled all his trays to the floor.

"What are you saying? That you think someone in my employ is stealing from little old ladies?"

"Who're you calling old?" Abby Ruth growled and pointed to his thinning hair. "I'd be careful of throwing stones because your house sure looks like it's made of glass. Now, get that stick outta your butt, and tell us what we want to know about your staff."

Oh, why hadn't Lil thought to search Abby Ruth before they walked inside? It wasn't beyond the woman to tote her Glock around in unexpected places. Her concealed carry permit could be a real menace.

"Look around you." With a royal wave of his arm, the caterer gestured toward the crystal chandeliers above their heads and the plush carpet below their feet. "This isn't exactly the Moose Lodge. People who work weddings like this are carefully screened," he told them, his poor face turning the color of his grapes.

"So," Abby Ruth said, "you're telling me that you ran a background check on each one of these canapé carriers out here?"

"They know they'll lose their jobs if they do anything to make a guest unhappy. I would *not* tolerate theft because that would most certainly make a guest unhappy."

"And you pay your temps so much that they wouldn't be tempted?"

Stella grabbed hold of Abby Ruth's arm. "Let's just go. We're obviously upsetting this gentleman."

It was true. The vein in the caterer's right temple had become prominent, and the way it was throbbing was alarming. It wouldn't do for their key suspect to fall out and die before they could finish questioning him.

"I think he's hiding something," Abby Ruth said.

From the way his hair was parted from right to left instead of front to back, Lil was pretty sure he might be hiding hair plugs. But bad hair wasn't exactly a crime. Perhaps a crime against nature, but not against Stella.

"Do I need to have you removed from the premises?" he threatened.

Before Abby Ruth could go all Texas Ranger on the guy, Lil waved her friends toward the exit. Then she smiled at the caterer again, reached into her handbag, and retrieved one of her shiny G Team cards. "If you hear of anything unusual happening among your staff—temporary or otherwise—I would appreciate if you would give me a call."

With the way he turned his back on her, she had a feeling the only place that business card was going was down the garbage disposal.

ONCE THEY WERE ALL OUTSIDE IN THE PARKING LOT, STELLA glanced back at the fancy building. "That wasn't quite as fun as I'd expected."

Yeah, well, it hadn't been quite as *easy* as Abby Ruth had expected, but it did remind her each chase brought a special thrill. Stella, on the other hand, did not appear thrilled.

"Every piece of the puzzle brings us closer to an answer," Maggie explained. "Don't worry. We're good at this investigating stuff. We have a proven track record."

Stella chewed on her lip. "I understand that caterer being upset about us thinking his people had something to do with my purse being taken, but he didn't have to talk down to me. I know what happened. I'm not crazy."

"No one called you crazy," Abby Ruth consoled her.

"In fact, I'm not the only one who's had a problem like this. My friend Virginia lost an heirloom necklace when we were at the governor's daughter's wedding at the governor's mansion back in April. Not to mention the time the bride's ring disappeared at the Cumberland Resort wedding last summer." Stella hitched her purse up on her shoulder. "Even if they did decide a pesky Muscovy duck was the culprit *that* time."

"A duck?"

"The poor groom followed that duck around for two days collecting poo but never did recover the rings."

"That's terrible," Lil exclaimed, covering her left hand with her right.

Abby Ruth knew wedding rings were a sensitive subject to Lil. She'd almost lost hers to a pawnshop when she'd been in prison camp. If it hadn't been for Maggie, they'd be long gone. "You didn't tell me about these other incidents before."

"Virginia's necklace was definitely lost or stolen at the governor's," Stella continued. "It's possible she lost it while flirting with a handsome young man, but I sincerely doubt it. Too many coincidences if you ask me. Now I'm wondering if it was foul play."

"Ducks. Fowl play. I see what you did there." Maggie chuckled.

"I wasn't joking."

"Sorry." Maggie stepped back. "I didn't mean to make light."

"A necklace went missing at the governor's mansion?" Abby Ruth was even more interested now. "Didn't they have security?"

"You know the governor?" Lil closed in on Stella. "I've always wanted to meet the governor."

Abby Ruth gave Lil a not-right-now look. "What kind of necklace?"

Stella's eyes flashed with excitement. "The most beautiful Paraiba tourmaline. It's a beautiful bluish-green stone. Absolutely stunning, almost neon the way it shines."

"Did they have security cameras at the governor's mansion?"

"I'm not sure about cameras, but they had security guards. Virginia was working overtime on those good-looking security fellows. She's such a flirt, but I think she scared them off because those boys were nowhere to be found after she cornered a cute florist man."

"The florist?" Good gravy, this purse thing was become more and more complicated, which made the blood pump through Abby Ruth's body in a way that reminded her she was alive and able to kick bad-guy butt.

"Yes, the florist. And no, Lil, I don't actually know the governor."

"I still can't believe you crashed the governor's daughter's wedding," Maggie mused.

"Best hors d'oeuvres and champagne in the state." Stella smiled wide. "He got my vote after throwing that kind of a party."

"I'm starving." Maggie's stomach let out a teensy growl. "What did they serve at the reception? I love shrimp puffs."

"Me too! They served those and oysters on the half-shell. Come to think of it, maybe that's what had Virginia in overdrive that night. Oh, and mini lobster tacos. Have you ever heard of such a thing? They were delicious."

Maggie moaned. "Not your low-budget tea sandwich party."

"It was just like on the Food Network. They even had maple bourbon candied bacon."

"Bourbon? If you like bourbon then you have to try my special tea," Maggie said.

"I can't wait. Now that I've rung the bell, I plan to partake in a few drinks now and again. Did I mention miniature gourmet barbecue bites with beer shots and salted caramel doughnuts with gold leaf on them? I couldn't drink the beer shots, but boy, those doughnuts were delicious."

Abby Ruth muscled her way between the two women. "Could we take a commercial break here for a minute?"

Maggie mouthed *sorry*.

"Do you think we could talk to your wedding-crasher friends?" Abby Ruth asked.

"No." Stella spun toward her. "Absolutely not. We're sworn to secrecy. They'd kill me if they knew I'd told anyone about our outings, because they're pillars of society." She covered her face with her hands. "Why did I ever mention any of this?"

Maggie placed a gentle hand on Stella's shoulder. "Don't worry. Your secret is safe with us."

"Like hell it is," Abby Ruth said. "Listen here, Stella. You tell those girls to suck it up. We need answers." When Stella took a step back, Abby Ruth quickly amended her words. "Just kidding. Now let's lighten up and get our heads right about this. This may not only be about you and your purse."

"My goodness." Stella blinked. "Why didn't I put that together?"

"Because we're professionals." Abby Ruth wrapped an arm around Stella's shoulders. "Maybe we could meet with your friend Virginia and bring up the missing necklace in casual conversation. Not even mention the wedding."

"I can't break her trust." Stella lowered her head.

"Or maybe you could get the information for us." With a casual movement that mimicked her tone, she waved everyone toward the truck, careful not to pin Stella with a probing look. "We can tell you what to ask about the necklace incident."

"I guess I could see what I can find out."

"Great," Abby Ruth said, but sometimes she wished she was a badge-carrying investigator so she could wield more power and push people to do what she wanted. Because the truth was she had a feeling that dastardly duck could've been the fall guy for the crime. Or heck, maybe a whole string of wedding-related crimes.

Her palms dampened at the thought of a bigger case. Now this was the kind of problem that deserved their attention.

If Stella wasn't willing to give up the goods on her wedding-crasher friends, then Abby Ruth needed to find another way to wiggle her way into the wedding world.

The answer was suddenly so obvious that she laughed aloud. Wedding? Her daughter was smack-dab in the middle of that world right now. Or she would be once Abby Ruth convinced her that hitting the justice of the peace wasn't a good idea. That it would absolutely break her mother's heart.

Two birds. One stone. With Jenny's wedding less than three weeks away, the timing couldn't be more perfect.

Meanwhile, Abby Ruth would stick close to Stella. That was the best way to get intel on the next wedding her friend decided to crash.

CHAPTER 7

The next day, Abby Ruth stood on the front porch of a beautiful old church with Ritter at her side. The former house of worship had been converted to a family home, her daughter's and Teague's home. She sucked in a deep breath, readying herself to play the role of a lifetime. Guilt-inducing momma.

For today, Abby Ruth had settled on her normal jeans and boots, but hopefully she'd softened the effect by wearing a silk blouse with a draped neckline and bell sleeves that Sera had brought her back from her last trip to California.

She'd thought about putting on a skirt, but Maggie had wisely pointed out that she didn't own one. And if Abby Ruth had tried to wear one of Lil's, it would've been so short that she'd look like she was auditioning for a job at Gary's Gallery of Girls strip club.

Jenny had borrowed one of Lil's suits when Teague was running for sheriff, trying to make them into some modern day Jackie and JFK. Abby Ruth was pretty sure the only thing that had accomplished was a hot time between the sheets for the young couple.

Ah, to be in love.

And why did her thoughts go directly to Red?

She didn't want to believe she was still in love with him, but her own heart seemed to be turning on her, calling her a liar.

Red had hinted a few times over the past few months that he'd be more than happy for her to take his equipment out of the bag any time she liked.

Normally, she liked a good roll in the hay as well as the next gal. But she sure hadn't felt very sexy lately. Radiation and chemo would do that.

Maybe it was time to consider moving past the friendship stage they'd been stuck in while she was sick. Then again, she couldn't see doing that until Jenny knew the truth.

But that wasn't the reason she was here this morning.

She knocked on the castle-size double doors, and what sounded like a herd of wild bison thundered on the other side. "I'll get it," Grayson hollered.

Panting, he pulled open the door with Bowzer by his side. Both boy and dog had either been playing in the dirt or eating chocolate pudding. Her stomach growled. She hoped it was pudding. As tempted as she was to swipe a finger over Grayson's cheek and find out, she thought better of it.

But Ritter gave Grayson's cheek a big lick then ducked when Bowzer came careening across the threshold toward him. The puppy chased Ritter around the yard. He'd probably cause the old dog to have a heart attack. For a fleeting moment, she felt bad for thinking about Ritter's end-of-life stipend. In a quick sprint, he turned the game back on Bowzer, sending the puppy in a somersault, head over tail, toward the backyard. No, Ritter wasn't even close to dying. For the first time ever, that dog looked as if he had enough energy to fetch, run, and track.

Grayson hugged his belly in a fit of giggles as he watched the dogs.

"Whatcha up to today, sport?" Abby Ruth ruffled his hair.

Grayson laughed. "Bowzer and me were helping Teague plant roses out back with something mom calls man-ure."

Thankful she hadn't sampled the "pudding" on Grayson's face now, she said, "Does your mom know you're in the house with that all over you?"

"Uh..."

Bravely, she took him by the shoulders and pulled him outside, then marched him around to the side of the house. Bowzer loped toward them and happily followed along, his tail thumping against her leg hard enough to leave a bruise. Touching as little of her grandson as possible, she led him toward the hose. She spotted Teague pushing a wheelbarrow from the shed. His dark hair gleamed in the sunshine, and although he normally wore a starched khaki sheriff's uniform and felt cowboy hat, today he was dressed in battered tennis shoes, cargo shorts, and a T-shirt screen-printed with a massive pig eating a barbecue sandwich. Clothing choice aside, her Jenny sure had nabbed herself a handsome man.

She called out to him, "I found this one in the house."

"Grayson," Teague scolded. "I told you this was a shower-with-the-water-hose day. That means no going in the house until you've been hosed off."

Grayson gave his soon-to-be dad a salute and took off across the yard, his arms and legs pumping.

"Sure you want to have another one?" Abby Ruth nodded toward Grayson before she thought better of it. Sometimes she forgot Grayson wasn't of his blood.

Teague's eyes were a touch sad as he watched the boy. "Do you think the baby will change the way I feel about Grayson?"

"Absolutely not. You love him like he's your own," she said. "Far as I'm concerned, he is yours. Besides, do you think your momma stopped loving you when your younger sister was born?"

His grin, when it came, was quick and wicked. "She was sorta ugly as a baby."

"There you go. Between you and my hideous daughter, it's obvious your baby will probably have to wear a paper sack over its head." She started to pop Teague on the shoulder, but he had as much "pudding" on him as Grayson had. "You'll love that new baby just like your momma and daddy loved every one of their four kids. I don't know what it's like, only having had Jenny. But I'm quite certain there's enough love in your hearts for as many babies as you might want to make. Don't worry about that."

His face softened. "I'm scared spitless."

The laugh she let out was deep and truly amused. "Of course you are. People like to pretend this parenting thing is a spin on a carousel. Truth is, it's one of those spider-whip rides that makes you toss your cotton candy when you stumble off."

"And yet you always want to get right back on, right?"

"Right, because kids may be hard work, but they're worth every bit of it." She pointed toward the house. "Jenny inside?"

"Yep," he said. "Back door is open. Go on in."

He grabbed the wheelbarrow again and headed for the flowerbed, and Abby Ruth found herself patting her hair as if she were primping for a date before she opened the back door. She called for Ritter, more to give him a break from the puppy than anything else. Plus, she could use a distraction to keep her calm for this discussion with Jenny.

Oh, for goodness sake. If you can beat cancer, you can handle this.

Somehow offering to throw her daughter a big hoopla of a wedding seemed scarier, though.

When Abby Ruth entered the house with Ritter at her side, Jenny was just closing the front door. "Did you knock at the front door earlier?"

"Yep. Why didn't you answer?"

"I was cooking."

Her boots thudding against the lovingly scarred wood floors, Abby Ruth wandered over to the kitchen counter. "What is it? Is it dead?"

Jenny poked at what appeared to be an over-baked chicken with the tip of her knife. The rainbow of color coming in from the former church's arched cathedral windows made the bird look as if it was covered with some type of iridescent bacteria. "I think so."

"I suggest takeout," Abby Ruth said.

Jenny's mouth dropped.

"Don't feel bad. Takeout is my best recipe. Must run in the family."

"I can cook," Jenny said.

She was much better in the kitchen than Abby Ruth had ever been, but some things were better left to the professionals. "Being able to doesn't always mean you should."

"You're right. I think this might turn into a Pizza Pie In The Sky night." Jenny set down her knife with a decisive clang. "So, what brings you by today?"

"Just decided I wanted to see what y'all have been doing with the backyard. Jenny…" She hesitated, feeling like ten kinds of fool.

Concern immediately filled Jenny's face. "Is everything okay? You're not feeling—"

"I'm fine. Bell rung, remember?"

Tears clearly visible in her eyes, Jenny came around the

counter and wrapped her in a hug. "I can't do this without you. Please stay well. This baby needs her mimi."

"And she'll damn well have one. But she won't have a proper daddy if you don't get yourself married."

Jenny sniffle-laughed. "Oh, he definitely wasn't proper the night we made this baby."

"He would poke himself in the ears if he heard you say that in front of me."

She pulled back, her grin lessening Abby Ruth's fear of her tears spilling over. "What about you and Red? Don't you think it's about time to let him have his improper way with you?"

Although she'd recently been thinking the same thing, this wasn't the conversation she and Jenny would have today.

"Jenny, I have a favor to ask of you."

"Anything you want, Mom," she said with no hesitation. Then she threw a look at the poor excuse of a baked chicken she'd made. "Except wrestle with that thing anymore."

"Better to let it die in peace. Speaking of which, I know you said that you and Teague planned to just do the justice of the peace thing, but I want you to reconsider."

"What?"

"Don't you want pretty pictures of your wedding day? I bet Grayson would love to be the ring bearer or maybe the best man. Both. Is that legal? I'll find out."

"Slow down, Mom. If I push this wedding off one more day, Teague will lose his mind. The only reason it's almost three weeks away is because I told him Sera couldn't be here any sooner."

"That's plenty of time to throw together—" Abby Ruth winced inside at her own words, "—put something nice together. Lil would really like to host the wedding at Summer Haven. She and Maggie are spiffying the place up as we speak."

"What has gotten into you? Teague and I just need to get married and be done with it."

"But he's the sheriff." Abby Ruth was willing to push whichever button would get her what she wanted. "You owe it to the county to let them join in the celebration. Let's give this marriage the start it deserves."

At that moment, Ritter decided to make himself at home, and before either of them could stop him, he had his paws on the counter and was lapping up the juice on the chicken.

"No!" Abby Ruth yelled, grabbing him by his collar and pulling him out of reach of the food. That was all she needed, a dog with some kind of food poisoning. "Sorry. He's got no manners. But you do, and you should have the wedding that Teague needs to secure his future as an elected official of this town."

Jenny took in a breath as if she was going to argue, then stopped. "Do you really think it's that important?"

"It would make so many people happy, including me. And Jenny, I'd really like to coordinate the whole thing."

JENNY FELT AS IF SOMEONE HAD PLUCKED HER FROM REALITY and dropped her into the middle of a cartoon—the kind where the main character shook her head so wildly that marbles rattled loudly inside. "What did you just say?"

Please tell me this is a dream.

"I want to coordinate your wedding. Sugar—" her mother wrapped an arm around her shoulders and strolled her toward the living room, "—y'all owe this to yourselves and to the community. I want to do this for you."

She dragged her feet, trying to slow her mom down, but there was no stopping the steamroller named Abby Ruth Cady. "There's no time, but I appreciate the sentiment." True, even though it was weird since her mom had never shown an interest in planning any kind of girly party, much less a wedding. "Maybe you could throw us a small celebration afterwards. Then everyone will be happy."

"That won't do at all." Her mom's voice was calm, almost sweet, but her eyebrow was arched up like a question mark, and her lips were pulled so tight Jenny could've strummed a D chord on them. That look on her mother's face put an icy fear in her. "Be reasonable."

As they faced off in the living room, Teague walked inside with Grayson at his side, both in soaking wet clothes head to toe.

"This town wants to see the two of you tie the knot. After all, Teague owes these folks his job and the food he puts on the table, scary as some of it may be." Her mom turned to Teague and speared him with the look that had made three-hundred-pound linebackers cry for their mommas. "Isn't that right, Tadpole?"

Jenny prayed he'd pick up on her telepathy and offer an intervention, but he was nodding thoughtfully. *Traitor.*

Abby Ruth poked Jenny in the shoulder, sending her quickly to a seated position on the couch.

"But..." Jenny didn't need to lift her head to know that her mother was looming above her.

"Here's how it's going to be. After my cancer scare last year, I don't want to miss one important moment of our lives. Your wedding to Teague is something I've been waiting for since you were in middle school together. This is way overdue."

Oh, she had not just played the sick card. How could Jenny argue with that?

"Teague?" Jenny looked at her husband-to-be. Surely he would stop her mom's insanity.

"I'm sure your dear momma will be thrilled to hear you're having a real wedding," Abby Ruth said to him. "I bet you anything she cried when she found out y'all planned to get hitched down at the courthouse, didn't she? I can call her for you, Tadpole. Let her know to make travel plans."

"That'd be great." Teague grinned, making Jenny want to tell him to go to his room in her best mom voice. Which she would the second she'd caught the breath her mom had verbally sucker-punched out of her.

Grayson ran to her side. "Can I be the ring barrel?"

"Ring bearer," Teague corrected him.

"You sure can, sport," her mom assured him. "I did some research. My friend Stella is an expert on weddings, and she recommended the best florist in Atlanta."

"Whoa," Teague said. "Winnie does everyone's flowers in this town."

Abby Ruth sputtered. "My point exactly. You need an even better florist. Extra special. Trust me, you're going to love it. I'll bring you samples."

"Mom, we owe it to our community to use local vendors."

"See, so you *are* in."

"I didn't say that." Sometimes Jenny forgot that her mom had been a shrewd reporter who'd been able to weasel the tiniest tidbits out of professional athletes. Times like this, she saw why her mom had been so successful in such a male-dominated field. She could run roughshod over the best of them.

"I have to run." With a suspicious grin on her face, her mom hustled toward the front door. "I'm picking up Maggie to go talk to the cake people."

"But you don't even know what we want," Jenny said, her heart sinking with the certainty that her wedding was now out of her hands. "Or how many people."

"I'm the wedding planner. I know everything." Abby Ruth gave Grayson a noogie on the head and waved over her shoulder as she walked out the front door.

Jenny sank into the couch cushions, letting them support her bulldozed body. "I can't believe that just happened."

"I don't know why. She's been doing that to me ever since I've known her." Teague sloshed over and pulled her up and into his arms, the water from his clothes seeping in to hers.

She pressed her forehead against his chest, cooling what felt like a fever of confusion. "What happened to our private little wedding?"

"Your mom has been through a lot. We should give it to her. My mother was disappointed when I told her there'd be no wedding."

The fight was slowly being sapped out of her. "But we said it would be small."

"Come on. Gives us all an excuse to get together. It won't be so bad."

She relaxed into his arms. "Sweet Jesus. There's no telling what kind of circus she'll put together."

"Maybe we can have doves fly at the wedding," Grayson said. "I saw that on television. It was so cool."

Jenny pressed her hands against Teague's chest, putting some space between them. "You know if Mom has us release doves that she'll try to shoot them out of the air."

Teague laughed. "With her aim, she'd probably get a perfect score. Think we should have a prize?"

"For sure. It would be a regular carnival." She glared at him. "You might want to wear Kevlar if you're making those kinds of comments. I'm not a bad shot either."

"I heard when women get pregnant they can get a little cranky. Is this a warning shot?"

"Don't push it, Castro."

CHAPTER 8

Now that she'd convinced Jenny that she was the perfect choice for wedding coordinator, it was time for Abby Ruth to put her new role to good work. Next step was to attend a wedding with Stella's crasher buddies. So she'd invited Stella out for an early supper at an Italian place south of Atlanta.

Stella walked into the restaurant and settled at the table with Abby Ruth. The drawing paper tablecloth crinkled as she scooted in her chair. "Goodness, we keep eating like this and I might gain back that fifteen pounds I lost."

Picking up a crayon the waitress had left, Abby Ruth sketched out a little bride and groom. "Well, a gal can't live on cake and champagne alone."

Stella was no dummy. She pursed her mouth and gave Abby Ruth a pointed stare. "I've told you all I know."

"But your friends—"

"Won't be my friends anymore if I spill their secrets."

If Stella wouldn't out her friends as wedding crashers, Abby Ruth would have to channel Sera's bang-up computer skills and do an internet search to make a short list of the best wedding venues within thirty miles of Atlanta. She'd sure rather do this the easy way, though. "Whatever you say, but you see, my daughter is getting married and I wanted to ask you about your favorite venues. Nothing but the best for my Jenny."

Unfortunately, the waitress strolled up about then and asked, "What can I get you girls?"

"Sweet tea for me," Abby Ruth said quickly.

"Me too." Stella set her phone on the table, then hung her purse from the handy dandy purse holder contraption she always carried around. "I'm going to run to the little girls' room."

Luck was on Abby Ruth's side, because darn if Stella's friend Virginia didn't text right after Stella turned the corner.

Abby Ruth's body might be aging, but she still had the eyesight of a twenty-year-old. Stella didn't, so her icons and font were super-sized, and it was easy to read the text from clear across the table.

VIRGINIA: ATL Botanical Garden Sat 1pm. C U There.

Aha, so that was the next wedding those women planned to attend for the teensy price of a ten-dollar donation. Excellent, because it was one of the top venues on Abby Ruth's list.

Stella returned to the table and glanced at her phone, then turned it facedown. They ate salads and pasta, and Abby Ruth tried to draw the meal out as long as possible, tossing out probing questions now and then. Unfortunately, Stella didn't offer up any information, so Abby Ruth would have to use the intel she'd gathered from the text.

Now that she had a true starting point for this investigation, she had to force herself to maintain the speed limit all the way home. Things were starting to fall into place, and she could hardly wait to talk to the girls to tell them they'd be attending a wedding this weekend. She'd even be willing to wear a frilly jacket. Hell, she'd put a flower in her best Stetson for this occasion, and normally she had a no-flower policy.

Except when she got home, Lil and Maggie had already turned in for the evening. What were they? Old ladies?

So she headed to the garage to check on Ritter. Strangely, his normally dusty coat was shiny, and a bandanna was tied around his neck.

"What happened to you? You look fourteen doggy years younger there, buddy," she said, giving him a scratch under the chin. She expected him to lean in to her touch, but he simply snuffled her palm and turned away. That's when she realized he smelled of…flowers?

Seeing as he wasn't all that interested in her investigative plans and the gals were already asleep, Abby Ruth spent a night dreaming of bad-guy take-downs. She woke up twisted in her covers as though a cowboy had taken a piggin' string to her with two half-hitches and a hooey.

She jumped from bed at the first ray of sunshine, raring to get going on the G Team's newest case. She hummed "Friends In Low Places" as she descended the stairs to feed Ritter. She opened the garage door, and he gave what looked like a yoga stretch. He didn't even get excited when she filled his bowl with kibble. Just sniffed and sat down by his meal.

"You okay, fella?" She kicked the toe of her boot against his dish. "Better eat." He lay down, his ears spreading out over each side of his paws. "Not hungry? Then come on inside with me for a while." He jumped to his feet and pranced alongside.

Back inside the house, it was obvious Lil and Maggie were already up from the chatter coming from the parlor.

Excitement two-stepped through Abby Ruth. She and the gals would waltz right into that wedding today and check things out. Maybe even solve Stella's case right out of the chute.

Although in a way she kind of hoped it might take a little longer. She was ready for some fun.

When she strolled into the parlor with Ritter behind her, it looked as if a magazine stand had exploded. Every tabletop was full of wedding paraphernalia. Magazines lay open, pages turned back to fancy finger foods, frilly dresses, and prissy decorations.

Abby Ruth lifted a roll of flimsy fabric. "What *is* all this?" She propped her hands on her hips, her right toe tapping.

Lil glanced up, a twinkle in her eye and a bright smile on her face. "Dear, we do have a wedding to plan, and less than three weeks to do it. Since you haven't done a cotton-picking thing, I thought I'd give you a hand. Time's a wasting."

She stood there, unable to look away from what was surely a train wreck.

"Or have you already forgotten?" Lil asked.

Ritter tromped across the room and lay down at Lil's feet. *Better her than me.* "No, I haven't forgotten, but it's one little wedding. This?" She swung her arm as if she'd turned the last letters on the *Wheel of Fortune* wall. "This could plan weddings for every debutante from Georgia to Texas, and we could probably toss in an Oklahoma bride or two."

"It's not as much as it might seem." Lil stacked a few of the magazines.

It didn't make things look any better to Abby Ruth. "I thought we were concentrating on the case."

"We are, but we can multitask. It's a good thing I have oodles of experience planning parties. You'll be tickled pink to know that the bridal show is in Atlanta this week too. We can solve for so many things in one place. It'll be perfect."

"Simple." Plans for Jenny's wedding were spinning out of control. "Let's keep it simple."

"We have to do right by Jenny and Teague though. I mean, some things you shouldn't shortchange," Lil said.

The muscle in Abby Ruth's jaw got a mini workout as she tried to maintain control. "I would never shortchange a thing when it comes to my daughter's happiness."

"We know that." Maggie laid a hand on Abby Ruth's arm. "Calm down. We'll keep the wedding simple. Simply beautiful."

She needed their help, but this…this was over the top. *Simple* to Lillian Summer Fairview wasn't in the same ballpark as Abby Ruth's concept of *simple*.

She'd been so hopeful they'd rekindle some fun and excitement with this case. She really hadn't thought about how they would juggle the investigation and Jenny's wedding. This mess was one helluva wakeup call about how complex a wedding was to plan. This wedding stuff wasn't going to be fun at all.

Lil frowned. "If we're hosting a wedding at Summer Haven, we *will* give it the attention it deserves. This is the most important day in a lady's life." Lil crossed the room carrying a glossy white hardcover book half open in her arms. "I've already filled some things in for you."

"What the heck is that thing? It's the size of an unabridged dictionary."

Lil tipped the fancy white book in Abby Ruth's direction. "It's a wedding planner, of course."

For heaven's sake. Thick as that book was, they could be organizing the logistics of the Super Bowl. Abby Ruth glanced at the contents. "I think we can mark off about half this stuff." She grabbed the pencil from behind Lil's ear and crossed off the bridesmaids' and groomsmen's tasks. "See, we're a quarter of the way done."

"Hardly, but we are well underway. We'll need the guest list, but I'm thinking one hundred chairs, give or take.

Maggie is checking into borrowing them from Dogwood Ridge Assisted Living and the bingo hall for free since she did some work for them both earlier this year. We have to watch our budget, right?"

"Budget?" Abby Ruth sped-read through the list. "I guess I better set one." Not that it mattered. She had a nest egg that would cover this wedding, and if it meant going into debt, she didn't care. Seeing Jenny and Teague finally together, the way it should've been long ago, was worth any price to her.

Lil flipped the page. The two facing pages were filled with yet more tasks.

"This is impossible," Abby Ruth said, suddenly overwhelmed with the reality of planning and hosting a wedding in just over two weeks. "All I wanted was to have some fun and get the G Team back in gear. Jenny's wedding planning seemed like a good way to get some information for the case. I didn't mean for it to be the shindig of the year. I can't believe I'm saying this, but I think I've bitten off more than I can chew."

"Don't be silly. We'll all help. I just got off the phone with Sera, and she's handling the invitations."

"And Darrell Holloway said we can use all his white twinkle lights. He'll get the Christmas boxes from storage this weekend."

"Lovely," Lil said, scribbling furiously in the fancy planner. "We can accent light the gazebo and drape twinkle lights through the trees. It will be magical."

Abby Ruth groaned. "It's a *June* wedding. Who needs Christmas lights?"

"White lights are all-purpose. Leave this to us. Also, I hope you don't mind..." Lil said cautiously, which told Abby Ruth she would *not* like whatever was to follow. "...but I called Jenny and asked her about the colors for the wedding and a few other things. She gave us carte blanche, so I'm thinking a soft blue would be nice. If that's okay with you, Abby Ruth?"

"I guess." What did she know about picking a color for a wedding?

"You should wear a blue dress," Lil insisted.

"I'm not wearing a dress."

"But—"

Abby Ruth raised her chin, which communicated better than a slew of words. Lil switched gears like a NASCAR racer on the last straightaway to the checkered flag.

"We'll deal with that later. Jenny doesn't want to write vows, so we're going traditional. A few I do's and done. Nothing to do there. Check." Lil checked off a couple more tasks. "And who will give the bride away?"

"She's her own woman. Skip that part." Abby Ruth's gut knotted. She sure as hell wasn't opening that can of worms right now. Forever if she had her druthers, but Red would never let that happen. And his deadline was ticking closer with every minute.

"You could walk her down the aisle," Maggie added. "That's very common these days."

"No," she barked the word and regretted it immediately. Even Ritter flinched, and she wasn't sure how well that hound could hear. The expressions on Maggie's and Lil's faces stabbed at her, making guilt rise. She dropped to the couch, head in her hands. Her friends didn't understand what was really going on here. "I'm sorry. I didn't mean to snap. But I need you to slow down all the walking-down-the-aisle stuff right now. It's more than I can take."

"We're here for you," Maggie said as she and Lil plopped down on either side of her.

"I can't do this."

Lil slapped the book closed. "Oh dear. I've overwhelmed

you. Please don't worry. I've planned a million parties. It's totally in my wheelhouse. Don't you worry about a thing."

"She really is the best," Maggie said, placing a hand on Abby Ruth's back. "It's short notice, but if anyone can do it, we can."

"You don't understand," she mumbled into her palms. What had made her believe today would be a great day? Old personal baggage was like an uninvited party guest, always ruining a good time.

"I think we do," Lil said gently. "Party planning isn't your thing."

"There's more." Better spit it out before she chickened out. "Jenny's father will be there."

Lil and Maggie looked at each other, then back at her. "Jenny doesn't know her father," Maggie said.

"But you do." Abby Ruth's voice went up an octave, her throat scratchy. "It's Red. Red is Jenny's father."

"What?" Maggie slumped as if all her bones had been sucked out of her skin.

"I can't believe I didn't see the resemblance before," Lil said. "The nose. Yes. Even more so in Grayson."

Abby Ruth nodded.

Lil sat back, her arms pulled tight across her body. "But he's been here since—"

"You don't have to tell me." She swallowed hard. "And if I don't tell her soon, Red will do it himself."

"You can't let that happen."

"She'll hate me."

"This is definitely a delicate situation. Jenny will probably feel betrayed. After all, Red has been a part of our daily lives and the community for the past year. And yet you never told her. Never told any of us."

Abby Ruth regretted that so many people's feelings were being hurt by her choice to keep the past in the past. What had seemed so logical all those years ago felt twisty, selfish, and complex now. "I never expected him to steal back into our lives." She didn't mean just as Jenny's father either. As much as she hated to admit it, Red had stolen back into her life and her heart too.

"The good thing is Jenny already loves him," Maggie said. "We all do."

"I'm not sure if that's better or worse." Abby Ruth closed her eyes. "He wants to walk his daughter down the aisle."

"Can you blame him?" Lil asked. "She's smart and beautiful. He has to be so proud of her. But I don't understand why he never tried to be a part of her life before now."

"He didn't even know about her until..." Abby Ruth swallowed hard. "Until he ran into us in Atlanta."

"You never told *him* either?"

"It was complicated, and I thought it was best for everyone." She raised a palm. "No lectures. No judgment. I can't change the past. Now I have to make it right."

"When will you tell her?"

"Soon." But her heart pounded so hard at the thought that she wasn't sure how she would break it to Jenny. If she hadn't found the right time all these years, how did she expect to do it now?

"You should talk to her immediately," Maggie offered. "We'll come with you."

"Not today because we have somewhere important to go." Abby Ruth was thankful for the diversion Stella's text had inadvertently offered her. "I found out Stella and her friends are hitting a wedding today. It's the perfect opportunity to look for a bad guy and shake him down." She jumped to her feet. "Let's go crash the wedding crashers at the botanical garden in Atlanta. This case is on."

"But Stella seemed dead set against us meeting her friends. How did you convince her to let us help?"

"Things just sort of fell into place," Abby Ruth hedged.

Lil put her hands on her hips. "She doesn't know, does she?"

"Don't give me that look." Abby Ruth avoided making eye contact with Lil. "Besides, I now know why Stella was so resistant to it. One of her friends, Virginia, is married to Sinclair LeFleur."

"Isn't Virginia the one Stella described as…flirty?"

"Yeah, but apparently *flirty* is putting it kindly," Abby Ruth said, followed by a snarky snort.

"She's married to the owner of LeFleur Publishing? Don't they publish books about family values and stuff like that?"

"That's the one." Abby Ruth loved it when she had their full attention. "And apparently, Penelope is married to Ted Wesley."

"He's one of the biggest TV preachers in history. Why on earth would these women crash parties? Certainly they could get an invitation to any event they'd like."

"Guess that's part of the fun. I think it'll be fun for us too. In the name of bringing justice, of course."

"Abby Ruth, you still have to tell Jenny about Red," Lil said. "Don't think switching the subject makes that go away."

She took in a breath. She was living with the consequences of decisions that had once seemed so cut and dry. They sure didn't seem so now. "I'll tell her tomorrow night."

Lil glanced away, and the lines etched across Maggie's forehead resembled kindergarten writing paper.

"I promise," Abby Ruth said. "By Monday."

"Fine," Lil finally said. "I know you're a woman of your word. So why are we still standing here? We have a wedding to attend."

CHAPTER 9

Saturday turned out to be a perfect day for a garden wedding. Lil had taken it upon herself to make sure they all looked presentable for such an affair. Even if that had meant an exhausting morning trying to coerce Abby Ruth into a dress, a failed attempt. At least she'd compromised and changed into a soft gray pair of trousers and one of Lil's few remaining designer blouses.

Lil had barely been able to contain her excitement on the long ride up to the Atlanta Botanical Garden. Not only was she getting the chance to dress up, gloves and all, but the anticipation of an investigation was exhilarating.

As they waited outside the garden until the wedding I-do's were done, timing their entrance into the reception with the rest of the guests, the reality of what they were about to do sank in. Anxiety in the form of sweat under the jacket of her favorite fitted suit—sea foam with an A-line skirt and worn with dyed-to-match pumps—had her squirming and struggling for a gulp of air.

"This feels a little unethical," Lil whispered to Maggie as

they wove their way through well-dressed wedding guests to a huge white tent in the rose garden.

"That's slightly funny coming from you, Lil," Maggie whispered back. "Relax. It's business."

"I know, but..."

Maggie placed her hands on Lil's shoulders. "This G Team thing is one for all, and you're the one who decided we should have an official identity. We aren't breaking any laws."

True. But it was still uncomfortable for Lil to use other people's social occasions to further her own agenda.

Up ahead, Abby Ruth was following a step behind Stella, who had yet to spot them. Lil and Maggie triple-stepped to catch up to Abby Ruth. Before their threesome could get to her side, Stella joined a group of women.

One was tall and slim with rounded shoulders. Another was possibly shorter than Lil herself, and that was saying something.

Maggie leaned over and said, "I could probably put that woman in my pocket."

Lil smothered a laugh and slapped Maggie lightly on the arm.

The third woman, a short-haired brunette with breasts rivaling Dolly's, had to be Virginia because there was no disguising a sexpot, no matter her age. She was balancing on four-inch heels, as pretty as you please. And not wedges or those square heels. These things were needle sharp and the color of a pomegranate. Her cocktail dress was made from a shimmery silver fabric and had a neckline that made it clear this was a woman who took care of her décolletage.

Once again, Maggie had a comment. "Wish my neck and cleavage looked like that."

"Not to be catty, but what you're looking at is either the result of an expensive French cream or a nip and tuck."

"Definitely not interested in the nip and tuck, and I'd

never remember to slap on pricey face goo even if I could afford it."

Lil gave her a quick hug. "It's a lot of work to look that nice, and let's be honest, you'd much rather spend time hammering nails."

"Amen."

By this time, she and Maggie had drawn close to Stella and her friends, but before they could devise a plan, Abby Ruth stormed right up to them.

That Texan would be the death of Lil.

"I can't believe it. Is that you, Stella?" Abby Ruth made quick work of inserting herself into the center of their group. "How long has it been?"

"Not that long." Stella's eyes had a wild and cornered glint to them. Rightfully so. Abby Ruth had that effect on most people, but rather than raise a fuss, Stella introduced everyone.

The taller woman's name was Juliette, and the fairy-sized one was Penelope. When Virginia reached out to shake hands, Lil could certainly see why someone might be tempted to take a jewel or two from her. She was wearing an emerald ring as big as a Greek olive.

Lil didn't have much good jewelry left after she'd had to keep herself afloat when Harlan died, but she knew paste when she was looking at it. None of the pieces Virginia wore on her hand, wrist, throat, or ears was a fake. If Lil had to guess, she was toting around at least $100,000 worth of jewelry.

Heck, that would make a nun look twice.

"So nice to meet you," she said to Virginia.

"Likewise." Virginia had one of those long Southern drawls that made every word sound like a song.

Maggie pointed to an empty table a short distance away. "Why don't we find a place to sit?"

Once they were all settled, with Abby Ruth on one side of Virginia and Stella on the other, they all smiled politely at one another. Awkward as that was, Lil could tell that Abby Ruth was itching to start questioning the woman. Abby Ruth wasn't one for small talk.

"Lovely reception," Lil commented, and that was no lie. Every nook and cranny had obviously been carefully planned. White ladder-back chairs decorated with pink pomanders flanked guest tables laden with silver and delicate china and beautiful centerpieces with mini-fountains bubbling over shiny iridescent stones.

Covered with fresh tea roses on a mirrored surface, even the cake table looked as if it could grace the cover of a magazine.

"Who knew we had friends in the same circles?" Abby Ruth said to Stella.

Stella's lips were twitching. "Indeed."

"I have friends everywhere," Virginia said as she scanned the crowd. She wiggled her fingers in a flirty little wave toward a waiter who couldn't have been more than twenty-five. "Well, you know *friends* can mean such a wide variety of things."

Abby Ruth leaned in, elbows on the table, which made Lil want to pick up a fork and poke her. So rude. "How so?" Abby Ruth asked.

"Well, you know. Sometimes a girl just needs a good party," Virginia said.

Abby Ruth did a pretty good fake appalled expression with rounded eyes and mouth. "Oh, you mean *those* kind of friends."

Lil was ready to award Abby Ruth the Oscar. If she didn't know this was a big fat fishing expedition she'd have bought the whole act. Standing-ovation-worthy performance for sure.

"Gonna have to be our secret." Virginia spread her arms out across the table, wagging her forefingers back and forth. "Don't you tell anyone."

"I'd never." Abby Ruth crossed her heart and flashed a wicked grin.

Excellent. They now had an opening to ask Virginia questions about her *friends*. Lil said brightly, "Who feels like having a glass of champagne?"

As she'd hoped, all hands at the table went up except Abby Ruth's. "Think I could get a Bud Light?"

"Of course," Lil said. "Stella, why don't you and I go get in line for the bar?"

"No," Virginia protested. "Standing in line for a drink will get us into trouble."

Abby Ruth nudged Stella. "Isn't that half the fun?"

Stella blushed. "You and I know it, but I wasn't talking about *that* kind of trouble. Well…" Looking across the group of women, she suddenly let out a breath. "We're all friends here. Conversations start in the drink line and well, we aren't exactly friends of the bride. We wouldn't want any problems."

"I don't much like her either." Abby Ruth played along.

"Or the groom," Virginia said, her gaze darting toward the wedding party's table.

"Oh." Lil nodded politely. No need to tell Virginia that the G Team had crashed the wedding too.

"Your secret is safe with me, but I'm ready for a beer," said Abby Ruth.

"Since our friends can't stand in line, why don't you and Maggie go then?" Lil said.

Although Abby Ruth grumbled, she rose from the table and followed Maggie to the long line of folks snaking around the portable bar.

Lil scooched closer to Virginia, "That's such a beautiful bracelet. Is it a family heirloom?"

"Not exactly." She touched the stone on her hand, then the ones around her throat. "My third husband, Marvin, loved me in green. And who was I to deny him a little pleasure?"

"Aren't you worried about wearing something that expensive? I heard you recently…"

Stella was making a chopping motion across her throat, a gesture Lil had no problem understanding. She wasn't ready for Lil to bring up Virginia's missing necklace.

They had to do something here. Maybe cut Virginia from the herd and get her alone.

Surprisingly, Maggie and Abby Ruth were back much faster than Lil would've imagined with that bar line. "That was quick."

Abby Ruth flashed her sharp smile to the table at large. "It's funny what flirting with an eighty-year-old man will get you."

"If you're not careful," Maggie muttered, "it'll get you another four hundred-year-old dog."

Oh, Lord. That was all they needed.

A waitress stopped and passed around generously sized glasses from a shiny silver tray. Lil lifted hers and took a sip. Not just sparkling wine, but excellent champagne. What a treat.

If they served wine this delicious at all the receptions, Lil figured the wedding crashers might ought to drop in at least a twenty in the card box, but she politely kept that to herself.

"So, Virginia, do you attend a good number of weddings?"

"More than I can count," Virginia said. "Better than hitting funerals. All you get at those are casseroles and fruit punch. Right, Juliette?"

Juliette said, "Everyone needs a hobby."

Virginia had already tossed back her first glass of champagne and was flagging down a waiter. Instead of selecting one glass from his tray, she took one for each hand. Well, this was good news.

Lil jerked her head toward the buffet table and said to Abby Ruth, "My that food smells delicious, but my bursitis is acting up. I don't want to hold the rest of you back though."

Thank goodness, both Abby Ruth and Maggie seemed to understand her hint and they encouraged Stella, Juliette, and Penelope to join them in checking out—in Abby Ruth's words—the vittles.

To Lil's luck, Virginia had somehow procured her fourth and fifth glasses of wine. She was chugging it back like fruit punch, smiling and waving at every man who walked by.

Goodness gracious, if she always indulged like this, it was no wonder the woman was missing jewelry. It wouldn't surprise Lil to see her jerk off her necklace, twirl it around, and toss it into the crowd.

"You mentioned you'd been married three times. Were all your husbands generous when it came to buying you jewelry?"

"Five."

"I'm sorry?"

"Been hitched—" she gave a polite little hiccup, "—five ti-imes."

"Oh my."

"But to answer your question, getting men to give me pretty things is my superpower."

"I can imagine you're very careful with your baubles then."

"Try to be, but sometimes things happen. Lost a necklace at a wedding not all that long ago."

"What happened? Do…do you think someone stole it?" Lil ventured, trying to draw out information.

Virginia's eyes went soft, and she heaved a sigh that threatened to let her girls loose from her neckline. "I can't really be sure. It may have slipped off during the hustle bustle, if you know what I mean, but he was *so* worth it. The Pettiway wedding. Lord, that was a good one." Virginia made eye contact with a passing waiter and gave him a wink. "Yes, indeed. So worth it."

Worth it? Stella had mentioned a flirtation with a younger man. It sounded like Virginia's MO at these weddings was to slip away and have a rendezvous with a man. Maybe one of her paramours had taken her necklace. "So it was someone you'd seen before?"

"No. I think maybe he was the florist. Calla and something. They're out of Atlanta. I remember thinking there wasn't anything flowery about him. He was more like a tree." Virginia fanned her face and took another drink of her champagne. "Tuck. Yes. That was his name. He was one sweet, sweet oak tree, if you know what I mean. Big. Strong. And his eyes were greener than leaves in the springtime." She shimmied her shoulders. "All my husbands have been either blond or dark-haired, but I had a yen for a ginger that night."

"A ginger?" Ooh, that matched Stella's description of Possum Boy. This information was promising. "Did he happen to have a mustache?"

She frowned as if having a hard time remembering. "No? Well, I'm not really for certain. No. Absolutely not. I prefer my men clean-shaven." She squeezed Lil's forearm. "I do hate a whisker burn. Don't you?"

Shoot, Virginia's gentleman didn't sound like a match to Stella's, but before Lil could ask more questions, an obnoxious hee-haw song came blasting out of a nearby speaker, and the DJ said cheerfully, "Now c'mon, y'all! It's time for that crowd favorite, the Chicken Dance!"

Four squawking blasts from an accordion had Virginia

rocketing from her seat. She grabbed Lil by the arm to pull her to her feet. "You heard the man, c'mon."

"No, dear, I couldn't." Lil tried to wrap an ankle around the leg of her chair, but that Virginia was one strong gal, yanking her right to her feet.

The woman had the audacity to slap Lil on the rear end. "Live a little. Get out there and shake your groove thing because ain't no man gonna take your poodle for a walk if it looks like he'd have to drag it around by a leash."

Why in the world did everything have to be about dogs these days? Her focus having slipped for a few seconds, Lil was dragged to the edge of the dance floor before she knew what was what.

"Lil!" Maggie hollered. "What're y'all doing?"

Virginia yelled back, "Get your fannies on the dance floor, ladies."

No way was Lil going out there and making a fool of herself alone. She gestured wildly for Maggie and Abby Ruth to join them. Abby Ruth refused, standing at the edge of the dance floor with her arms folded, but the rest of the wedding crashers boogied their way into the crowd.

Virginia was a steamroller, cutting through people to lead them to the middle of the dance floor. Lil was almost decapitated by one man's wayward elbow, but she ducked at the last second and her hip spasmed. "You know what, I think I'll just go sit over—"

Virginia jerked her forward, and the group of them somehow made an unlikely circle around the bride, groom, and what appeared to be a set of their parents. Lil had never participated in this Chicken Dance before in her life, but elbows were flapping, hands were quacking, and people were doing a funky wiggle all the way to the floor.

"Twist it, sister!" Virginia said to Lil.

So she did, and goodness did her bursitis object to that,

but then it became kind of fun. Still she sidled closer to Virginia as she clapped and turned with the beat. They needed more information about the man who'd taken her jewels. Lil swung her arms and spun around, colliding with a handsome young man who caught her by the hands.

"Oh, I'm so sorry." She steadied herself against his strong biceps, circled by a tattoo of some kind of flower. Normally, she wasn't impressed by young men who put ink on their bodies, but this gentleman's blue eyes flashed with intelligence, and his smile made her legs woozy.

He brushed a hand through his dark hair before putting his hands under his armpits and flapping. "Go, girl!"

Lil wiggled her bottom and turned her focus back to Virginia. "Have you bumped into your handsome ginger friend again?"

"Not yet, but I'm counting on it. You see a lot of the same people at these things." Then she flapped, shook, and spun like a human mixing bowl.

That was too bad, but Lil still had some good information to share with the girls. Just as she was giving the I've-got-what-we-need signal to Maggie, Virginia had somehow danced her way out of their circle and in between an older couple. A shimmy and shake, and then Lil could not unsee the way that woman did a rodeo grind with the father of the bride.

As anyone would expect, the mother of the bride didn't cotton to all that. She yanked Virginia away from her husband and shouted above the music, "Who is this woman? Who invited this floozy?"

The Chicken Dance music faded away with a squawk of the speakers, and the place went silent. The mother of the bride glared at Lil and the rest of the wedding crasher circle. "I don't recognize a single one of you. Steven," she said to the groom, "were these ladies on your mother's guest list?"

The groom looked them over and gave a definitive head shake. "Never seen them before in my life."

Lil had hoped to never have a law enforcement professional of any type ever take her by the elbow again, but before she could twitch an eyelash, a big burly man wearing a blue sport coat and an earpiece gripped her arm, and his colleagues were doing the same with the other women.

She had to hand it to Burly. He moved a lot quicker than she would've expected of a man his size.

Burly was herding them off the dance floor when Abby Ruth tried to intercede. "What are you doing with my friends, sir?"

"Out of my way, lady."

Abby Ruth stood her ground, but Burly snagged her by the hand and pushed her along with the rest of them.

In no time flat, Lil and the other ladies found themselves outside the botanical garden and in the parking structure across the way. They stood staring at one another until Virginia broke into laughter. "I do love weddings."

Stella looked over at Lil, Maggie, and Abby Ruth with a smile and a shrug as if to say *see why we love this.*

Maggie leaned in and whispered to Lil, "At least we tried."

Oh no, dear. We did more than try. I got exactly what I came for.

When Lil and her friends piled into Abby Ruth's dually in the parking lot, she said, "Never in my life did I ever think I would meet a woman more forward than you, Abby Ruth. No offense. But that Virginia woman takes the cake."

"None taken. Damn," Abby Ruth grumbled, "that reminds me I wanted some of the German chocolate triple-decker groom's cake."

Maggie clicked her seatbelt into place. "Forget about the cake, what about the information we needed from Virginia?"

Lil smiled and tapped her temple. "I have it all right here.

I think I know..." She clapped her hands, and the feel made her gasp. Something was terribly wrong. "Oh, no. This can't be happening."

Maggie twisted in her seat to check on her. "What's wrong, Lil?"

"My rings!" She rubbed her fingers, her very naked fingers. "My wedding rings are gone."

CHAPTER 10

Saturday might've gone down in Abby Ruth's list of best days ever if it hadn't been for Lil getting robbed right under their noses. After the wedding, Abby Ruth had been hog wild to find the greedy numbskull who'd swiped the rings, but Lil had insisted Jenny's wedding needed to take priority. Unfortunately, wedding planning wasn't nearly as fun as crashing a wedding.

Could one culprit be skulking around ripping off so many wedding guests? Hmm…probably not a bad gig if you could get it.

She opened the garage door. "Ritter?"

But not a single ear flop or tail wag. Great. Just as she was getting used to him, he'd up and died on her. Wouldn't that just beat all. "Ritter?" But a walk through the whole garage didn't turn up any sign of him, dead or alive. He must've gotten out somehow.

With no luck finding Ritter, she moseyed around Summer Haven and across the lawn to where Maggie was overseeing the crew Sera had hired to work on the gazebo.

"Mags," she asked, "have you seen Ritter?"

"Lil let him out this morning. She said it was too hot to keep him cooped up today."

"I guess I should've rigged up a fan out there. I bet she's mad. Where is she?"

Maggie never took her eyes off the workers. It had to be killing her not to be the one wielding that hammer. "She went somewhere to look for bubbles."

"Excuse me? I thought we were planning a wedding here, not a playdate."

"That's what you do these days when the bride and groom leave—you blow bubbles or toss birdseed."

"What happened to good old rice?"

"Sera heard it can hurt birds."

"Bull crap. It's not like birds have boiling water in their stomachs. I swear, Facebook has made everyone an expert on urban myths. Birds are probably more likely to burp up soap bubbles. Dang wedding will look like an episode of *The Lawrence Welk Show*."

Maggie was barely paying attention to her because she was so intent on watching every move made on the gazebo.

"I can't believe Lil is working on this wedding when we should be finding her rings," Abby Ruth said. "If we don't track them down soon, they'll be back in a pawnshop."

"I think she's concentrating on the wedding so we don't notice how upset she is about losing them."

"We'll get them back. This may have started out about Stella, but it's now become twice as personal. I wish I'd witnessed the crime. I'd have made a citizen's arrest right then and there."

"You probably would've gotten us all arrested too," Maggie said with a smile.

Abby Ruth couldn't argue with that. Thank goodness

they'd only been kicked out of the reception. If she'd had to call her future son-in-law to come bail her out of jail in Atlanta, it would've been a real embarrassment. And she could hardly go to him for help in recovering Lil's rings after crashing a wedding either.

Just as well. They could handle this situation as they had all the others in the past.

A huff and moan made Abby Ruth look toward the house. Ritter had just settled his old bones down into a hole he'd dug near Lil's treasured Chevalier de Malte irises. Which was, of course, when she came bumping up the drive in Maggie's little truck. When Lil got out, her arms were full of enough boxes of bubbles to keep the birds in Summer Shoals burping for a good long time.

Abby Ruth strode out to help her carry the load to the porch. "Lil, we need to get back on the case or we may never find your rings."

Lil set her purchases on the porch, then settled into a rocker and gazed out at the flurry of activity in the gazebo. "I've been thinking about that. The prettiest blue-eyed boy bumped into me while we were dancing. He had opportunity."

"You have a clear description then!"

"Don't get too excited. He didn't look a thing like the people Stella or Virginia described. He did have a tattoo, but it wasn't on his neck. It was around his arm." She tapped her fingers against the arm of the chair. "Besides, my young man was a wedding guest or he wouldn't have been on the dance floor."

"It's enough to make my head hurt," Abby Ruth said.

"Maybe this thief is disguising himself," Lil said.

"Something's sketchy here, that's for sure," Abby Ruth mused. "But we're gaining ground, and we need to look closer at all these wedding vendors. Right now, it looks like our guy works for both the caterer and the florist, or he might've been a guest."

"What if Stella's purse ending up by the caterer's supplies was a coincidence? Maybe the man she thought looked suspicious was completely innocent."

"That still leaves us with Virginia's guy and your blue-eyed boy," Abby Ruth said. "You're sure you still had your rings on when you hit the dance floor?"

"Positive."

"None of us ever spotted a redheaded guy the entire night. So I think you're right. Your wedding ring perp either had to be someone on the dance floor or one of the security guards who tossed us out."

"I think we have to start with Virginia and her tête-à-tête with the florist. Before she got too loopy on champagne, she mentioned the flowers at that wedding were done by Calla & Company out of Atlanta."

"Why didn't you say so before now?" Abby Ruth turned toward the gazebo and yelled, "Mags, stop supervising. We've gotta hit the road!"

Maggie had a quick conversation with one of the workers then jogged over to Abby Ruth. "What's up?"

"Following a lead. Let's go." Abby Ruth motioned for them to follow her to her truck.

Lil hustled into the passenger seat of the truck, and off they went to Calla & Company florist to see if they could spot a man who looked like anyone they had suspicions about.

"How much further is it?" Maggie asked after an hour.

Abby Ruth glanced down at the navigation screen on her phone. "Says we'll be there in fifteen minutes."

"I brought some snacks along to hold us over," Lil

announced as she handed packs of nabs to Maggie and Abby Ruth.

"I have to say, it's moments like this when I don't entirely miss Sera. That trail mix she used to make with anise in it was an acquired taste." Maggie opened the pack and bit into the neon orange snack. "Give me a good old-fashioned peanut butter cracker any day."

"She means well," Lil said, passing out a pack of wet naps to each of them. "A good Southern girl should never leave the house without a stash of nabs, though."

Abby Ruth tucked the wet nap into the cup holder. Nothing a good swipe of her hands on her jeans wouldn't take care of, but she'd trade a pack of peanut butter crackers for a good Slim Jim any day of the week. At least the nabs would quiet Lil from wedding talk for a few minutes.

"There it is." Abby Ruth pointed toward Calla & Company, which took up the whole corner.

"Oh, dear," Lil said. "This will be a pricy choice. I bet this would cost four times more than flowers from Winnie."

"We don't have to buy anything here. We just need information, so follow my lead," Abby Ruth said.

They piled out of Abby Ruth's dually with Lil clutching a folder full of flower ideas.

The front of the store had three large windows on each side of the front door—each dressed in a different color and theme.

"Aren't these flowers lovely?" Lil ogled the display of seasonal floral wedding bouquets and pew arrangements to match.

"Good enough. We can price some." Abby Ruth yanked open the door.

"This is what I imagine a dewy-fresh morning at a flower market in the south of France smelling like," Lil cooed. "The intoxicating aroma of roses, freesia, lilac, and peonies in the air. Or heaven. I bet heaven smells like this."

"Seriously?" Abby Ruth couldn't hide her sneer. "I hope it smells like fresh-cut grass and dirt when it's kicked up after a slide into home plate."

Lil's head-shake wasn't wasted on Abby Ruth. "We might not be going to the same heaven."

Soft music filled the air, and across the way a man stood on the other side of the counter wrestling a four-foot-tall floral arrangement into submission.

Maggie leaned in and whispered, "Winnie's shop isn't a sixth as big as this one."

"Size isn't everything," Lil said.

"Like hell." Abby Ruth snickered.

Lil shot Abby Ruth a look that would've shamed anyone else. "Winnie does lovely work."

"Wasn't arguing with that." Raising a shoulder in the flower arranger's direction, Abby Ruth asked Lil, "He look like the guy you danced with?"

"No, my gentleman was broader in the shoulders, I think."

It was possible he could still be Virginia's guy, so Abby Ruth swaggered toward the man. "Can you help us?"

"Yes," he answered without making eye contact. He continued to fuss with the arrangement. His hair was strawberry blond, but dang it, she needed to see his eyes. "What can I do for you?"

"My daughter is getting married. I'm looking for someone to arrange the bouquet for her. I loved what you did at the Pettiway wedding a while back. Do you remember that one?"

"Bridezilla with a flower allergy. I wish I could forget that customer. Four-foot cascade of the most ridiculous combination of flowers. A myriad of roses in deep reds, corals, and pinks. Then she added random silk posies to my perfect fresh design. An utter mess." Nose in the air, he sputtered in disgust.

"Maybe something a little smaller than that. And all white." *Nothing like that at all.* "Do you own this place?"

"I do."

Now she could tell the man's eyes were hazel, which got her pretty much nowhere seeing as they probably changed colors depending on what he was wearing. "Ever go out and set up the weddings yourself?"

"Of course."

From somewhere behind her, Abby Ruth heard a rough cough made to sound like a word that rhymed with "pool sit." She whirled around, but all she spotted was a doorway at the back of the building.

"We're in the market for some wedding flowers," Lil told the florist. "Actually, my cousin is the one who recommended you. You might remember her. Virginia? She was at the wedding too."

"Ma'am, I meet hundreds of people each week. I can't possibly remember them all."

Abby Ruth stepped into his personal space and cupped her hands in front of her chest. "Virginia's a hard one to forget, if you know what I mean."

His expression was completely blank. This wasn't looking promising, but she tried another tactic. "How do you feel about jewelry?"

"It can work. I did a wedding bouquet with a cameo broach in the center of a peony one time. It was quite lovely. And for the wedding you're talking about, we did huge rhinestones in the middle of each daisy. How's that sound?"

"Hmmph." Sounded too glitzy to her. She rolled her eyes and caught a glimpse of a young man with a beard toting a box of yellow flowers. Sometimes the hired help saw more than people realized. Maybe he could shed light on his boss.

"Keep him talking." With a quick swing of her elbow, Abby Ruth nudged Lil toward the flower shop owner and darted into the storage area to follow as the other man left the shop. The late-spring sunshine glinted off his bald head. Why did so many young men shave their heads these days? Didn't they realize that stuff would fall out soon enough?

He placed the flowers in the back of a delivery van and swung himself inside the cab.

Before he could back out, Abby Ruth darted up to the driver's side window and knocked.

He glanced over, surprise clear in his apple green eyes. He rolled down the window. "Can I help you?"

"I think you can, Mr..." She let the question dangle out there.

He stuck his muscular arm out the window to shake her hand. "My friends call me Kenny Ray."

"Abby Ruth. I'm curious. Did you deliver flowers to the Pettiway wedding?"

"I honestly can't remember. They all run together, you know?"

"So I guess you didn't happen to see your boss with a very sexy buxom older woman, a short-haired brunette wearing sky-high heels at the wedding that day?"

"Yeah, the boss man was at that gig." He laughed, the sound slightly forced. "He has a thing for the older ladies if you know what I mean."

"And why would I know that?"

"I didn't mean... Well, umm." The guy reddened.

"How about you? Did you ever *talk* with her?" With the cougar movement these days, anything was possible, even if he didn't really fit Virginia's description other than his eye color.

"That woman is at a lot of our weddings. She's hit on me a

few times, but she's old enough to be my grandmother. Besides, I like long, lean brunettes."

Did he just wink at her? "Did you see anyone else with her? Maybe a guy with redder hair than your boss?"

"You must mean Dicky."

Dicky? She cocked an eyebrow that never failed to convince men to spill their secrets. "Tell me more about this…Dicky."

"He's the DJ."

"Where could I find him?"

"Probably every wedding we're at. Elisabeth, the owner of E-lite Wedding Planning, always hires the same vendors."

"When's the next wedding?"

"In a couple hours. The work never ends around here, and I'm running late. Do you need any more help?" He reached out to adjust his side mirror, and a smudge of black dirt peeked out from under his watch band.

"Got everything I need," she said. "Thanks."

Lil and Maggie walked outside as Abby Ruth watched the delivery guy pull out of the parking lot.

"I think the florist is a dead end," Lil said. "He just doesn't seem the type to canoodle with Virginia, and he's doing quite well with this business. Why would he steal from his customers?"

"Delivery driver doesn't agree, so let's keep Mr. Calla on our radar. But honestly, I'm not feeling it. Got a new lead, though. Apparently, the DJ from that wedding is a ginger too."

"A DJ?" Lil groaned. "Please, no more dancing."

"He also said the wedding planner from E-lite Wedding Planning hires the same vendors every time," Abby Ruth said. "Could be our link."

Lil brightened. "If E-lite Wedding Planning has any credibility in the wedding industry at all, they'll be at the bridal show. It's the show of the season. We could pay them a visit. We might be able to sneak a peek at their vendor list while we're at it."

"Perfect." Abby Ruth pressed the remote to unlock her truck. "I think we have a plan." They chugged down the road and entered the highway.

When they finally took the exit toward Summer Shoals, Abby Ruth made a hard right turn into a cemetery, sending Lil and Maggie careening to the side of the truck.

"What are you doing?"

"I forgot we needed flower samples for Jenny," she told Lil. "I promised her. Remember?"

"We're going all the way back?"

Abby Ruth threw the truck into park and jumped out. She pulled a knife from the front pocket of her jeans and began a quick and dirty pruning of the flowers planted on either side of John Smith's headstone.

"Stop that!" Lil called out. "Oh my word! If you're stealing flowers from those graves, we're surely going straight to hell."

Abby Ruth jogged back to the truck. Once inside, she tossed a handful of assorted flowers into the back seat, and they landed smack dab in the middle of Lil's lap. "Jenny needs to know we're making progress and be in a good mood before I break the news about Red."

"You're probably right." Holding tight to the ill-gained bouquet, Lil leaned over the seat. "Do you want us to come with you?"

"Sure." Having Lil and Maggie around might be a way to assure that Jenny didn't completely go crazy on her. If Jenny never forgave her, Abby Ruth couldn't blame her, but at least she'd always have her friends.

. . .

Abby Ruth marched up the steps to Jenny's house and rapped her knuckles on the front door. Bowzer barked inside as they waited for several minutes. "Jenny's car is here."

"She couldn't sleep through all that barking," Maggie said.

"Got that right."

Jenny finally pulled open the door, and in the light from the huge pewter chandelier suspended over the living room, her lank hair and the bags under her eyes were obvious.

"It's two o'clock in the afternoon. Why are you still in your pajamas?" Abby Ruth pushed past her. "We brought you some flower samples, and I have something to tell you. Something important."

"What's up?" One hand pressed to her forehead, Jenny closed the door and shuffle-stepped into the living room.

But Abby Ruth couldn't bring herself to blurt out the news that Red was her father yet.

Lil lifted a soft pink peony under Jenny's nose. "What do you think about these?"

"Pink isn't my color."

"Don't they smell delicious?" Lil asked.

Jenny held up a finger in front of her face, then darted from the room.

The retching sound from down the hall was unmistakable.

"First trimester sickness." Efficient as always, Maggie marched into the kitchen and opened cabinets one by one. "Does she have some ginger ale?"

"Cold rag on her forehead," Lil added.

"Only thing that helped me keep from tossing my cookies when I was pregnant with her was penne pasta with butter on it." Abby Ruth went into the kitchen and grabbed a cast iron skillet, filled it with water, and set it on the stove. With a twist, the flame glowed blue under the pan. "Maggie, can you find some noodles in the pantry and get them cooking?"

"In a skillet?"

"They cook faster this way."

"I'll take care of it."

Abby Ruth tapped lightly on the bathroom door Jenny had disappeared through. "How are you, sugar?"

"Mom, this is so awful. I was never sick with Grayson."

She opened the door and sank to the floor next to Jenny. "Every pregnancy is different. I bet you're having a girl this time. I was sick as a dog when I was pregnant with you. Everything I swallowed, you were in my stomach free-throwing back up for a three-pointer."

Jenny laughed and ran a hand through her sweaty bangs. "I thought little girls were sugar and spice."

"That's a myth." Abby Ruth winked. "Ask me. I have a daughter. The best one in the world."

"Thanks, Mom." She lurched for the toilet and heaved again.

Abby Ruth ran a washcloth under the sink and held it to her daughter's neck. "You'll be okay."

"I know. Sorry," Jenny croaked out. "What did you need to tell me?"

"Umm..." Abby Ruth leaned against the bathroom vanity. Gaunt and tired, Jenny stared up at her from the cold tile floor. "I—"

Maggie poked her head inside the door. "I have that pasta made for you."

"Thanks." Abby Ruth put her hand out for Jenny and pulled her up. "I was just going to tell you that I had the perfect morning sickness cure. Works on all the Cady women. Pasta with butter. Come on."

"It sounds awful right now, but I'll try anything." Jenny shuffled out to the kitchen and slid into one of the chairs.

Maggie put a small bowl of macaroni noodles slathered with butter in front of her.

"Go ahead. It's the only thing that worked for me. For us." Yeah, those early days of Abby Ruth's pregnancy had been awful for more than one reason—heartburn and heartache.

Jenny took a tentative bite and sat quietly. Then another. "I think it's helping. Thank you so much."

"Jenny, there's nothing I wouldn't do for you."

CHAPTER 11

"As much as I hate to say it, we have to hit the big wedding show that Lil was yammering about the other day," Abby Ruth said to Maggie as she stared into her first cup of coffee for the morning. And it did pain her. The last thing she wanted was to walk around an exhibition hall the size of Alaska with starry-eyed brides-to-be. She'd rather donate her wisdom teeth.

"Of course we do," Lil said as she swept into the kitchen, hair perfectly curled and bluer than it had been the day before. She was dressed in snazzy yoga-type pants and a flowing sweater in a sassy green. More Sera's style, but then again, the Californian had rubbed off on them all. Lil's tennis shoes gleamed white against the wood floor. "How else are we going to finish the plans for Jenny and Teague's wedding?"

Lil placed the huge white wedding planner book on the table, then poured herself a cup of coffee.

Abby Ruth hated that doggone thing with a red-hot passion. "This isn't about my daughter's wedding." She shoved the planner out of her line of sight. "It's about finding who is apparently going around preying on old ladies."

"Takes an old lady to know one," Maggie said cheerfully, handing a plate of pancakes and bacon toward her.

"You better be glad I love you so much," Abby Ruth shot back. "I swear, if we can just concentrate on finding the DJ, I will get back on track with Jenny's wedding."

The pang from not telling Jenny about her dad hit Abby Ruth mid-chest again. But Teague had mentioned that Jenny was still struggling with the early pregnancy pukes. He'd been shoving as much pasta and butter down her as he could, but the stuff wasn't a complete cure-all. If they didn't watch out, Jenny might have a pasta gut too big for her dress come wedding time. Soon, she'd be out of her first trimester, and if she was anything like Abby Ruth, that sickness would vamoose faster than a losing team's fans. She hoped that would be the case.

"The wedding will come together," Abby Ruth said.

"Forgive me if I don't completely believe you, dear," Lil said. "It's clear as day you're shaking in your boots about this whole wedding event, even though we told you there's no reason to be."

She'd much rather concentrate on bad guys. Thinking about what the delivery driver had mentioned, she dug into Maggie's fluffy buttermilk pancakes. "I have a feeling about this DJ. He's our guy."

"How can you be so sure?" Maggie asked.

Abby Ruth patted her midsection. "A Cady knows these things."

"Perfect." Lil scurried around the kitchen, snatching up magazines and other stuff from her stash of wedding samples. "Then it won't take us long to nail him, call the police, and move on to the real work we need to do."

"You're the one who was all fired up for us to become the

G Team," Abby Ruth protested, disappointment settling over her. She needed something, anything, to distract her from keeping secrets from her daughter.

Lil pursed her lips disapprovingly. "I still don't know what to make of the wedding crashers, and I wouldn't put it past Virginia to have simply misplaced her necklace."

"She did seem like the type of woman who might misplace—" Maggie made air quotes, "—a lot of things she wears."

"My bet is on her underwear," Abby Ruth cracked. "But that doesn't make her a liar."

"I'm not accusing her of lying." The edges of Lil's smile drooped. "But we *do* know two things truly happened."

"Money disappearing from Stella's purse and someone nabbing your rings."

"Yes. And right now, the DJ and E-lite Wedding Planning are our best leads, so we need to attend the bridal show to make Jenny and Teague's wedding the best we possibly can. And if we get information to help get my rings back, all the better."

"That's fair," Abby Ruth said. "Worst is we hit a dead end. If that happens, we'll skip around the whole place picking us as many samples as will make Jenny happy." Quickly, she finished off her breakfast and wiped her mouth. "The bridal shindig starts at ten sharp. We need to get on the road."

She headed for the front door, with Maggie right behind her. Lil fell in step with them and then they were on their way to Atlanta. Right on schedule.

Abby Ruth was plenty accustomed to big structures. After all, she'd seen Red play baseball in the Astrodome many times. But something about the Atlanta Convention Center made her anxious. Probably because there was a lot of froufrou stuff in there she had no idea what to do with. Little trinkets and glitter and crap.

Beside her, Lil clapped her hands in complete joy. "I can't wait!"

"The DJ first," Abby Ruth reminded her and pointed at Maggie for good measure. "If either of you get distracted and start wandering off, I will yank you back like a wayward sheep."

And holy guacamole, when they paid their entrance fee and strolled inside, it was worse than she'd imagined. White flowing fabric was draped from the industrial fixtures fourteen feet above. Here and yon, balloons were tied into elaborate bundles.

"Is that a bounce house?" Maggie pointed to a structure made from balloons that did indeed look like a contraption people rented for kiddie parties.

"I wouldn't try it," Abby Ruth advised. "Those don't look like commercial-grade balloons."

On another corner, someone had fashioned a white bird so big it resembled the offspring of a swan that had canoodled with Sasquatch. "What is all this stuff?"

"Decor, dear." Lil gazed around, the closest thing to avarice that Abby Ruth had ever seen in her eyes.

"You really love this, don't you?"

Lil's smile was both sad and reminiscent. "If I hadn't been so busy trying to be the perfect wife to Harlan and the perfect matriarch to Summer Haven, maybe I would've found a career I loved, like wedding planning."

"I'm pretty sure this is what hell would look like for me."

"Your personal hell would be a place with no guns or whiskey."

"You know me so well." She craned her neck to look around. If there was one vendor in this place, there were a thousand. "How are we supposed to find our ginger DJ Dicky in all this?"

Lil handed over a thick pamphlet. When Abby Ruth shook it open, it looked like a map of Six Flags on steroids.

Lil said, "All the music vendors, including harpists and ukulele players, are on row D-6."

"No harps," Abby Ruth said and took off in the direction of row D. She led the way through streams of people, the vast majority of them women, oohing and aahing over stuff like an accordion player and what appeared to be a choir of eunuchs, if their smooth faces and pretty looks were any indication.

What was wrong with the traditional organ player?

"I see the sign over there." Maggie pointed to a swath of red plastic with the name DJ Dicky emblazoned on it.

"Excellent." Abby Ruth pivoted and strode in that direction. Sure enough, when she made it to the booth, a man—dressed in a leather vest, a backwards ball cap, and enough gold chains to sink a ship—was chatting with a gaggle of rapt young women and telling them about the hottest first dance songs of the year. It was hard to see his hair color with that hat pulled low, so Abby Ruth circled around the other women to get behind DJ Dicky.

Didn't take much to flick his hat from his head.

He spun around and hunkered down in a strange attack crouch. "What the hell?"

"Are you always this touchy?" She stooped down to pick up his hat and gave him a good look up and down. She picked up the hat and waved it around. Huh, Red Sox. She wasn't surprised. He looked like a Sox fan.

But he was a redhead, and that made her heart happy.

She nodded at his pose, one only a person who'd never practiced martial arts a day in his life would think was correct. She was tempted to chest-bump him just to see how he'd respond. "Maybe you get violent and rob old ladies?"

"What?" He straightened, which was when she noticed he

barely came to her chin. Diminutive DJ Dicky. "Who are you and why did you knock off my hat?"

"To get your attention," she said, as if it were the most rational thing in the world. "Because it's hard to compete with fifteen girls whose cleavage is still exactly where God intended for it to be."

He tried to turn back around, but she out-juked him. "Do you know an extra-friendly curvaceous gal named Virginia?"

"Who? Lady, you're crazy, and if you don't leave now, I'm calling Security."

"Lord, not that again," Lil said. She and Maggie had made their way into the booth and were distracting the young women.

"Sir, I'm sorry we just barged into your booth," Abby Ruth said, "but we have a few important questions to ask you. If you answer them to our satisfaction, we'll be on our way and you'll never have to see us again."

"Please tell me you're not some bridezilla's family."

"Did you work the Pettiway wedding?"

"Yeah, I work any wedding E-Lite Wedding Planning coordinates." Pushing his chest out like the only rooster in the henhouse, he tugged on his vest. "Pretty sure Elisabeth has a thing for me."

"Of course, what woman could resist you?" Abby Ruth wanted to laugh aloud, but she needed to save her energy to either take down this jerk or walk the rest of the way through this exhibition hall. "Do you know what Paraiba tourmaline is?"

He shrugged. "A musical instrument?"

He was either playing dumb or he had no idea about the type of necklace Virginia had been wearing. "Do you remember seeing a group of four middle-aged women at that wedding? One who might've had her assets on display?"

His eyes lit with interest. "You mean the old chicks who

like to shake it on the dance floor, drink a bunch of wine, and dip bananas in the chocolate fountain?"

"Sounds like them," Maggie said.

"One of them dirty danced with every man on the dance floor."

"Definitely them," Abby Ruth said.

DJ Dicky leaned against his table, finally loosening up a little. "Yeah, they are a hoot."

"What about you?" Abby Ruth asked him. "Did you do the hootchy-kootchy with the well-endowed gal?"

"She did a shimmy around me when I played Marvin Gaye's 'Sexual Healing,' but then she found a better mark. An old guy who looked like he could be a sugar daddy." He stopped laughing. "That didn't hurt my feelings."

"And when you saw her, was she wearing a big necklace with green stones?"

He stared up at the ceiling then snapped his fingers. "Yeah, I remember thinking the way she was dancing around, that rock could put out a guy's eye."

He was a dead end. Abby Ruth said to Lil and Maggie, "I don't think he's our man."

"Not your man for what?" he asked.

"Wait a minute." Lil stepped around Abby Ruth to ask DJ Dicky, "What about the wedding planner you work with. Is she here today?"

DJ Dicky hooked a thumb in the direction of more booths. A lot more booths. "She wouldn't miss this. She picks up boatloads of business at these bridal shows. She's in booth R-1800."

"Next stop, the wedding planner," Abby Ruth announced.

Staring out the front window of Summer Haven and watching Grayson practice his fastball with Red, Jenny nibbled on a bowl of pasta and butter. The crazy concoction had been a lifesaver. She mentally counted down the days until the end of her first trimester. Dr. Broussard said the morning sickness—afternoon, in her case—should ease up by then. Couldn't come soon enough.

Meanwhile, her mom and the grannies had been sweet enough to stash enough cooked pasta and butter in every refrigerator to get her through the first trimester. Thank goodness, because when that icky feeling came Jenny had no time to boil water or cook noodles. If she could figure a way to dehydrate the stuff she'd do it, but for now she'd resorted to carrying a baggy of it in her purse for emergencies.

Grayson thought her pasta in a bag was gross, probably the start of his being embarrassed by anything his parents did. She watched him tug on the front of his ball cap, a frayed one that had once been Red's. Grayson swore it was his good-luck hat and was the only reason he had such a golden arm these days.

Red had been so generous with his time, helping Teague coach Little League since he'd moved to town. He'd also taken quite a shine to Grayson, practicing one-on-one almost every afternoon.

Jenny had to admit that up until recently Grayson hadn't been much of an athlete, but something had come alive in her little guy since they'd moved to Summer Shoals. Being athletic herself, it made her happy to see Grayson finally enjoying sports.

She chomped pasta until her uneasy stomach calmed.

In the kitchen, she washed out her bowl and put it back in the cabinet, straightening every dish on the shelf. She'd been in nesting overdrive the past two months, a welcome side effect to her condition.

Which was good for Summer Haven because the whole place was in a state of chaos. It was clear her mom and the others had been one hundred percent focused on planning her wedding. Had to be if the wedding clutter in every corner of the room from kitchen to parlor was any indication. She straightened and neatened her way through the room.

She grabbed a handful of Jordan almonds and chomped on them as she flipped through a couple of the magazines. Several pages were dog-eared.

A siren rang out from her phone. Teague's ring tone. "Hey, babe," she said.

"How are you feeling?"

"Good now. I was looking at the plans for our wedding. Mom is out of control. If they do half the stuff they have printed out or marked in these magazines, it'll be one hot mess."

"How bad could it be?"

"You mean besides the note here about the chicken dance and a conga line?"

"I might need to practice."

She could imagine him rolling his arms and sticking out his foot with a sexy flex of his hips. "Funny. Admit it, you regret not letting me put my foot down on Mom planning our wedding."

"It'll be fine. As long as I walk away at the end of the day with my grandmother's ring on your finger and you and Grayson in my life until death do us part, I don't care what road takes us there."

"I'll remind you of that."

His laugh made her smile. He was so easygoing, and she hoped Grayson would learn that from him.

"I'll be late tonight," he said. "Town meeting."

"No worries. I'm over at Summer Haven. We're eating with Mom tonight."

She hung up the phone, returned to the parlor, and sat

down on the couch. Being pregnant had really knocked the stuffing out of her lately. She stretched out on her back, picked up the glossy book Lil had insisted she look over.

As she flipped through the pages of the wedding planner she was surprised at the number of notes in the borders. Checkmarks and scratch-outs littered the hefty list of tasks.

She scanned them with interest.

Every possible detail was on the multi-page list. Santa's list of naughty and nice around the world was probably shorter than this.

Color: Blue.

Flowers. White roses and Texas bluebonnets.

"Tasteful." Maybe this wouldn't be as bad as she thought. As long as Mom didn't sneak in "The Aggie War Hymn" as the wedding march.

Under the heading Mother of the Bride, the MOB dress had been scribbled out. Her mom's doings, no doubt. She'd never expect her mom to wear a dress to her wedding.

Under Father of the Bride, a check mark filled the box next to boutonnière. She squinted at the penciled words to the right. *Red walks Jenny down aisle?*

Why would Red Jensen want to walk her down the aisle? He was great with Grayson and he was Mom's close friend, but that was just weird.

She glanced up as Red and Grayson zoomed past the front of the house. Grayson's arms pumped furiously, his hands clenched into fists except for the first two fingers on each hand. Those stuck out straight as if he were punching a hole in the air with every arm swing.

The kids in her high school had teased her nonstop about running with her fingers pointing out like that. It wasn't intentional, just the way she'd always run, and Grayson had naturally adopted the same habit.

The guys zoomed by in one last sprint, and Jenny's breath caught.

Red's fingers were pistoled in that same action as he raced Grayson.

Red *Jensen?*

She glanced back at the list.

Red walks Jenny down aisle?

The breath she'd yet to release seemed to grow in her chest, making it feel as if she didn't have enough room inside.

How obvious was this? As obvious as the nose on her face…and the first name on her birth certificate, the one with no father listed. Jensen Elaine Cady.

She wasn't sure how long she stood there staring out the window, the world a blur in front of her as her mental calendar swished backward to her birth year.

Was it possible?

Her tears blurred the outline of Red through the curtains. Her stomach swirled, but this wasn't morning sickness. A baseball soared through the air between Red and Grayson, and her heart jolted at the slap of leather against leather when Red caught the ball.

Her own impulse to slap something made her tremble. She marched out the door, and with all the adrenaline rushing through her, she must've slammed the door, because both Red and Grayson spun in her direction.

"Hey, Mom!" Grayson waved then pounded his fist into his glove.

"Just a second. Hold it right there." She held her hand up like a traffic cop toward her son. "Grayson, I need you to go inside and do your…" Her first inclination was to say *homework*, but school was already out for the summer. "… chores."

"What chores? Mimi doesn't ever make me—"

"Miss Lillian has cookies in her jar."

Those were the magic words. Grayson shot across the yard.

Jenny watched until Grayson dashed through Summer Haven's front door.

She turned and stalked straight toward Red.

All this time, she'd viewed him as Red Jensen, the baseball star. Now she saw him through a new lens. She considered the curve of his cheek and the cleft in his chin, just like Grayson's. The straight nose, like her own. The strong calves that Jenny had always attributed to her years of ballet and gymnastics.

"You're my father, aren't you?"

Red's jaw dropped and his mouth moved in a chewing motion, but no words came out.

CHAPTER 12

Outside DJ Dicky's booth, Abby Ruth scoured the big fold-out convention center map until she found the listing for E-Lite Wedding Planning. She had a good feeling that this wedding planner might be the key to the wedding crashers' missing items. "This way, girls."

"Excuse me." Lil squirmed between a group of giggling twenty-something women as she tried to keep up. If it weren't for her bright green jogging suit, she'd disappear in this crowd. "Excuse me."

If Abby Ruth ever had to be around this much chiffon, bubbles, beads, and rhinestones again, it would be too dang soon. Who knew there were so many ways to wrap up birdseed to throw at a wedding?

Finally, she stopped at booth R-1800.

The booth reeked of froufrou, shimmering in layers of silver and creamy white. She was afraid to touch anything for fear she might get it dirty.

A cream-on-cream settee sat catty-cornered in the booth. Literature lay neatly displayed on a mahogany coffee table, complete with silver tea service and pastel-colored macarons. She was tempted to snag one to see if they were real, but she restrained herself.

Everything about the booth said high dollar. A slide show projected images of perfect weddings. Lush flowers, beautiful couples, colossal cakes, and catering spreads to feed hundreds.

As soon as she laid eyes on the wedding planner, she didn't have fond feelings for her. If she had to trust her Texas instincts, she'd swear this lady was a problem right down to her dyed hair and boots too fancy to be functional.

A thirty-something blonde, with pinup-girl good looks and a pretty scarf tying up her curls, stood at the wedding planner's shoulder as she ticked off wedding must-haves to a young couple. Poor kids were probably being suckered into a wedding day that would cost more than a yacht.

"I'm so excited to be working with you." The young bride-to-be shook the wedding planner's hand with such vigor it looked as if she was pumping water out of an old well. "And you of course," she said to the pretty girl. "You don't know how long I've been planning for this day. It was worth moving my wedding date to be able to have you plan my dream wedding. Plus, more time to save up enough money for everything I ever wanted."

"It is the most important day in your life." The wedding planner cast a gaze down her nose. "You really can't put a price on that. Ask my assistant, Honey."

Honey was an appropriate name for the pinup girl, who was smiling sweetly. "It really is a once-in-a-lifetime event. I would do—am doing—anything to have Elisabeth plan my wedding. She's the best."

"Elisabeth is the one I want to coordinate our wedding." The bride-to-be grabbed her fiancé's hand so hard it looked as if his knees were buckling a bit. That was one determined gal.

Abby Ruth's heart gave a squeeze for that poor sucker. His knees would surely buckle when he got a whiff of the price tag this snooty woman was going to lay out.

"And although one can't put a price on perfection, I will." The woman's haughty laugh made the young woman giggle nervously.

"Here it comes," Abby Ruth mumbled under her breath.

If she hadn't had such a strong feeling that this wedding planner might point them to who had taken advantage of Stella, she'd be so out of here.

Instead, she plastered a smile on her face, waiting her turn to make good on her promise to Stella and Lil.

The wedding planner scribbled furiously on a fancy three-fold brochure, then passed it to her dutiful assistant, who handed it to the couple. It was as if the wedding planner was too good to touch commoners like this young couple.

"Elisabeth will give you the wedding of your dreams and more," Honey said in a voice so sweet it was almost like a song. "If you'll fill out this card, we'll have what we need."

The bride-to-be scribbled on the glossy card in a hurry and passed it back to the assistant, who raised a finger, "Oh, wait a second. We have a gift for you." She disappeared behind a silky curtain near a giant video wall, then breezed back with a organza pouch. "A little something to start your planning off right."

"Thank you." The bride-to-be half-skipped down the aisle with her fiancé in tow.

Her brightly painted lips pursed, the wedding planner turned toward Abby Ruth. "Now, how can I help you ladies?"

Abby Ruth had a feeling the woman thought that made her look like she had high cheekbones. It wasn't working though. She just looked ticked off.

"We need a wedding planner," Lil chimed in.

"Not just any wedding planner," Abby Ruth said. "The *best* wedding planner."

The woman lifted her nose even higher into the air. "Then you've come to the right place. I'm Elisabeth. With an *S*." She extended her hand toward Abby Ruth.

"Well, hello, Elisabeth with an *S*." Abby Ruth played out the *S* like a hissing snake. "I only want the best, but I'm not a real trusting gal. I like to have references. I assume you have plenty, including some of the vendors you work with?" Abby Ruth planted the seed, praying it might be this simple to get her hands on a list of other possible perps.

But the wedding planner gave Abby Ruth a suspicious once-over. "Of course I have references from my clients. However, I never share my vendor list. You won't have to worry about any of that because I handle it all. When is the big day? I'm assuming this is a second wedding for you?"

Abby Ruth laughed. "Not my wedding. My daughter's, and the big day is June fifteenth."

"Have you set a budget?"

So this was how they were going to play it, huh? "Money's no object."

"Lots of people say that, then I find out they're thinking twenty thousand." She tilted her head. "Heck, you can't plan a decent bachelorette party for that these days."

Abby Ruth tried not to choke. What planet was this woman living on? Finally, she wheezed out, "What budget do you recommend for a wedding?"

"No less than sixty thousand."

Holy guacamole! "Let's make it seventy then," Abby Ruth said without so much as a quiver.

With interest gleaming in her eyes, Elisabeth waved them to follow her. Her assistant rushed ahead and moved the curtain to the side, revealing a meeting room set up just behind the giant video wall. Back here, the table was simple but elegant, and a chandelier hung over it. Maggie eyed the electrical work.

"Let's see." The woman's pink-and-white French manicure glinted under the bright fluorescent lights as she flipped through a shiny silver-bound book with fancy calendar pages in it—each full of handwriting that looked like calligraphy.

"Yes, I'm available then. We'll have to get busy though. Just a year to plan. That's tight."

"Not really," Abby Ruth said.

"Not really?" Her laugh was a pompous puff of air. "Oh, yes, I see what you're saying. It will be *me* that will be busy. No worries, though. I have the perfect team to help me. What are you thinking? Simple? Extraordinary?"

"I want the works," Abby Ruth said. "Everything and all your best vendors."

The woman's eyes sparkled with greed. "I do love a woman who knows what she wants. My assistant will take your deposit before you leave today, but let's go ahead and set up a date to chat about the particulars. Shall we meet next month? Maybe the twentieth at two?"

"That won't work at all. The wedding is the fifteenth."

"You mean June fifteenth of *this* year?"

"Yes."

"I couldn't possibly do that." Elisabeth sniffed and slapped the calendar closed. "I'm highly sought after. People hire me years in advance. We can't help you."

"Why not? I thought you had the perfect team." Abby Ruth enjoyed challenging this woman.

Her nostrils flared. "You clearly are *not* my kind of client."

Lil and Maggie backed against the wall as if worried Abby Ruth might throw a punch at the woman if she dared say no. She hoped it wouldn't come to that. "Money is no object. Surely you can fit us in."

The woman pushed her fancy book to the side and stood. "Even if I wanted to take your job, I'm already double-booked for that day. Honey is taking care of the other wedding." Elisabeth's jaw pulsed. "Something I've *never* done before."

The young assistant blushed.

"And all my vendors are booked. You might try the Knights of Columbus or Moose Lodge folks. They're probably more what you're looking for."

"No," Abby Ruth said, feeling the hot rush of blood run up her neckline to her ears. "That wouldn't do at all."

She did a little Texas two-step to the right to block the woman's escape, and just as she'd hoped, Miss Snooty dodged her and peeked around the video wall. "I have another guest so I'll have to ask you and your friends to step out."

"Shoot," Abby Ruth said. "I think I dropped my pen. If you'll give me a sec to find it, we'll be on our way." *On our way to taking over one of your June fifteenth weddings for my daughter.*

The wedding planner stepped out to greet her next sucker...er...client, and Abby Ruth stage-whispered to Maggie, "Flip through that book and find out who's getting married on the fifteenth."

Maggie gave her the okay sign, and Abby Ruth hovered in the entryway to the meeting area to block Miss Snooty's view.

A moment later Maggie and Lil whisked past Abby Ruth, and the wedding planner turned to see Abby Ruth standing there. "You're still here," she chided.

"I wanted to leave my number. Should anything open up, please call me. I had my heart set on you orchestrating this wedding for us." Abby Ruth held her cool and sashayed out of the booth, disappearing into the thick of the crowd.

Maggie and Lil were waiting for her at the end of aisle R.

"Did you get the couples' names?" she asked Maggie.

"Sure did, both the one Elisabeth is planning and the one Honey is handling."

"Perfect!"

"I Googled them." Maggie beamed with pride. "And I found both brides on Facebook."

"Great work. Let's contact the bride for the wedding the assistant is coordinating. I have a feeling she'll be a lot easier to handle."

"And less likely to get your boot in her butt," Maggie said with a chuckle.

"True."

"I bet they're here," Lil mused, turning a circle as if she could take in the entire conference center and spot the bride with her X-ray vision.

"The bride-to-be's name from the wedding Honey is handling is Hannah Huckleberry. I sent her a friend request and look—" Maggie flipped her phone around, "—she already accepted me!"

Huckleberry? No wonder the girl was getting married.

Think, think, think. What will entice a couple who's obviously into this wedding crap to ditch the big hoopla and cancel their date?

Something niggled at the back of her brain, something about Red.

Aha! Got it!

Abby Ruth grabbed the phone from Maggie and typed in a private message to the bride. *You've just won an exclusive all-inclusive beach wedding and honeymoon getaway from the G Team. Message back that you're interested, then meet the woman in the bright green outfit at the center of aisle R.*

She quickly outlined her plan to Lil and Maggie. And it didn't take sixty seconds for Maggie's phone to blow up with a stream of excited responses from Miss Hannah Huckleberry. "They're on their way!"

A moment later, a young lady came barreling down aisle R with a muscled guy who looked as if he'd spent his share of hours on a football field or in the gym. Perfect. "Are…are you the G Team?"

"Yes, dear—"

"Congratulations," Abby Ruth rolled right over Lil's chitchat. They needed to get down to business. "You were chosen from thousands of bridal couples."

"I never win anything! I mean we don't. My goodness, this is so exciting. Isn't it, Brandon?"

Brandon stood there with his mouth half-open like he wanted to say something but was afraid. She felt for him. This place was about to suck the life out of her too.

"But everything is already planned," he said. "We have people traveling in from out of town." He turned a shrewd stare in Abby Ruth's direction. "Is this some kind of scam?"

Kid was smarter than he looked, but she had no intention of scamming them. Red would just have to loan her his condo for a week. No big deal. He'd do anything for her.

Lil nudged Abby Ruth, and she rolled on with the details—condo with an ocean view, a private luau for two, bodysurfing lessons, and more.

"It sounds so perfect." Hannah bounced with excitement.

"You have to commit now," Lil added. "Or we pick another lucky attendee."

"I don't know what to do. We have the cake, the caterer, the photographer, the DJ, the works!" Hannah's gaze darted around the convention center. She bit down on her lip, then turned to her fiancé, but Brandon's head-shake said he wasn't about to get into the middle of it. "Why couldn't this have happened before we paid all those deposits?"

"We'll handle the wedding planner and any additional cancellation fees." *C'mon, you two. Stop waffling and say yes!*

"I don't know," the bride said. "Oh, gosh, what do we do? My parents would be so disappointed."

"Not really," the groom said. "Your dad tried to get me to take money instead of the big shindig, remember? You were the one who wanted the whole fairytale wedding."

"You think we should get married in Hawaii?"

"Surfing over a stuffy dinner and dancing? Sure do. Can we get married on the beach?" he asked Abby Ruth.

"At sunset if you like."

The young girl grabbed her fiancé's arm. "Did you hear that?"

"I did."

"And I can get you a private tour of Aloha Stadium while you're there. You know, where the Pro Bowl is played," she tossed in to sweeten the pot.

"I'm in." He spun back to his bride-to-be. "I mean, if it's what you want."

"You're right. Dad's been trying to talk us into running off anyway, so we'll blame him!" She smiled at Abby Ruth. "We are so in."

"Great. Then we'll need some information from you." Abby Ruth held out her hand, and like a mind reader Maggie slapped a small spiral notebook and a carpenter's pencil into her palm. Prepared friends were invaluable.

Then she led the young couple to a table behind a row of empty booths. She quickly collected information about the wedding, documenting it all in Maggie's notebook.

Abby Ruth shook hands with the couple and congratulated them again. She handed them a G Team business card. "Hang on to that. We'll drop off your prize package within the week. Remember to keep this under wraps."

"Thank you so much."

"Best wishes. And aloha!"

"Aloha," the young couple sang out as they walked arm in arm straight out of the conference center.

"You're a genius. We can hire E-lite Wedding Planning now," Lil said.

"Like hell. I wouldn't hire that woman if she didn't cost a dime." She waved the list of Brandon and Hannah's wedding details in the air. "I have a better idea."

"Why does that always worry me?" Lil asked.

"Wait right here."

Maggie and Lil settled on a white bench next to one of the huge pillars in the convention center.

Abby Ruth squared her shoulders and headed back to booth R-1800.

As she rounded the corner to the wedding planner's booth, she spotted Elisabeth with an *S* being escorted off by a good-looking man in a three-piece suit.

Things are falling into place.

As soon as they made it through the front hall doors, Abby Ruth forged her attack on Honey. "Excuse me, may I have a word with you?"

Honey turned, recognizing her immediately. "I'm so sorry Elisabeth couldn't work y'all in. I know what it feels like to not get what you want for your wedding. In fact, that's why I'm working with Elisabeth. So I can have the wedding of my dreams."

"Really?" Abby Ruth put on her listening ears. She had no idea what her plan would be, but somehow she needed to commandeer the Hannah and Brandon wedding and use it to her advantage.

"Oh, yes. She plans dream weddings."

"She's a piece of work. How did a nice young lady like

you end up working for someone like that? She must be paying you one heckuva salary."

Honey's cheeks reddened. "She's not paying me at all."

Keep it zipped, Abby Ruth. Let her spill the story. There's a loophole here somewhere.

"She said if I worked by her side for two years that she would consider reducing her fees for me."

Abby Ruth choked. "Two years of helping at these shows?"

"No. Helping with every wedding, event, and meeting. I don't have the means to afford her fees any other way."

Aha. Willing to think outside the box to get what she wanted. This Honey was Abby Ruth's kinda gal. "If you could help me with one little thing, Elisabeth wouldn't have to know, and I think we could both come out better for it."

Honey bit down on her lip and glanced in both directions, then motioned toward the meeting room behind the curtain. "Maybe we should chat."

Twenty minutes later Abby Ruth was cruising down the R aisle feeling as if things were finally going her way. Now if Lil and Maggie had just stayed put, they could get the heck out of here. Finally, the crowd thinned and she saw them sitting on a bench with sampler plates all around.

"We were beginning to wonder if you were coming back," Maggie said lifting a plate of hors d'oeuvres. "Here. Try some."

Abby Ruth helped herself to a fried mushroom.

"You didn't get into a scuffle with that wedding planner, did you?" Lil's brows pulled together.

"No ma'am. Quite the opposite. We have a deal with Honey. I mentioned to her that we happened to know Hannah and Brandon and had recently heard they won a big wedding trip to Hawaii."

"Why would you do that?" Maggie asked.

"Because that poor girl is working like an indentured servant for Elisabeth to possibly give her a discount on her own wedding. But I mentioned if she would be willing to simply transfer the vendors over to the wedding we're hosting and keep the switch out of Elisabeth's fancy scheduling book, we'd pay Honey to take care of the change and wouldn't breathe a word to Elisabeth. The idea of extra jingle in her pocket perked Miss Honey right on up. And..."

"And what?"

"I might've mentioned the possibility of her using Red's condo for her honeymoon."

"I wonder how Red will feel about you turning his condo into a time share," Lil said.

"I'll handle him," Abby Ruth said.

"I'm sure you will." Lil exchanged a smile with Maggie, who responded with, "I think he might be very happy to have you indebted to him."

"Stop, you two. This is in the name of justice, and I do believe our investigation has just kicked into high gear."

CHAPTER 13

Red stood in front of Jenny, speechless. Seconds ticked off, turning into minutes, as he avoided her stare and fiddled with the change in his pockets. It was the first time she'd ever seen him look anything less than a self-assured pro athlete.

He reached for her hand. "Jenny, you have to understand—"

She jerked away. "I don't have to understand anything. For some reason, you and my mom thought it was best for me not to know my father. And you've been right here for months. It's not like you didn't have a chance to tell me." She stepped away from him, needing more space to keep herself from lashing out at him physically. "My whole life has been one big lie."

"Don't you think that's a little dramatic?" His voice softened.

"Dramatic? You don't get to say that." Even if she hadn't been pregnant and overwhelmed, she had every right to be upset. "You cheated me out of a family."

"Your mom was—"

She shushed him. Nothing he could say right now would turn down the static in her head or disperse the red haze in her brain. "I need you to do one thing for me."

"Anything," he said without a second of hesitation. Probably because of the guilt he felt.

"I need you to take Grayson home for me. There's a pan of baked spaghetti in the fridge. You can pop that in the oven and both have dinner."

"Are we okay? What are you planning to do?"

She didn't know what the chain of events would be, and she really didn't know if they'd ever be okay, but she knew exactly how the evening would end. With one helluva come-to-Jesus meeting between her and her mother.

Four hours later, she was waiting in a rocking chair, the motion making her queasy. The porch was littered with an empty bag of peanut M&Ms, a few Slim Jim wrappers—her mom was sure to fume over that—and an empty half-gallon of butter pecan ice cream. She'd wanted a glass of nerve-calming wine, but that wasn't an option right now, so she'd had to settle for fat and sugar to dull the pain.

And now she was paying for it all. She covered her stomach with her hands as if she could calm it through force of will.

Like she'd had any control over that part of her body since she and Teague had—

An arc of light cut across the front of Summer Haven, slicing through the summer twilight, and her gut cramped. They were home. "Please, everyone," she said to her midsection, "just stay in your seats until this plane has safely landed, okay? I really need to get through this conversation without yakking on my mom's boots."

The baby and the ice cream seemed to listen to her, both settling back into their proper places.

When her mom, Maggie, and Lil all climbed out of the

truck, they were smiling but moving slowly as if they'd had a very full day. Lil glanced up and must've caught sight of Jenny rocking on the porch. "Jenny, you should've been at the wedding show—so many pretty things. Balloons, harps, and—"

"And a bunch of birdseed holders," her mom cut in. "Do you really want people chucking birdseed at you?"

They hesitated on the steps, their gazes darting from the greasy bags, the ice cream tub lying drunkenly on its side, and the inside-out wrapper with a single piece of green candy clinging to it—dammit, she'd wanted that last M&M.

"Are you sick?" Maggie hurried toward her, holding out her hand in that age-old let-me-check-you-for-fever gesture.

Jenny shook her head hard enough that it made the ice cream reconsider a trip back to the top of the pipe. But she knew what had them concerned. Her red-rimmed eyes, lank hair, and clammy cheeks.

She breathed through the nausea and croaked out, "*Sick* doesn't begin to describe what I'm feeling right now. Could you and Lil please go inside? I need to talk with my mother."

"But, dear," Lil protested, "you really look like you're running a fever."

"I. Am. Not. Sick." She repeated her words slowly, enunciating them carefully. But if those two lovely ladies didn't get their butts inside quickly, Jenny was going to blow. And it wouldn't be pretty.

It would be decidedly ugly.

"Please let Mom and me have some privacy."

Maggie put her arm around Lil and scurried her inside.

Smart woman that Abby Ruth Cady was, she hesitated on the top step, watching Jenny like she might a baby rattlesnake. "Something's obviously wrong."

"You think?" Jenny laughed, a harsh sound, because if she

didn't laugh, she would start crying again and might never stop. Dammit, she was a grown woman. Why was she this torn up over the news of her father? The fact that she didn't have one had stopped bothering her years ago. At least she'd thought it had.

Then this.

Her mom bent at the waist and cleaned up Jenny's mess, picking up the candy package and beef jerky bags without glancing up. Yeah, she knew something bad was going down. Once she had everything stuffed inside the ice cream tub, she set it near the front door. Then she picked up the wedding planner from the rocker next to Jenny's and carefully lowered herself as if she was afraid there might be a bomb strapped to the chair's seat.

"Just tell me, Jenny. Is it something with the baby?" She reached and tried to grab Jenny's hand, but she wasn't ready for any physical contact and shifted away. "Did something…happen?"

"The baby is fine. Assuming I didn't put her into a lard and sugar coma."

"Then what's this all about?"

Jenny fixed her gaze on her mom's face. "This is *all about* Red Jensen being my father."

THE AIR IN ABBY RUTH'S LUNGS COULDN'T HAVE WHOOSHED out with more force if someone had marched across her chest wearing combat boots. Her mind blanked, went black like when the electricity failed in the dead of winter.

Then the thoughts and excuses and pleas swirled so fast in her brain, making her dizzy.

"Don't deny it, Mom. I've already confronted Red."

All she could do was push out two words. "I'm sorry."

Jenny cocked her head to the side in a smart-ass way Abby Ruth hadn't seen since her daughter was an angsty hormonal teen. And far be it from her to point out how Jenny's hormones might be affecting her attitude right now. Abby Ruth wasn't an idiot.

"What exactly are you sorry for, Mom? Are you sorry for leaving my birth certificate blank? Or maybe telling me that you didn't know who my father was when I was a little girl?" With every word, Jenny's voice rose in pitch and volume—up and down like she couldn't control herself. "Or possibly letting me watch an untold number of Astros games without mentioning that my dad was the pitcher? Or, gosh, could it be that you have allowed me to live in the same small town with Red Jensen for the past year and never said a damn word about how you apparently hopped into bed with him at some point and I was the accidental byproduct?"

Abby Ruth leaned in and pointed a long, thin finger toward Jenny. As much as she loved her daughter, she wouldn't let her make what she and Red had once shared sound like some tawdry one-night stand. "I did not just hop into bed with Red. It wasn't like that."

"How long did the two of you date?"

"We didn't date, not exactly. You see—"

"So you're saying it was only sex? Mom, women have every right to have physical relationships, but I don't understand why—"

"Jenny..."

Something in Abby Ruth's warning tone must've clued Jenny in because she said, "Oh, Mom, you loved him, didn't you? That's even worse."

Abby Ruth lowered her head.

"It's obvious he cares for you. How long have the two of you been in love? And why couldn't you tell me the truth, if not raise me together? I don't understand. He's obviously a good man."

"The absolute best," Abby Ruth said.

"Then how could he..."

Before Jenny could finish that horrible thought, Abby Ruth grabbed her hand and held on tight. "He didn't let you down, Jenny. Until recently, Red didn't know about you."

"What?" By the way Jenny was clutching her other fist against her chest, it was obvious that bit of news had sideswiped her.

"I never told him I was pregnant."

"W...why?" The way Jenny's voice stumbled over that one word made Abby Ruth nearly choke in response.

"We never meant to fall in love, but we did. He was married, which was bad enough. But he was also married to a woman with a chronic medical condition. At the time, she needed him far more than I did."

"Did you think about whether or not *I* would need him?"

"Of course I did. But I was a grown woman who had a good job, and I knew I could provide for you."

"Dinner on the table every night isn't the same thing as a parent's love."

And that cut through Abby Ruth like a jagged saw blade, ripping flesh and feelings. "I love you with everything inside me."

"Just not enough to tell me who my dad is. I'm not some breakable six-year-old child. I'm a grown woman with one child of my own and another on the way. Did you think I was so fragile, so weak?"

"No," Abby Ruth insisted. "Red and I went our separate ways after the night he told me his wife's condition had worsened and that he needed to honor his marriage vows. That's exactly the reason I couldn't put more anchors around him."

"Great," Jenny scoffed. "Now I'm not just gaining three pounds a week, I'm an anchor. Big enough to drag a man down to his death."

"A bit of an exaggeration, don't you think?"

"You still think you did the right thing, don't you?"

"I don't think it, I know it. It was a complete fluke that Red ever walked back into my...our lives."

"Did you ever intend to tell me?"

"Hell, I hadn't planned to tell *him,*" she mumbled, then caught Jenny's horrified expression. "Look, I planned to tell you the other night when I came over, but you were a little busy trying not to heave."

"Handy."

"Dammit, Jenny." Abby Ruth jumped from her seat, the wedding planner slipping from her lap and thudding to the porch. In that instant, she'd released her daughter's hand. One that had curled into a tight fist. "I did the best I could. Was that always good enough? No, it absolutely wasn't. I remember that time you wanted me to make you a Pocahontas costume for Halloween and I couldn't sew to save a life. You ended up wearing a paper sack and fringed cowboy boots. Lots of times I downright sucked as a mother. But tell me this, before today, were you happy? Consider yourself moderately well adjusted?"

"That doesn't matt—"

"Of course it matters. You're the same woman who got out of your bed this morning. Now you happen to know something that changes your perspective on the world."

"No, Mom." With deliberate—and brittle—movements, Jenny pushed herself up from the rocker. "It changes everything."

The calm chill in Jenny's words froze its way through Abby Ruth's bones. "What are you saying?"

"I'm saying forget about being involved in my wedding. I have no interest in you planning it." She kicked the white book that held every detail about her wedding, sending it sliding across the porch. "In fact, I have no interest in talking with you for a long while. If ever."

CHAPTER 14

Lil stood at the base of the stairs looking up toward Summer Haven's second floor. It wasn't like Abby Ruth to sleep this late. Usually, she was up and at 'em. "Do you think we should wake her? It's ten o'clock."

Maggie leaned forward, listening. "After what she said about her and Jenny's fight last night, I bet she tossed and turned until early morning. I hope she's okay."

"I've never seen her in that kind of state, and I was afraid of the same thing." Lil patted the balustrade. "But we also can't coddle her. She needs to get out of that bed. If not, she'll just lie in there feeling sorry for herself, and that certainly won't help anything."

"If you say so." Maggie's forehead creased. "You don't think she'll do something crazy, do you?"

Honestly, the thought had crossed Lil's mind too, but Abby Ruth was a strong woman. Action was a better medicine than wallowing in whatever was making you miserable. She knew that firsthand. So even though it pained her knees a little, she marched up to the Sweet Vidalia Room and knocked twice on the door. "Abby Ruth, it's time to get up. You've slept for long enough."

Not a peep from the other side.

So Lil rapped again, harder this time. "Abby Ruth Cady, it's midmorning. You need to get out of that bed."

"Go 'way" was the mumbled response from inside.

"Since Summer Haven is my home, I doubt that will happen, so why don't you get on your feet and get dressed?"

"Don't wanna."

For Pete's sake, it looked as if she was going to have to take this stubborn old Texas bull by the horns. Normally, Lil was very respectful of her roommates' privacy, but desperate times called for boldness. So she opened the door and swung it wide. Then she hit the light switch before bustling around the room, opening the drapes to let the spring sunshine flood inside.

Abby Ruth groaned and turned over.

Ha. Like that would stop Lil. She grabbed the end of her own grandmother's Jacob's Ladder quilt and yanked it from Abby Ruth's lean body. Her man-style pajamas were woggled around her calves and creased all over. A sneer touched Abby Ruth's lips, which made it apparent the creases didn't stop with her clothes. Her face looked as if a bunch of drunk semi drivers had raced across her cheeks all night.

Poor baby.

But not so sad that Lil was about to let her hide in here today. They had things to do—a wedding to pull off and a bad guy to take down. Nudging the mattress with her hip, she said, "When I was a girl, if I was throwing a fit—not a regular one, mind you, but a bad one—my momma would threaten to toss a glass of ice water on me. That's all it took to straighten me up right quick."

"I'm not throwing a fit," Abby Ruth said into her pillow.

"Well, then pull yourself together," Lil said. "Don't think I won't resort to Momma's tactics. It only takes one time. Shocks the very breath out of you, and yes, I'm talking from experience."

At that, Abby Ruth opened one eye. "I think I would've liked your momma."

"Once she got past some of your sharper angles, I think she would've liked you too."

"Why are you here?" Abby Ruth asked.

Rather than sitting on the edge of the bed to comfort Abby Ruth, Lil yanked the comfy feather pillow out from under her head. "Because wallowing in this bed all day won't accomplish anything. It sure won't fix things with Jenny."

But Abby Ruth just lay there. "Pretty sure nothing in this world will fix things between Jenny and me."

Lil clucked her tongue. "This isn't like you. Where's the woman who'll fight with her own shadow if it comes down to that?"

"Jenny has a right to be mad at me. I can't blame her."

"Can't say I blame her either, but it's up to you to fix all this. None of us can help in that regard." It occurred to Lil that this might not be the best avenue to light a fire under Abby Ruth's behind. "But that's not why I'm here. We have a case to solve. If you don't get dressed and get on the ball, we're never going to track down that scoundrel who's targeting the wedding attendees."

"I could care less about that guy now."

"That may be so, but I care a great deal because my rings are missing. Plus, you promised that sweet couple, Hannah and Brandon, a free destination wedding and honeymoon. You can't let them down."

Abby Ruth groaned.

"If you don't care about anything else, the least you can do is help me get my rings back."

Abby Ruth turned her face away, but not before Lil spotted the guilty look in her eyes.

"And with all the ado last night, I'm assuming you haven't spoken to Red yet."

"His number is in my phone," Abby Ruth said. "Why don't you give him a call and bring him up to date?"

Lil pulled her hands to her hips. "No."

"What?"

Lil sucked in a steadying breath. Abby Ruth wasn't used to people refusing her demands, and if her balled fists were any indication, she was ready for a fight, but that was better than the woman lying around in a heap of a pity party all day. "You started all this. One secret that's snowballed over the years."

Abby Ruth rolled her eyes. "I get it. It's huge now."

"The least you can do is talk with Red about it yourself. Good Lord, woman. You can fix this if you two put your heads together."

Abby Ruth thrust her arm out as if asking Lil to pass her the phone.

Instead, Lil grabbed Abby Ruth's cell and slipped it into her pocket. "And you owe him the courtesy of doing it face to face." She went to the wardrobe and pulled out a starched pair of Wranglers, a bright yellow shirt, and Abby Ruth's favorite pair of cowboy boots. "Get dressed."

"Ugh," she said from the bed.

"If you're not dressed and downstairs in twenty minutes, I'm coming back with the ice water." With that pronouncement, Lil strode out and shut the door behind her.

When Lil returned to the foyer, Maggie said, "Any luck?"

"I have a feeling I may have motivated her."

Sure enough, Abby Ruth was downstairs nineteen and a half minutes later, pouring herself a cup of now stale coffee with jerky motions. The glare she shot on her way out of the room would've intimidated Lil a year or so ago. Now, she knew that Abby Ruth had a big bark, but she was a caring mother and a good friend at heart.

The front door slammed, rocking the pottery on an open shelf, and Maggie said, "Whoa, she was not happy."

"Of course she wasn't, but she was in motion. That's all that matters right now."

ABBY RUTH KNOCKED ON RED'S FRONT DOOR, THEN WALKED inside before he could answer. They hadn't exactly gotten to the walk-on-in stage in their relationship, but this was a desperate time, and it wasn't as if Red would care about her barging in.

Sure enough, he looked up from Teague's old recliner, the *Summer Shoals Dispatch* spread out on his lap and a cautious smile on his lips. "Good morning. How are you?"

"How do you think I am? I'm paying the ultimate price for keeping a lifelong secret from Jenny. Our daughter hates me now." She held out a hand to stop him from butting in. "Please don't say you told me so. That's the last thing I need."

"Ru, you know me better than that. I never wanted things to end up this way. I know I was pushing you to tell Jenny, but this...this isn't good for any of us." He ran his fingers through his greying hair. "The look on her face..."

"I can't listen to that right now." She pressed a palm against her chest, trying to ease the pain that had settled where her heart was supposed to be. Her normal swagger had vamoosed, and all she really wanted was to curl up and hibernate until things could miraculously change. "I swear I've never felt worse."

"Then why are you here?"

"I need your help."

"Anything." With quick movements, he folded the

newspaper three times into a perfectly creased rectangle and set it on a side table. "You know that."

Amazing, after all she'd kept from him, that he was still willing to support her, no questions asked. "I need to borrow your condo in Hawaii for a week."

"Running away won't fix this."

"It's not for me. Is it available the week of June fifteenth?"

"For Jenny and Teague. That's a great idea. Why didn't I think of that?" He stood and pulled her into a hug. "It's something we can give her together as her parents."

She pressed her palms against his chest and kept some distance between them even though what she really wanted to do was lean in and rest against him. But she couldn't afford that right now. Fixing things with Jenny was priority one, but a getaway to Hawaii wouldn't smooth away the pain Abby Ruth had caused her daughter. "She won't ever forgive me."

"Yes, she will. Give her time." He tipped up her chin and met her gaze. "She's getting married. She's pregnant. Her whole life shifted on its axis. This situation with her finding out about me on her own isn't perfect, but we're all adults. It's not like she's fifteen and this is getting hurled at her. We can work this out."

"If she was fifteen I could send her to her room and make her cooperate."

"Somehow I doubt that. She is your daughter, after all."

She couldn't suppress a smile. "She is that."

"You Cady girls are tough customers, but there's nothing deeper than your loyalty to who and what you love. You forgave me after all we went through years ago, and I've forgiven you for not telling me about Jenny."

"I've royally screwed things up. You do know that I was trying to protect you both, don't you?"

"Yes, and Jenny will too once she has some time to cool

down. Trust that to work in our favor. A trip to Hawaii won't hurt either."

"I don't think I was clear about the condo. I don't need to borrow it for Jenny and Teague's honeymoon either."

"Do I even want to know what you're up to this time?"

He'd been right there for the takedown of the G Team's last big case, but did she really want him to be involved in this one? He'd probably try to talk her out of the investigation, or tell Teague, and right now the case was all she really had.

"Probably not."

He went to the desk under the window and pulled out a leather folio from the second drawer. He thumbed through it and pulled out a card. "Here," he said. "Call the property manager and let her know the details. The account codes are all right there. Whatever you need is yours."

"Thank you."

"What are you going to do now? About Jenny, I mean."

"I have no idea. She won't accept my phone calls. I hate to upset her any worse than I have. For the first time in my life, I'm out of ideas."

He didn't bother to try to pep talk her. He knew her well enough to know some rah-rah speech wasn't what she needed. Instead, he placed a gentle kiss on her brow. "I'm here for you, Ru, and I always will be."

CHAPTER 15

Abby Ruth waved her hand through the buttery-smelling haze hanging in Summer Haven's kitchen. On any other day, she'd consider the scent a good sign and would grab a plate and napkin. Because it meant Maggie had cooked green tomatoes in the cast iron skillet to make fried green tomato and pimento cheese sandwiches, but today Abby Ruth had no appetite at all.

"Come on in and sit down," Maggie sang out and gestured toward where Lil was sitting at the kitchen table. "I have your favorites."

Maggie was a believer in comfort food when things went wrong, and Abby Ruth just didn't have the fight to argue today, so she took a seat.

Maggie slid a plate in front of her then joined them at the table.

Abby Ruth pretended to nibble and enjoy the high-calorie concoction while slipping bites to Ritter every time Lil and Maggie engaged in conversation. Lil had become strangely willing to let the old hound dog have occasional house privileges.

The doorbell rang.

"I'll get it," Abby Ruth said, waving the rest of her sandwich at Ritter under the table. He snagged it and swallowed it in one hungry bite, but when she made a hasty exit from the kitchen, he stayed behind. Guess he figured snacks were all she was good for these days.

She hustled toward the foyer, anything to distract her from thoughts of her daughter never speaking to her again. When she pulled the front door open, to her surprise, there stood Stella and her friends. What in the world? "Hi, there. I didn't know we were expecting visitors."

"Lil did," Stella said, breezing past her into the foyer. "We need to talk to the three of you."

Abby Ruth stepped aside to let the other ladies enter as well. Thank goodness for a diversion. "Is everything okay?"

"Hardly." Virginia sashayed past Abby Ruth. "My, this place is lovely." She sauntered over to the portrait of Lincoln William Summer. "Who is this good-looking hunk of Southern man?"

"My late father," Lil said, her smile obviously strained as she approached their guests with Maggie behind her. "And although he was handsome, he was a very faithful husband."

"Too bad for him." Virginia tossed her short hair back, her eyebrows waggling as she gave the portrait a second glance.

Lil scowled at the woman.

Abby Ruth placed herself between the two women, just in case things got catty, and asked Stella, "So what brings y'all here?"

"Well, when Lil called to say the three of you were still looking into the missing items, I knew I had to tell my best friends everything," Stella said. "It wasn't fair to let y'all continue the search for Virginia's necklace when she hadn't agreed to it."

"Oh, darlin'," Virginia drawled. "Some secrets are good for the soul."

"Not secrets between friends."

Lord, if that was the truth, Abby Ruth and her best friends probably had some little black spots on their souls.

"Anyway," Stella continued, "when I finally confessed why y'all showed up at that reception, we realized we're not the only ones who've had bad luck at these weddings."

"Really?" Maggie gestured from behind Lil. "Please come in and have a seat in the parlor. This story sounds like it deserves a batch of my special tea."

They paraded into the parlor and took seats.

Juliette spoke first. "When we compared notes from our shenanigans, we realized some of the things that have happened may not have been accidents after all."

"What do you mean?"

"A couple of weeks ago I slipped a hundred-dollar bill to a sweet bartender one night to get us drinks and bring them to the table, but he never came back with the drinks or the money."

"You know about my purse," Stella said.

"And my necklace," Virginia added. "And I recently overheard a woman mention that her earrings went missing after she danced with someone at a wedding last month. Didn't think much of it until Stella put the pieces together for us and told us you ladies suspected these losses might be related."

"Yes." Lil nodded, a slow and thoughtful motion. "My wedding rings went missing between the time we left the table to do the chicken dance and when we were tossed out on our fannies."

"Your wedding rings?" Virginia said, sounding sincerely distraught. "That's a real crime! Insured or not, you can't replace sentimental pieces. No amount of money can soothe that loss."

"Did you file an insurance claim on your missing necklace?" Abby Ruth asked Virginia. Now that was a motive she hadn't considered. Was it possible these ladies were committing insurance fraud?

"Heavens, no. I didn't tell a soul about it disappearing. My husband would kill me if he found out I was crashing weddings. That would be hard to explain."

Abby Ruth was relieved to hear the excuse. She hadn't really pictured Virginia as that type of schemer. A husband stealer maybe, but not a thief or a liar. Abby Ruth glanced around the room. "I hate to say this, but I'm beginning to wonder if older women are the target."

"I certainly hope not. How about you?" Lil asked Penelope. "Anything odd that you can recollect?"

"I've got nothing. I'm just here for moral support."

"What are the odds that three out of four of you would lose something at a wedding?"

"Apparently pretty good," Penelope said. "We just need to be a little more careful. I think we're so worried about not blowing our cover as wedding crashers that we're getting careless."

"Not the case," Virginia said. "I'm never careless."

Lil sat down in the chair across from Penelope. "No jewelry missing after a wedding?"

"No. I always wear my classic pearls." She ran her fingertips across the necklace. "My father brought these back from Spain for me."

"How about money out of your wallet?"

"Never. I don't carry a purse into those parties. I just tuck some money in my bra."

"Good idea," Lil said. "Nothing out of the ordinary? Ever?"

"No. Not unless you count the fact that my nephew's twit of a bride didn't send me a thank-you note for the high-dollar silver service I gave them. Of course, kids these days don't know good manners."

"So true," Lil said.

"And that was a very expensive gift. I bought it at Everything Elegant Bakery & Gifts. They only carry top-of-the-line items."

"I told you not to spend so much money on them," Virginia said. "Probably won't be his last wedding."

"I love that place," Lil said.

Maggie added, "They bake the cakes for the weddings E-lite Wedding Planning coordinates too."

"How do you know that?" Abby Ruth asked.

"If you'd given more than a passing glance at the vendor list from that sweet couple you're sending off to Hawaii, you'd know all this too." Lil pursed her lips. "When I called the bakery, the young lady helping me mentioned it. I can't help it if people open up to me more than you."

Fair enough, but since Jenny had fired her, Abby Ruth had been even less inclined to look at all that wedding paperwork. She was fine with Lil checking in with the vendors and gathering the information on what Hannah Huckleberry had set up with them so they could integrate it into the plans for Teague and Jenny.

"Isn't Everything Elegant Bakery & Gifts the place that wraps everything in shiny paper and ribbon?" Maggie asked.

"Sure do," Stella said. "Almost as on brand as a Tiffany blue box these days, at least around Atlanta."

"When we were at that wedding with y'all, I remember seeing several gifts from Everything Elegant," Maggie said.

"They have an excellent online registry," Penelope jumped in. "My nephew's wedding planner insisted they use it. He'd have much rather registered at Bed, Bath and Beyond or

Lowe's, but that money-grubbing bride of his wouldn't hear of that."

"Interesting," Abby Ruth said.

"I swear the cheapest thing on that registry was over a hundred bucks," Penelope said. "Seriously, no thank-you notes. That makes me smoking mad."

"Thank you so much for sharing all this with us," Lil said.

Stella glanced around the room at her friends, then settled her gaze on Abby Ruth. "Do you think you can help? I mean, I'd hate to think others are getting swindled and someone's getting away with it."

"You can believe we'll handle it," Abby Ruth said. Wasn't like she had anything else to do since she wouldn't be at Jenny and Teague's wedding. "I'll be on this full-time until we resolve it. Stella, have you remembered any other details?"

"No, but I was able to have the credit card charges removed. I still can't believe that someone bought almost two hundred pounds of birdseed."

"That's suspicious as heck. Who could possibly need that much?" Abby Ruth muttered the words, then it struck. Maybe a wedding planner would need a kajillion pounds of that stuff. She sure did seem like the common denominator in all this.

"We have to run." Virginia hopped up and shimmied her skirt straight. "Afternoon wedding at the tea house in Cartersville. I love those cucumber sandwiches."

"You love the *waiters*," Stella added.

"Well, they seem to love me too. I do hope that cute man will be playing the piano again. When he sings 'Forever Young,' I absolutely melt."

"I hope they serve the Italian wedding cake from Everything Elegant. It's my favorite."

Stella leaned in to Abby Ruth. "We see a lot of the same workers at these things. It's like visiting family. They kind of have our backs because we tip them. Probably why we don't *normally* get kicked out. "

"Sorry about that," Abby Ruth said.

"That was Virginia on champagne. We all know to never let her drink it. Not your fault."

After a mess of hugs and goodbyes, they walked the ladies to the door.

Abby Ruth closed the door and turned to lean her back against it. "Are you girls thinking what I'm thinking?"

"Wedding planner has opportunity," Maggie said. "Does she have motive?"

"We need to figure that out," Lil said.

Abby Ruth nodded slowly. "I still think she's up to no good."

Maggie's lips spread into a wide grin. "I'll get the paper and the markers."

LIL GRABBED ANOTHER PLATE OF COOKIES FROM THE KITCHEN. She and the girls would need fuel to work through the logic surrounding this mess of a case.

Ritter whimpered at her bedroom door as she walked by. She'd gotten to know the difference between his sounds for attention and his whimper to go out and do his business. This was the latter. She quickly set the cookies down and whisked him outside. He ran out to the yard, took care of things and came straight back to the door.

"You're such a sweet boy." She gave him a head scratch and led him back to her room. "Now you stay quiet." She clicked the door closed and rushed back to meet the girls.

Maybe they were out of practice, because these wedding thefts sure seemed harder than their last case. Hopefully, they still had their crime-solving edge because it would be a crying shame to let all that pretty G Team stationery go to waste.

It was high time they got back in gear.

We can do this. She returned to the dining room to find Abby Ruth sitting with her elbows on the table, her body leaning toward the long stretches of paper Maggie had affixed to the wall. Still made Lil wince when they taped it to her flocked wallpaper, but Maggie had assured her painter's tape wouldn't do any damage.

Maggie was brandishing a marker close to her nose, waving it back and forth like one might a wine cork.

"Maggie Rawls, are you trying to get high?"

"Good Lord, no. Sera sent us a package of these markers from California. The red one smells like strawberries. A bunch of fruit flavors. I was hoping the brown smelled like chocolate, but I think it's figs or something. If you write with them all at once, it's like you're making fruit salad."

Lil had to experience this for herself, so she picked up a bright green marker. Sure enough, it smelled like key lime. Yum. Reluctantly, she capped it again and set it aside. "Okay, since Sera isn't here to direct us, we'll just have to muddle through ourselves. Let's start with a list of all our suspects."

In her bold print, Maggie labeled a column with "PPs". "Possible perps," she explained.

"Excellent."

"My bet's on Elisabeth with an *S*," Abby Ruth said. "I just can't warm up to a woman who's that much of a snob."

"Or her assistant, Honey," Lil added.

"Not likely," Abby Ruth said. "That little gal is as sweet as her name. Plus she's helping us."

"No one is innocent until we clear them," Maggie said.

"Okay. Put her on the list." Abby Ruth's mouth twisted like she'd swallowed a glass of unsweetened lemonade.

"But all the wedding crashers believe the culprit was a

man." Regardless, Maggie printed Elisabeth's name at the top of the list, followed by Honey's. "And I think all the vendors had opportunity." She wrote out each on a new line.

Everything Elegant Bakery & Gifts

Calla & Company - flower shop

Touch of Class - caterer

DJ Dicky

Lil pointed at the paper. "Stella described the man she suspects as a red-haired man with a mustache."

"And Virginia said hers was a young, hard-bodied ginger, clean-shaven with green eyes." Maggie talked as she wrote.

"I don't like the way that Elisabeth woman acts," Abby Ruth grumbled. "I'm not willing to let her off the hook just yet."

"Hmm," Lil mused. "She's a tall woman. What if she's disguising herself as a man?"

"That's a pretty good point," Abby Ruth said. "I wouldn't put it past her."

"Maggie, go ahead and jot down what we learned from Juliette and Penelope."

Once that was done, Maggie made another column with the heading "Reception Venues."

"They were all pretty upscale."

"I have a feeling the wedding crashers pick those on purpose," Lil said. "After all, the food, drinks, and entertainment are all first rate at those events. Maybe that's the same MO the thief has."

"So this dude knows the people there might have bucks," Abby Ruth added.

"Exactly."

"He's not completely stupid then."

Lil decided not to point out that if he was an idiot he shouldn't be that hard to catch, and they hadn't caught him yet. "Then let's talk about the crimes themselves."

At the top of the paper, Maggie wrote "Thefts" in bold block letters with a flourish on the tail of the *S*.

"Stolen cash and credit card from Stella's wallet."

Maggie wrote on the wall. "Didn't she say the only fraudulent charge was bird seed?"

Abby Ruth tapped a finger to her pursed lips. "Maybe the thief is one of those birdseed bag vendors from the bridal show."

"That's not as farfetched as it might sound." Maggie scribbled the notes on the wall.

"Yes, she did say that," Lil agreed. "We also have the one missing necklace."

"And your rings," Maggie said.

Lil had tried to keep her anxiety to herself, but her wedding rings weren't only a symbol of her marriage to Harlan and a family heirloom. Maggie had gone to great lengths to recover them when Lil had nearly lost them, overextending her loan to the pawnshop. Those rings represented the strongest friendship of Lil's life.

"What if Penelope never got a thank-you for that expensive silver service because it was never received? What if it had been stolen? We might factor that in too," Abby Ruth added.

"All those things would be pawnable," Lil said. "I guess I should tell y'all that I did alert Rick at the pawnshop to be on the lookout for my rings."

"Smart of you," Abby Ruth said.

"Even Virginia's fancy necklace?" Maggie asked.

"A thief certainly wouldn't get top dollar for it at a place like J&R Pawn, but he could turn it into cash. I'll get the descriptions of the other items to Rick, too." He'd be able to spot her rings immediately since they'd once graced a prominent spot in one of his display cases.

"Yeah, that's what this sounds like it's all about," Abby Ruth said. "Someone trying to score quick cash."

"Maybe he's just trying to make ends meet," Maggie said. "It's hard to blame him for that."

"But why steal from older women then? If he were any kind of man at all, he'd realize they might be on fixed incomes."

"People do get desperate," Lil pointed out. "And lots of people think we make easy marks." After all, she'd certainly been taken for a ride like that once herself.

"I want this guy to come for me," Abby Ruth grumbled. "I'll show him an easy mark. Right between the—"

"That's enough. We don't need to stoop to that kind of violence." Her own words made Lil smile because she had a feeling the last man they'd taken down—right here at Summer Haven—would warn others that older folks were not easy targets. Duct tape and an eighty-mile-an-hour fastball could convince a man.

Maggie stepped back and gave the wall a careful once-over. "I'm just not seeing a real pattern right now except for the wedding coordinator, her preferred vendors, and the wedding crashers."

"And we have no idea if other people besides the crashers have been targeted. It's not like we've canvassed all the guests at one of these things."

"Maybe we should do that," Maggie suggested. "We could pretend to do wedding guest satisfaction surveys or something."

"Dear, I hate to burst your bubble," Lil said, "but we have a wedding coming up of our own."

"We can still pull the next string we have," Maggie insisted.

Lil picked up the yellow marker, which made her crave

banana pudding. "Looks like that means we need to head into Atlanta to talk with the bakery folks as soon as we can."

Maggie grabbed the iPad and poked around on it. By the way her expression melted, she wasn't happy with whatever information she'd found. "There's no way we can get there in time today."

"Just as well," Abby Ruth said, rising from her chair. "I doubt one day will make a difference. Right now, I need to get my head right about all this stuff with Jenny. I'm going down to Earlene's Drinkery. Holler if you need me." With that, she strode out of the room, and a few seconds later the front door banged closed.

"Have to say I always thought taking Abby Ruth down a notch or two might be a good thing," Lil told Maggie, "but I can't stand seeing her like this."

CHAPTER 16

Her heart still heavy because Jenny had been true to her word about not talking to her, Abby Ruth glanced up when Teague slid into the booth across from her at Earlene's Drinkery. He glanced at the plethora of plates scattered across the table. "Couldn't decide?"

"I figured this called for wings, nachos, and fried pickles."

"Good thing I'm starving." He pulled a small plate toward him and piled it with all the greasy, fattening food. "Besides, all Jenny's been able to stomach is that damn pasta. I appreciate you curing her puking, but what I wouldn't give for a big steak right now."

"Gah," Abby Ruth said. "When I was pregnant with Jenny I couldn't abide the smell of charred beef."

"Pregnancy must suck," he muttered.

Once he had his plate filled, a nacho teetering atop enough chicken wings to look like a graveyard, Abby Ruth said, "I need your help. Jenny won't take my calls. I've wanted to come by the house, but my heart breaks at the thought of her slamming the door in my face."

Teague licked the sauce off his thumb and sat back. "I'll be honest. She's been so upset, I'm not sure she'd answer the door. She feels betrayed."

"She wouldn't listen to my side of the story. Not really. I wish—"

"Teague Castro!" A strident voice came slicing through the drift of cigarette smoke in the watering hole. "I want to give you a piece of my mind."

Abby Ruth looked over to see Winnie—the owner of the Love 'Em or Leave 'Em Florist here in Summer Shoals—hustling across the room toward them as fast as her chubby thighs would carry her. Over the sound of Hank Williams, Jr. wailing from the jukebox, Abby Ruth could hear the *scritch scritch* of Winnie's polyester pants rubbing together. With the way she was stalking toward them, it was obvious she was one angry woman.

"Uh-oh," Teague said in a low voice.

"What's going on?" Abby Ruth noticed Desi Fanning trailing Winnie, her glossy red braid bouncing with each step. Desi owned the local bakery, Icing On The Cake.

Desi'd had her share of bad times, but that woman always put her best and most hopeful foot forward. Even when her ex-husband had gone half-crazy a while back, she'd found a way to make things work for her and her daughter. Besides, she was an amazing baker, making the best éclairs this side of the Mississippi. Which was only one of the reasons she and Jenny had hit it off the first day they'd met.

Desi wasn't as fired up as Winnie, but she didn't look happy. Her eyes held a sadness and hurt that Abby Ruth recognized immediately.

Winnie stalked up to the table and plopped an arrangement of some weird tropical flowers and little pink roses down hard enough to shake Teague's mountain of chicken wings. One teetered and tumbled, but he was dexterous and snagged it before it landed in his lap.

Then Winnie propped one fist on her round hip and wagged her finger close to his nose. So close that Abby Ruth was surprised he did nothing more than smile up at the florist. "I can't believe you, Teague Castro. We've embraced you as one of our own. Heck, half the time I forget you're from Texas." She spit out the word like it was a piece of lint on her tongue. "We elected you as our sheriff, our sworn peace provider, and this is how you repay us? Give him a piece of your mind, Desi." She pulled the bakery owner around to her side so she stood close to Abby Ruth.

Desi slid a three-layer cake iced in what appeared to be buttercream frosting onto the table and flashed a crooked, apologetic smile. She wasn't totally comfortable being here, but it looked as if she had an honest-to-goodness beef with Teague as well. "What Winnie is trying to say is that all the local Summer Shoals business owners are disappointed in how you're handling your wedding. We've heard rumors that you're bringing in a florist, baker, and caterer from Atlanta."

Teague wiped his mouth and set aside his napkin. "Ladies, is it traditional for the groom to make all the decisions about a wedding, or any of the decisions for that matter?"

"You're the sheriff," Winnie said, as if that had a damn thing to do with little pink roses.

It was time for Abby Ruth to come to her future son-in-law's defense. "I'm the one you want. I'm in charge of Jenny and Teague's wedding." Or at least she had been at one time.

The way Winnie and Desi goggled at her would've been funny if this wedding plan was moving along smoothly, but it was a train wreck all the way around. "You?" Winnie choked out. "You wouldn't know a daisy from a dandelion."

"Wrong," she said, keeping her voice even. "One has a black center with happy colorful petals. The other one you make a wish on and get mad when someone blows it all over your yard. After all, they're weeds." And Sera sometimes made bitter-tasting tea out of them. Blech.

Winnie's shoulders dropped, making her abundant bosom land on the tabletop. As if they didn't already have enough stuff cluttering up the small space. "Then why in the world would you hire people outside Summer Shoals? We're not backwoods here. We're more than capable of handling a classy wedding out at Summer Haven." Her eyes widened with some Winnie-like realization. "Maybe that's it. Lillian Summer Fairview doesn't think we're good enough to throw a party at her home. She's always been a little stuck up—"

"This wasn't Lil's decision," Abby Ruth cut in. "It was mine and mine alone." She really didn't need to add to Lil's somewhat uppity reputation in town, especially with Winnie, who was a gossip queen. "My girl's been living in Boston for a lot of years. I just thought she'd be happier with big-city vendors."

And that totally took the wind out of Winnie's sails. This. This was why weddings were a damn menace. There were lots of rules and expectations, fluffy crap that made no sense, and people got their feelings hurt.

But she certainly couldn't explain the real reason she'd hired outside vendors in front of Teague. He'd have a conniption fit if he caught wind of Abby Ruth and the other gals dabbling in more crime solving.

"Tell you what," she said brightly. "We haven't figured out the groom's cake yet. Desi, why don't you take care of that?" Looked like she'd be tossing a perfectly good German Chocolate out the window. "And I'd like to be sure Jenny's bouquet is extra special. Would you handle that for us, Winnie?"

Winnie's foot went to tapping, much like Abby Ruth's did when she was agitated. Darn, that was way more annoying than she'd ever realized. Obviously, her concession to include Winnie in the floral arrangements wasn't cutting it.

Winnie said, "It's not just me and Desi who are heartbroken. Bunches of people just knew they'd be involved when Jenny and Teague finally got around to tying the knot. And when I heard from Angelina Broussard that Jenny was expecting, I assumed my phone would start ringing off the wall for wedding flowers."

Abby Ruth restrained herself from rolling her eyes. Most of the time, she loved living in little bitty Summer Shoals, but sometimes she missed being one of several million people in Houston. Anonymity had its benefits.

Like when she and Red had been seeing each other years ago. Thank goodness no one had been suspicious of the affair when she'd gotten pregnant with Jenny. If they had, she and Red would've been found out for sure.

"Fine," Abby Ruth said, "what would soothe your pain and suffering?"

The hollow-eyed greed in Winnie's face made Abby Ruth wince. Whatever was coming would put a big ol' dent in her wallet, she had no doubt.

"My cousin Sharma Lee recently opened a dress shop on the other side of town. She has a lovely assortment of bridal gowns. Dresses for mothers and guests too. As luck would have it, she's open late on Thursday nights. It's hard for small businesses to get off the ground. Sure would help if you were to spend a couple thousand dollars in her store."

The nacho Abby Ruth had just popped in her mouth caught in the back of her throat. Two. Thousand? Luck wasn't exactly how she would describe that chunk of change. What was Winnie expecting her to buy—a dress sewn with pure gold thread?

Teague reached across the table and whacked her on the

shoulder, just hard enough so she could swallow the nacho and wheeze out, "Jenny only needs one dress."

"Well, when you consider the bridesmaids, the mother of the groom, and the mother of the bride, it does add up."

Far as Abby Ruth knew, Jenny didn't plan on having any attendants. Besides, it wasn't clear if Abby Ruth herself was still on the guest list. But she said, "I'll get over to your cousin's shop as soon as I can get around to it. Can you text me the address?"

Winnie did a little electric slide around Desi and pulled Abby Ruth out of the booth so fast that she almost ended up on the floor. "No time like the present. Why don't you go on down there now?"

With a sly grin on his face, Teague slid Abby Ruth's half-finished beer over in front of himself. "Don't worry about these wings, Abby Ruth. I'll make sure they're well taken care of."

Yeah, she hoped they gave him a big case of indigestion. Still, she hip-bumped his shoulder as Winnie herded her toward the bar's front door. "Later, Tadpole."

He toasted her with her own beer and took a big drink. He was a smart-ass, but she loved that boy.

Once they were outside on the sidewalk, Abby Ruth turned to Winnie, "I'll head over to your cousin's place right now." Surely that would satisfy this bulldog of a woman.

But Winnie just smiled, highlighting the dimples in her rounded face. "Perfect. Then I'll follow along."

CHAPTER 17

Abby Ruth pressed speed dial to Summer Haven as she walked down the street and whispered into the phone, "Lil, it's me. Desi and Winnie were down Teague's throat about not using them for the wedding." Glancing over her shoulder, she added, "I need y'all to get down here to Sharma Lee's dress shop and help me pick out dresses to take to Jenny."

"We're in the middle of putting Jenny loves Teague stickers on the bottles of bubbles. Do you know how hard it is to get those things on straight?"

"No time for that," she snapped, lifting her arms to cool the sweat pooling under armpits. Winnie was still behind her. Was that woman going to follow her all the way there? "Meet me and bring Maggie with you."

"Calm down," Lil said. "We're on our way."

Abby Ruth entered the shop and was met with a suspicious look from the shop owner. No surprise…dresses weren't Abby Ruth's thing, which any woman could see in a hot second. Maybe she should've waited until Lil arrived.

"May I help you?"

"I need to pick up some wedding dresses for my daughter to try on," Abby Ruth said.

"What's the last name?"

"It's the Cady-Castro wedding," Winnie told her cousin. "Abby Ruth is a little behind on things."

"You should have scheduled something. Is your daughter on the way?"

"No, and we're trying to keep this a surprise. Bad luck if the groom hears about the dress and all that," Abby Ruth said.

"It's only bad luck if the groom *sees* the bride-to-be in the gown. We're very careful about that here."

"We can't take any chances. We'll pick out a few dresses and take them to her." Abby Ruth swept a gown to the right on the rack, snickering at the next one. Good Lord, a gal could suffocate in that much chiffon. Made her feel itchy all over just looking at it.

"That's not the way we operate here." Sharma Lee took Abby Ruth by the elbow and hustled her back toward the door.

Winnie plopped into one of the chairs. "What made me think this was a good idea?"

Lil and Maggie rushed inside the shop.

Abby Ruth jerked away from Sharma Lee and turned on her. "Do you want to sell a dress or not? I can certainly go over to Clarksville or Atlanta and pick up dresses. In fact, Atlanta has offered to deliver them too. Right, Lil?"

Lil's eyes went wide with a what-have-I-missed expression, but she smiled that society girl smile of hers and said, "Absolutely. Hello, Sharma Lee."

Abby Ruth should've known Lil would know the dress lady. "She doesn't want to let us take dresses out of the shop for Jenny to try on. What kind of— "

"I can't believe we hadn't heard about your new shop," Lil

said in her most patient tone. "You know I'd never want to take my business anywhere but here. But—"

"I have a full tank of gas. I can go to Atlanta right now," Abby Ruth added.

Lil tugged on the peplum of her dress. "Sharma Lee, I hope you can help us with this teensy-weensy favor. You know I'm good for it."

"I'm happy to help," Sharma Lee said as if Lil was the most influential and charming woman in the world. "Now what kind of dress are you looking for? And what size?"

Abby Ruth stepped forward. "Size six. None of that big poufy stuff either."

Lil added. "Traditional, maybe."

"Or something kind of modern," Maggie said. "I could totally see her in something flowing like a Grecian style, or maybe that high-low hemline."

"Oh no." Abby Ruth said. "My daughter is not wearing a mullet bridal gown."

"Sounds like you need an assortment of styles. I can show you some of the more popular dresses."

Abby Ruth whipped hangers from left to right. *Whish whoosh whish whoosh.* Suddenly, she stopped and pulled a gown from the rack. A simple flowing skirt with a sleeveless lace-and-beaded bodice. Classic and classy. "This is the one."

An hour later, Maggie and Lil were wrestling yards of white fabric into the crew cab of Abby Ruth's dually. She drove to Jenny and Teague's, with Maggie and Lil following in Maggie's truck.

She parked just out of sight of Jenny's house. Then she loaded her arms with five dresses and hauled them down the road. Once there, she quietly slipped up to the front porch and hung the gowns on the light, which made it look as if a giant ghost had just taken up residency. Maggie and Lil came trudging up, their arms filled with the last seven dresses.

"You don't know what this means to me. Thank you." Abby Ruth's palms were clammy as she reached for her friends' hands. How had she gotten here, where she was worried about how her own daughter would react if she found her standing on this front porch?

"You're coming in too, aren't you?" Maggie asked.

"No, it would just upset her. She doesn't want me here. That's fine. This is her day, and her happiness is all that's important to me."

"She still loves you," Maggie said. "She's your daughter, and y'all will get through this."

Abby Ruth shuffled down the steps from the porch, then snuck around the corner of the house where she could watch without being seen.

Ding dong. Dingdong. Dingdongdingdongdingdong.

The doorbell woke Jenny from a fitful dream about wedding flowers with people's faces where the centers should be. She had to stop snacking on bread-and-butter pickles before lying down on the couch.

She pulled herself up from the cushions and answered the door. A pile of white satin, charmeuse, chiffon, and organza nearly assaulted her. Sequins scratched at her skin and somehow a bugle bead found its way into her nose.

"Surprise!" came from somewhere beyond the fluffy fabric.

"Lil? Is that you?" Jenny pushed the door wide. "What is all this?"

"We've brought wedding dresses for you to try on."

"We?" A sizzle crept up Jenny's spine. Was her mother behind one of these giant heaps of hoop skirts?

Maggie pushed Lil forward then stumbled in behind her.

"Scoot on out of the way, Jenny. We're coming through. There are more on the porch too."

Jenny scrambled back, peeking around the cloud of dresses, thankful there was no sight of her mother in the white cloud. "Where did all these come from?"

"Sharma Lee's new dress shop. Your mother can be very persuasive."

"*Persuasive* isn't exactly the word I'd use to describe her." The words that had been going through Jenny's mind about her mom lately weren't nice ones, so she gave Lil a closed-mouth smile. Enough said.

Lil pulled a thick white book out from under the dresses and pressed it into Jenny's hands. "We thought you might want this back."

The wedding planner felt heavy, kind of like the way her heart had been since she discovered the truth about her father.

She set it aside while Lil spread the dresses out around the room. Three on the couch. One on each chair, and some hanging off the stair railing.

"I'd planned to wear a simple dress I picked up in New York last summer. This is overkill."

"Don't you want to look like a princess for Teague?" Lil asked. "After all, he's your true love, your perfect match. You don't want to regret one detail of your wedding."

Jenny picked up a dress with big poofy sleeves and a big-ass bow on the back. "I don't want to hurt anyone's feelings, but there's no way that I'm wearing this."

"Okay, not your style." Maggie said, snatching it from her and hugging the dress to her chest, but Jenny saw the disappointment in her eyes.

What would it hurt to try them all on? It would obviously make these gals happy. They were like family to her, and the last thing she wanted to do was alienate them. It wasn't their fault her mom had kept a secret from her.

She did want to look like a princess on her wedding day because marrying Teague would be the second best day of her life. Grayson would always be her first best. She smiled to herself. Well, when this baby was born, she'd have two first bests. "I'm sorry, you two. I'm just a little cranky and feeling fat."

"You're not even three months pregnant yet," Lil said. "You are still skinny as a rail."

"I don't feel skinny." But she pushed aside her skunky mood.

"Maybe a bridal dress-up will make you feel better, dear."

"Anything to get my mind off being sick," Jenny agreed. She could use some fun in her life right now, and she hated to disappoint Lil. "Let's try them on in the den. I have a big mirror in there."

One by one, Lil and Maggie helped Jenny get in and out of the stack of dresses. Everything from huge to hugging to a mini-skirt number the dress shop owner had told Lil and Maggie was all the rage for brides Jenny's age.

Jenny picked up a simple dress with a sheer skirt, more full than an A-line, but it was the bodice that stole her breath. Intricately beaded on delicate lace, it would look like pearls against her skin. "This one is gorgeous."

"Quite elegant," Lil agreed.

Maggie slipped the hanger from the dress and let the gorgeous fabric drape into Jenny's arms. She stepped into the dress, and Maggie went to work on the five tiny buttons that held it all together just above Jenny's rear end.

Jenny turned to the side then back to the mirror.

"That's it, isn't it?" Lil clapped her hands. "I can see it in your eyes. You're positively glowing."

"It's beautiful."

Her fingers ran across the fabric, then across the tiny beads that added a dash of elegance to the gown.

Maggie tugged at the fabric, pulling it straight. "Jenny. It's perfect."

Jenny nodded. For the first time, she felt like a real bride. A fairytale kind of bride.

A sudden movement in her peripheral vision caught her attention. The unmistakable black and gray of her mom's spiky hairdo bobbed just above the windowsill at the far side of the room.

Jenny's heart broke again, because she knew this was the dress her mom had picked out for her. Yes, she was still so mad at her mom, but a tiny voice inside reminded her of all the years when it had been just the two of them against the world. They'd made a good mother-daughter team, and she hated that it suddenly seemed as if they were on opposing sides.

"This is the only gown your mother picked out," Maggie said, confirming Jenny's thoughts. "She knew it was the one."

"I'd skip the veil," Lil said. "It would take away from the simplicity of the dress. Maybe an updo with your hair, and some small flowers. You want the back of your dress to show."

"I think so too," Jenny said, glancing back toward the window. She caught her mom gazing longingly at the dress. Then she looked up and realized Jenny had spotted her. That wistful look in her eyes vanished and her mouth tightened, but Jenny knew her mom well enough to understand what she was seeing was a defense mechanism. Her mom didn't want her to know how much this wedding meant to her too.

How in the world would they get through this?

Jenny's instinct was to turn her back, but with a tight feeling around her chest, she glanced over her shoulder and gave her mom a little wave.

CHAPTER 18

Another morning. Another road trip. Hopefully, to Lil's way of thinking, another lead.

She and the other girls had been back and forth to Atlanta so many times over the past few months—for Abby Ruth's cancer treatments and now for all the wedding hullabaloo surrounding this case—that Lil had almost every landmark and billboard memorized up Interstate 75. Every time they took this road her stomach growled, begging for breakfast at the Cracker Barrel, and there were at least four on this route.

After a quick stop to drop off the Hawaiian destination wedding and honeymoon package details to Hannah and Brandon, they were on their way.

On the bright side, an investigative trip to Everything Elegant should mean cake. Maybe even some coffee or hot tea, and that was almost as good as hash brown casserole.

They followed the GPS directions on Abby Ruth's phone. *In a quarter of a mile, you will reach your destination on the right.*

Lil scanned the horizon. "There it is," she said, pointing toward a large building with pretty metal awnings.

They drove by the storefront in search of a parking spot.

The store windows were framed with sparkling lights. On the right was a display of wedding gifts wrapped in pearlescent paper and tied with looping organza bows. The front left corner was dedicated to the bakery. A beautiful table set for two with dainty china and delicate wineglasses looked like a scene straight out of a romantic movie. Between the two settings, a seven-tier cake was decorated with swoops of white and lavender icing. So pretty.

Although it was midafternoon, the parking lot overflowed with cars. "Don't people work in this town?" Abby Ruth said.

Maggie sat forward in her seat. "Business is booming. That's for sure."

"This is not your everyday cake shop," Lil said. "This bakery does treats and homemade bread too. Not to mention the gift shop. I'm sure that draws in a lot of traffic." Her kind of place.

Maggie got out of the truck. "The smell is making me drool. Can we sample cakes for Jenny and Teague while we're here?"

"Too late," Lil said. "I talked with Honey and she said we'd have to make do with what Hannah and Brandon chose because it was special order—a six-tier violet-infused cake."

"Violet-infused—what does that mean?" Abby Ruth snarled. "Violet is a color. Not a flavor."

Maggie tsked. "I don't know, but from the looks of those cakes in the window, these folks are doing some pretty elaborate stuff with their baking and decorating."

Abby Ruth eyed the cakes in the window. "How bad could a pretty cake taste?"

"You're right," Lil said. "Nothing we can do about it now anyway."

"We need to hit both sides. First we'll ask if they've had an increase in returned gifts or anything strange with the registry process. Then we'll move on to the cakes." Abby Ruth walked on without waiting for an answer.

Maggie flashed Lil a quick look. "She had to save the best for last, didn't she?"

"Think of it as incentive for getting the job done."

When they strolled inside, they set off a doorbell that played the "Wedding March." The shop smelled of fruit, chocolate, and old money. People were everywhere. Mothers and daughters pored through catalogs, and young couples tasted cakes trying to make decisions for their big day.

Lil jabbed her elbow into Abby Ruth's side and pointed to a corner table. "Look."

A rusty-haired man wearing a batter-smeared apron sat at a table with Honey and her boss. Elisabeth looked coolly professional in pumps, skirt, and a sleeveless top that left her toned arms bare.

"Elisabeth with an *S*," Abby Ruth mocked, tilting her nose in the air.

"That's not what I meant," Lil said. "Look at the man sitting with them."

Abby Ruth visibly perked up at the sight of the man. "Do you think he's the baker?"

"Seems to be, with the way he's dressed."

"He fits the profile of our suspect, too. With him and that suspicious Elisabeth sitting at the same table, we need to get over there and—"

Lil held out her arms in order to clothesline her friends. "Slow down. We don't want to be conspicuous. Let's wander over to the gift shop and pretend to be real customers."

"But—"

"Don't worry. They look like they'll be here for a while."

Maggie stopped just out of sight of the table. "I'll stay by the door and keep an eye on them while y'all get started."

Lil and Abby Ruth wandered over to the side of the store

that made up the gift shop. The walls were lined with bakers' racks full of unusual items, a cute way to tie the two places together. The well-organized space was divided into sections like a house. Bedroom, kitchen, bath complete with a clawfoot tub filled with spa essentials, closets of organizers, and outdoor goods under a pergola. Very clever. Someone had an excellent eye for merchandising.

Some shelves were filled with traditional items too, like crystal candlesticks and silver serving pieces. Intricate handmade sculptures by Georgia artists were placed throughout the room.

"Let me know if you need help." A man's voice came from behind a rack of organic bamboo towels in muted tones of brown, green, and blue. "I'm John Erik."

"Thank you." Abby Ruth waved a hand. "When you get a moment, I need to set up my daughter's registry."

"No problem."

But the next thing Lil knew, the man was walking away from them toward what she assumed was the storeroom. "Young people have no sense of customer service these days."

"Maybe he had to pee."

A few minutes later, a woman approached them. "John Erik mentioned you needed some help."

"Thank you. Yes, I need to set up the registry for my daughter's wedding."

"I can help you." She pulled an electronic tablet out from her apron and started clicking away. "What's the groom's last name?"

"Castro. Teague. T E A G U E." Abby Ruth patiently gave the information to the woman, who seemed to be in no hurry at all.

Out of another pocket, she pulled out a taser-like contraption. "This is for you. Just select the items she wants to add to the list."

A wicked grin crossed Abby Ruth's face. "Sweet!" She gripped the scanner like a pistol. "Right up my alley."

"So it is," Lil said.

"If you can't find what you like in the store, we have the catalog you can scan barcodes from," the woman explained.

Abby Ruth spun the barcode scanner on her pointer finger like Annie Oakley. Oh, goodness. Lil would need to keep a close eye on this process.

"You'll be able to check the registry to see what's been purchased or put on hold all the way up to the wedding date."

"Isn't that handy?" Abby Ruth scanned a meat cleaver. *Ding.* "So, how often do gifts get returned? And can people return them for cash or merchandise?" she asked so casually that Lil momentarily forgot finding out those details were the real reason they were there.

"We have a full cash return policy within thirty days of the wedding, as long as you're registered with us. Otherwise, merchandise returns only."

"I see." She walked over to the first aisle with Lil at her side. She scanned a two-hundred-dollar chef's knife and a margarita machine. Then she picked up what looked like a whiskey barrel. "Hey, do-it-yourself liquor."

"Don't you dare scan that." Lil said.

"Like a moonshiners beginner's course," Abby Ruth said. "But I could see how some folks like my friend here might take offense to it. You probably get a lot of these coming back."

"Our returns are extremely low. We only offer the highest quality housewares."

Abby Ruth's phone buzzed, and she pulled it from her pocket. "Excuse me." She grabbed Lil by the arm and made hasty spin. "Maggie just sent a 911 text," she whispered.

"Gotta go. Thank you." Abby Ruth tossed the gun back to the woman. "That should get us started."

They hustled over to the bakery side where darned if it didn't look like Maggie had just tripped over Elisabeth's bag on the floor and tried to catch herself by snatching a handful of the woman's hair.

Lil hurried to Maggie's aid. "Are you okay?"

"I'm fine." But Maggie suddenly went off-kilter again, grabbing for the wedding planner's arm and pulling her to the floor. In an awkward attempt to stand, Maggie used Elisabeth's body as a sort of ladder. Once on her feet, she weaved and stumbled off to the side to land on a bench near the window.

Elisabeth rubbed her head and frowned up from her less-than-graceful perch. "You three again?"

The baker hopped up to help Elisabeth to her feet.

While they were occupied with brushing off the wedding coordinator's designer skirt, Lil asked Maggie, "What in the world is happening here?"

Pulling Lil away a few steps, Maggie winked and whispered, "I was checking to see if she was wearing a wig."

"Good work, Mags." Abby Ruth chuckled. "One heck of an act you put on. Had me convinced."

"Maybe." Maggie's dejected exhale didn't bode well. "But she's not our baddie."

Abby Ruth's mouth twisted and her eyes went squinty. "How can you be so sure?"

"She's a woman."

Oh, goodness. "Mags, you didn't…"

"I did, and I can tell you those are God-given boobs that woman is wearing."

Abby Ruth stomped her foot. "I was so sure she was involved."

"At least we've marked someone off the list. That's a step in the right direction," Lil said. "Now we need to get close to the baker. Maybe we can just wait until Elisabeth and Honey—"

Maggie suddenly waved her arms behind the assistant, then pointed to her own wrist. Then to the woman.

What was Maggie trying to get across? Something important by her vigorous gestures.

Honey's sleeves were rolled back. Gracing the woman's wrist was a tattoo in the shape of what looked like a hummingbird on a scrolling vine and a bright yellow flower.

"Girls, it's time for us to go," Lil reined Maggie in and shooed Abby Ruth out the front door.

"Why did you pull us out?" Maggie said. "The little wedding assistant had a tattoo. So did the guy you think snatched your rings and the one Stella thinks could've taken her purse."

"She doesn't fit the profile at all," Lil said. "Not her gender, height, nor hair. Not everyone who has a tattoo is a suspect. Heck, if that were the case, we'd have to strip-search half the population of Georgia. Besides, all these tattoos are in different places—neck, biceps, wrist." And they wouldn't find her wedding rings and the other missing items by running down dead-end trails.

"She has a point," Abby Ruth said.

"What if they aren't real? What if the thief wears different temporary tattoos to avoid suspicion?"

"Even if that were the case, Honey can't be more than five-two, tops." Lil didn't have to have been on as many cases as Maggie and Abby Ruth to recognize *that* difference.

"And Elisabeth obviously wasn't wearing a disguise," Abby Ruth added, her entire body seeming to collapse on itself. "Lil's right. Let's just give it up. What's done is done."

"We do not give up," Maggie announced. "Since when were we quitters? What is wrong with y'all? We're the G

Team, and I think we should give a little thought to all the tattoos."

Abby Ruth didn't smile. Didn't snicker. Didn't even raise that eyebrow like she was known to do. "Get real. We're just bored women with business cards."

Maggie and Lil were silent for a three-beat.

"Speak for yourself," Maggie said. "We've solved some pretty important cases, and we are good at this. I think we're closing in on the real culprit. We can't give up now. We need to tail Honey."

"I don't think so." Abby Ruth's lips puckered.

Maggie's eyes brightened the way they did when she got an idea she loved. "We should set up a sting to see if she's involved."

"We don't have time for all that," Lil said. "We have a wedding in just over a week."

Maggie tapped a finger to her lips. "As will Honey."

"What exactly are you suggesting?" Abby Ruth demanded.

An idea buzzed in Lil's brain. "If she *is* involved, we could take her down that day."

"We know what this thief has hit before," Maggie said. "Jewelry. Cash. We can bait them at Jenny's wedding. It's the perfect setup. I know you like Honey, Abby Ruth, but I think she's involved. I feel it."

"No. No way." Abby Ruth's mouth was a mutinous line. "I've already put my relationship with Jenny in the toilet. If you can call her waving at me a positive step, I'm taking it. I'm not doing anything to add to the strain."

"Look," Lil said. "Don't bite off our heads just because your personal life is in a bit of a mess."

"A bit of a mess?" Her eyebrows near to her hairline, Abby Ruth glared at Lil. "Really? We need to put a stop to this investigation. It was my idea, but we're making mistakes. There's too much at risk. I say we stop right here and now."

"You don't get to decide everything, Abby Ruth, and you can't fire Honey and lose all those vendors at this late date."

Abby Ruth said nothing.

That was what Lil thought. "Then wait here." Lil pivoted and hotfooted it back toward the bakery.

"What are you doing?" Abby Ruth yelled.

Lil put on more speed and slipped back inside the building before Abby Ruth could catch her. She scanned the space to find Elisabeth standing across the room talking on her phone. Thank goodness Honey was sitting by herself.

Lil hurried over to take advantage of the opportunity. "Honey?"

The blonde girl looked up, her expression wary. "Do I know you?"

"We spoke on the phone. I'm Lillian Summer Fairview."

"I see. The Castro wedding." Honey gulped noticeably and cast a wary glance at her boss. "We really shouldn't be talking about this now."

"I know," Lil whispered before raising her voice to say, "We were able to get a flock of doves—are they called a flock?—and I thought you might like to see the release for events you plan in the future."

"Well…"

To make it look good for Elisabeth's benefit, Lil took out a G Team card and scribbled Summer Haven's address on the back along with the wedding date. "In fact, we'd love for you to come on out *early.*"

"The wedding coordinator is always on site early," Honey explained.

Lil gave Honey a wink. "The wedding is at four, but you'll want to get there extra, *extra* early. You don't want to miss seeing all of Summer Haven." That should allow them time to eyeball Honey before any of the guests arrived or festivities began. "I'll show you around myself."

"Thank you. That's so nice of you."

"I'll see you there, dear." Pride in setting a trap warming her bones, Lil strolled up to the bakery counter.

Elisabeth glared at her as she returned to the table where Honey was still seated.

Oh yes, this would work out perfectly. Lil smiled and ordered three organic chia seed dog treats for Ritter. The lady behind the counter packaged them and rang them up.

"Seven-fifty, ma'am," the store clerk said.

Lil almost choked but handed the woman a ten dollar bill. Goodness, that was more than the bakery in Summer Shoals charged for three delicious toffee crunch cookies. But Ritter deserved a special little something after all. She tucked the goodies in her purse then headed to the door.

"Ta-ta," Lil called as she passed Honey on her way out.

She climbed into Abby Ruth's truck. "Let's get a move on."

Abby Ruth pulled out of the lot and glared a hole into Lil. "What were you doing in there?"

"Eyes on the road, please." Lil let out her breath once Abby Ruth turned her attention back to driving.

"You stirred up something, didn't you?"

"I simply invited Honey to come see the doves before the wedding starts."

"I told you—"

"You're hoping to catch her at something before anyone arrives. Smart, Lil!" Maggie said.

"I still don't like it," Abby Ruth grumbled.

"You just do your thing," Lil said, risking a pat to Abby Ruth's leg. "Be the mother of the bride and leave this case to us."

"You think you can do this without me. Or Sera?"

Lil was pretty proud of herself for luring Honey to Summer Haven well before the wedding. Wouldn't Abby Ruth be impressed with Lil when she solved this case without her? "You're willing to drop the case right now anyway. I guess we'll see. If not, what have we lost?"

When Teague walked in the door that evening, Jenny had worked herself up into a lather. For days, she'd tried to distract herself from the swirl of conflicting feelings inside her, today by playing outside with Grayson and Bowzer, but every time she looked at her son, all she could think of was seeing him run alongside Red.

Red Jensen.

Her dad.

Teague shrugged out of his weapon harness and went to lock it away in the gun safe they'd installed immediately after buying the place. Then he walked over with that cocky swagger she loved and pulled her into his arms.

Thank goodness for this man. How would she be handling this whole having-a-father thing if Teague weren't around? Her ex-husband Daniel wouldn't have given her an ounce of understanding, even if he'd cared. Cared? Even if he'd listened to her. By the time they'd split, he'd quit hearing her.

Teague Castro would be an ear for her for the rest of their lives.

"You okay?" he asked.

Those two words made the tears well up and close her throat. Just when she'd been doing so well the past couple of days. She blew out a steadying breath and leaned back so she could look up into his face. "Lillian and Maggie came by yesterday."

"More wedding details?"

"You could say that." When they'd bustled in with those armloads of white dresses, she'd been struck dumb. She'd expected to walk down the aisle in a nice dress or cocktail suit, but she'd never considered a real wedding dress. It was as if she'd convinced herself she didn't deserve to be a bride again. "They brought over a truckload of wedding dresses."

"I'm not surprised. Winnie cornered your mom when we were having a bite to eat at Earlene's Drinkery."

Now she pulled all the way out of his arms. "You saw Mom?"

"Just because you're mad at her doesn't mean I am."

Needing to move, she walked around the kitchen island, picked up a dishcloth and began to clean out the sink. She hated cleaning the sink. "She came with Lil and Maggie."

"Your mother didn't mean to hurt you. You know that, right? It's complicated, but everything with Abby Ruth Cady always is."

"She didn't come to the door, didn't ask to come inside. At first, I didn't realize she was with them. They stripped me down and made me try on every dress."

"Did you find one you liked?"

She smiled, but it felt sad on her lips. "I fell in love with the last dress I tried on, and when I had it on, I glanced out the window and Mom was looking in. Maggie told me it was the only dress Mom picked out."

"Please tell me you didn't take it off and send it back just because of that."

"No! I knew it was mine the second I slipped it on. What should I do, Teague? I love Mom, but I'm so mad. So hurt." She slapped her hands against her thighs. "Half of me is desperate to have her at the wedding. And half of me wants to push her away."

He came closer and leaned against the bar. He studied her so intently she felt as if he were looking inside her. A man in law enforcement made for a very observant lover. "She's only ever wanted what was best for you."

"How is not telling me about my dad best for me?"

"Jenny," he sighed. "Sometimes the people who love you the most keep secrets for a reason. When they know something that will definitely hurt you, they may decide to keep it to themselves." He glanced down at the floor and back up quickly, but Jenny was pretty observant too and saw the flicker of anxiety rush across his face.

The man she was about to marry was also keeping something from her. And this wasn't the first time. His past secrets were the reason she'd married another man, the reason she and Teague had lost a decade together. "What is it? It's about Melinda, isn't it?"

"What? What does my ex-wife have to do with your mom?"

"Nothing that I know of, but I'm pretty sure she has something to do with that guilty expression you just tried to hide."

"I haven't given her more than a moment's thought in years."

"Then what were you thinking about?" She hated asking the question, but she was electrified with pregnancy hormones, and she *was* unusually needy these days.

"That I wish I could've kept you from feeling this pain, but I wasn't surprised you discovered Red is your dad."

"What do you mean? Why wouldn't you have been surprised?"

He reached out to run a gentle hand down her arm. "Because I've suspected it for a long while now."

The dullest pain hit her heart. She stepped back so quickly that she caught Bowzer's tail under her heel, and her feet slipped out from under her. One minute she was stable, and the next, nothing was beneath her.

But she never hit the floor.

Somehow Teague got his hands on her and cushioned her against his chest as his back slammed into the kitchen cabinets. As soon as she got her bearings, Jenny scrambled backwards in a dizzy crabwalk and pulled her feet underneath her on the floor.

Bowzer came over and climbed into her lap, resting his head on her knee. She stroked his soft yellow fur, taking modest comfort in the silky feel against her fingers.

Keep breathing. Maybe you heard Teague wrong.

She looked up at the man she loved. His eyes were shadowed, misery and worry etching his face in a way that told her she'd heard exactly what he'd said. "How? How could you have known? And not told me?"

He hunkered down next to her, and Bowzer whined. The pup was smart and sensed the tension between them. "Does it really matter? What matters now is that you have two people who love you, Jenny. They love you, and they both live right here in Summer Shoals. You have every right to be surprised. Shocked, even. But I'm not sure you have the right to act like a child."

He couldn't have hurt her more if he'd reared back and punched her in the heart. "You think I'm being silly? Petty? That I'm throwing a tantrum just because I enjoy it? Let me assure you that I'm not enjoying a damn thing about any of this. How could you have kept this from me? You knew I still had questions about my dad."

"It wasn't my story to tell. It was a suspicion. Call it an occupational hazard. Believe me, I have to dig around in a lot of stuff I'd rather not. I don't want to do that with my own family."

"Really?" she said sweetly, but inside she was withering, turning into a crumbling black mess she didn't recognize. "If that's the case, then I guess you'd be better off without a family."

Teague went still, so still he looked as if he wasn't breathing. "What are you saying?"

"That I can't marry a man I can't trust to share everything with me—the good, the bad, the pretty, the ugly."

"Jenny—" he reached for her, but she shied away from him, "—you can't be serious—"

"I wish it could've been different—" she scrambled to her feet and turned away from him so she wouldn't cave, "—but the wedding is off."

CHAPTER 19

The ride home yesterday from the Everything Elegant Bakery & Gifts shop had been a long one for Lil with all the tension in Abby Ruth's truck. She was still refusing to move forward with their investigation, and Lil hadn't been this riled up since Angelina Broussard wielded her Bartell County Historical Society powers to try to have the bronze marker removed from Summer Haven.

Lil would not allow Abby Ruth to dictate what the G Team worked on. No, ma'am. After all, Lil had been the one to turn their criminal chasing into a business. Maybe they hadn't made any real money yet, but they'd righted wrongs, which gave them all purpose.

Disagreements between Abby Ruth and her weren't new. Heck, Abby Ruth sparked a competitive spirit that Lil hadn't felt since her days on the intramural badminton team at William and Mary. Was it that sense of competition that had driven her to start sneaking Ritter into the house? At first, she'd agreed to letting him stay because his presence had nagged at Abby Ruth so much. But then that rascally dog had stolen Lil's heart. Besides, he could help them with G Team jobs. A good bloodhound could track trails a week old. Call it a business decision.

Lil glanced at the bracelet that Sera had given her, the symbol of the G Team's unity. Sera would be in town tonight, thank goodness. If Abby Ruth wanted to give up the case, Lil, Maggie, and Sera would take it totally undercover.

Wasn't as if they hadn't worked on cases behind Abby Ruth's back before. Lil felt a spark of empowerment. She went into the dining room to find Maggie staring at the wall of clues they'd brainstormed so far. "You're thinking what I'm thinking, aren't you?"

Maggie turned and smiled. "Probably. That pesky thief needs to learn a thing or two."

"Do you think that sweet girl Honey has something to do with all these thefts?" Lil asked. "After all, she's not a man, and she doesn't have red hair."

"Something about her tattoo reminded me of how you described the one on the man's arm who took your rings. And we need to get those back."

Yes, her heart pinged every time she held her bare left hand out in front of her, but she forced a smile and said, "That's not what's important. It's the principle of the thing now."

"But Abby Ruth does have a point." Maggie flopped down into one of the fruitwood chairs. "If we mess up this wedding, Jenny may never forgive her."

"That won't happen." Lil paced by the columns of paper stuck to the wall that Maggie had written their case notes on. "We'll work carefully. Keep things quiet. Besides, there's so much going on at a wedding that no one will ever know we're multi-tasking. It's the perfect setting for our bad guy hunt to go unnoticed."

"I'm not sure. It's awfully risky," Maggie mused. "What if something goes wrong?"

"It's not like this thief has been violent or anything. Besides, with you, Sera, and me in the know, we'll have everything under control. I'll wear jewels as bait. I have a few left. I might be able to get Rick down at the pawnshop to loan me something extra special this greedy person won't be able to resist."

"And if it's cash the thief is after, we could set up a box for donations at the wedding."

"Now you're thinking." Lil smiled. Darn, the G Team was a group of smart, shrewd women. "Jenny didn't want one of those, but how can she refuse if it's already there?"

"It'll be my gift to Jenny and Teague," Maggie said. "I'll design something special." Maggie picked up a piece of paper and pencil and began sketching. "I'll work on it tonight. I can router some little dollar signs and scrolled hearts into the wood. I'll paint it white with silver accents. It'll be so pretty she won't think of refusing it."

"No thief could resist that."

"For sure." Maggie got up and crossed the room. "I have another idea. Wait one second."

Lil went through her list of last minute to-do's while Maggie slammed and bammed upstairs, then clomped back down.

Maggie came back in the room carrying a big Lego box under one arm and Scrabble under the other.

"There's no time for games," Lil said.

Maggie placed the Scrabble board face down on the coffee table. "I agree." She pulled out a handful of Grayson's brightly colored Lego bricks and popped a few together in the shape of a house. "This is Summer Haven."

"A war board?"

"Exactly!" She plucked out a dozen mini-figures and lined them up in rows. "Guests. Bride's side, and the groom's side."

Lil snapped four white blocks together and positioned it to the side of Summer Haven. "The carriage house."

Maggie put more blocks around the board. "The garage. The gazebo. Where the wedding chairs will be. The table for gifts and the cash box will be over here." She dropped a few green blocks in that corner.

"We can put Sera on watch over the gifts to be sure none of them gets nabbed," Lil said.

"We'll bait two handbags and leave them in plain sight." Maggie rubbed her hands together. "And we'll have surveillance covering everything. Bruce and I talked about it. It's totally doable. He could monitor the activities from upstairs. There's a perfect view from up there, and if anything looks suspicious he'll communicate to me through a tiny earpiece."

"You're not serious," Abby Ruth said from the doorway, making Lil jump in surprise.

"This will work, and we won't interrupt the wedding at all. Since there's only one way in and out of the property, if the thief takes the bait during the wedding, we nab him…or her…and hold him until *after* the ceremony. Then we turn the bad guy over to Deputy Winston after the wedding."

"Perfect." Lil rubbed her hands together. "I think this is a solid plan."

Abby Ruth shook her head. "I'm having second thoughts about all this."

"You agreed," Lil protested.

"Not really," Abby Ruth shot back, taking four long strides to the wall and ripping down the paper and list of suspects. "I decided we will *not* ruin this wedding just so we can have a little fun solving a mystery. This sting can wait until the next wedding the crashers attend."

Maggie took a breath, pushed back her chair, and stood taller than Lil had ever seen her. "First of all, you started this.

You invited our entire list of potential perps when you made that deal with the couple at the bridal show."

Abby Ruth started to speak, but Maggie lifted a finger and barreled on. "Secondly, we don't do this for fun, Abby Ruth. You know these cases are more than that. We're helping people, and we're a team." She raised her arm into the air, letting her bracelet jangle. "You are still wearing your bracelet, aren't you?"

"Of course," Abby Ruth bit out.

Lil braced herself for the explosion sure to come.

"Then I know you would feel awful for the rest of your life if we didn't try everything we can to find Lil's rings."

Abby Ruth swallowed hard and looked away. "If Honey is our culprit—which I don't think she is—y'all better corner her or the real thief before either Jenny or Teague gets wind of what you're up to."

"What do you mean, *y'all*?" Maggie asked. "You know you won't be able to resist taking this woman down."

"Honestly, I don't know if I'm even on the wedding guest list."

Maggie quickly rounded the dining room table and folded Abby Ruth into her arms, which was awkward since the Texan was a head taller. "Don't you worry about that. She may be upset now, but she'll want her momma there to see her walk down the aisle."

Taking a shuddering breath, Abby Ruth finally relented. "Fine, but no drama. None."

"We won't need drama because Honey won't be able to resist the bait. All we need is to give her the opportunity."

"We're on it. Nothing will go wrong," Maggie said. "I'll make sure of it. I've been online looking up new surveillance techniques. Bruce is helping me with the equipment that we'll need."

"That'll cost a fortune," Abby Ruth said.

"It's not all that expensive. Plus, we can use the cameras and stuff on other cases later."

Abby Ruth ran a hand through her spiked hair. "If anything happens to y'all, or this wedding, I won't forgive myself."

Lil said, "We'll be careful, but this is personal. You do want me to get my rings back from that woman, don't you?"

Abby Ruth's nod was slow in coming, but it was all the yes Lil needed. "You seem so sure that Honey is the bad guy, but I'm not."

"She does have a tattoo and the opportunity," Lil said. "What do we even really know about her?"

"But…" Abby Ruth's eyebrow did the doubting question-mark maneuver.

Maggie said, "*If* she's not the one, we'll have enough traps and surveillance to uncover the real culprit. We have this under control."

"I don't know. What if things go wrong? We haven't yet worked a case that hasn't gone a little sideways. The thought of ruining Jenny's big day makes my head feel as if a marching band is on parade in there."

"Something we really haven't thought of," Lil said, "is that guests at this wedding might be hit."

"Oh great," Abby Ruth groaned. "We invited every suspect on our list, and Honey is the so-called coordinator. What were we thinking? This wedding is doomed."

"And it's not like we can somehow un-invite them. We have problems regardless." Maggie paled.

"Can you imagine how it would look if several people are fleeced while they're attending the sheriff's wedding? It could completely kill Teague's reputation. Ruin his chance of reelection next time around," Lil said. "This could end up bad. Very bad."

"Bad? Bad doesn't begin to describe it. If that were to

happen, he and Jenny might have to up and move. I want my daughter, son-in-law, and grandbabies nearby. And I've grown right fond of Summer Shoals." Abby Ruth went stubbornly silent.

Lil let the uncomfortable silence hang.

"Okay," Abby Ruth said finally. "I'm trusting y'all to bring justice discreetly. We have to keep this whole thing extremely quiet. Nothing memorable. Absolutely no wild take-downs."

The sudden sound of the front door opening and banging against the foyer wall made Lil jump to her feet, but before she could investigate the source, Sera bounded into the room. "I'm home!"

"You're early." Maggie dropped a handful of Lego bricks onto the Scrabble board, then ran toward Sera.

"I wanted to surprise you."

"You did!" Maggie hugged her, then stepped back to look over Sera's yoga pants and flowing tunic. "You look like the Sera we met and fell in love with."

"You mean instead of the wife of a famous Hollywood legend who dresses like she's headed to some society function?"

"You always look lovely, dear," Lil said.

"You too, Lil. Abby Ruth, you look like your old self."

"I'm good. Healthy as can be, if not a little stressed out."

"What's going on?"

"This calls for a whole pitcher of my special tea," Maggie said, waving toward the kitchen.

They followed Maggie's lead and took their places around the kitchen table.

"I'm so glad to be back. I've missed you girls like crazy." Sera smiled, reaching toward Abby Ruth to her left and Lil to her right. They each wore their G Team bracelets, which warmed Lil's heart.

Maggie filled four glasses with tea and set them on the table. "The G Team isn't the same without you here. You came back just in time."

"You're talking about the case, aren't you?" Sera's eyes were wide with excitement.

"Of course! You tell her," Lil said to Abby Ruth, hoping that retelling their progress might reignite some of her enthusiasm for the chase.

Abby Ruth brought Sera up to date, not leaving out a single detail, including the Chicken Dance when Lil's ring was stolen.

Sera reached for Abby Ruth's hand. "It'll all be okay. Jenny loves you, and we love you. We have this, just like we always do."

One hand on top of the other, they didn't need to utter a word to know things were under control once again.

AFTER THEIR LITTLE BONDING RITUAL OVER THEIR G TEAM bracelets, Sera announced she needed to check on things at the Gypsy Cotton Gallery. Before she left, she gave Abby Ruth a hug, her skinny yoga girl arms surprisingly strong and reassuring. "It'll all work out. Believe it. Send that thought out into the universe and it will happen."

So Abby Ruth sent a mental telegram to the universe: *Can you please whack Jenny Cady upside the head and let her know she needs to call her momma?*

Abby Ruth's cell phone rang and displayed Jenny's number. Whoa. Apparently Sera had brought some really good mojo or karma or whatever with her from California.

Thank goodness Jenny was finally ready to talk. They'd get through this. After all, Jenny was a Cady, and they were sensible folk.

"Hello?" Abby Ruth answered eagerly.

"Mom?" At the sound of Jenny's muted tone, Abby Ruth's heart dropped.

"I'm so glad to hear from you. Jenny, about all the—"

"I can't talk about everything right now. I called because I need a favor. Today."

"Absolutely. Anything you need." Lord, this whole thing had turned into an emotional roller coaster. One minute Jenny hated her and the next she was asking favors.

"Could Grayson stay with you for a couple of days?"

"Are you feeling okay? If you're still sick, maybe you should make an appointment with—"

"I'm not sick, at least in the way you mean." Her words wobbly, Jenny sounded close to tears. "Heartsick, maybe."

"Sugar, let's sit down and—"

"I need a few days away from everything—you, Red, this house, Teague."

A cold feeling raced over Abby Ruth, and she jumped out of her chair to pace a circle around the kitchen. "What do you mean you need to be away from Teague?"

"I called off the wedding."

"What?" That cold feeling flashed to below-freezing. "Why?"

"I think you know."

Okay, enough was enough. She had to stop tiptoeing around her daughter and get things back on track, so she steeled her voice. "I have absolutely no idea. None. This isn't like you, Jenny. What in the world is going on?"

"Apparently, a lot of lies of omission."

"You might be angry with me, maybe even with Red, but now you're pushing everyone away, and that makes no sense."

"Teague knew," she said on a ragged sob. "He knew that Red was my dad."

Yeah, Abby Ruth had had her suspicions that Teague had

his suspicions. But they'd kept their thoughts to themselves. "I never told him."

"Then how?"

"He might be the sheriff of a relatively small Georgia county, but Jenny, he's a damn good law enforcement professional. The man is observant and smart."

"The real point is he knew—"

"Suspected." By this time, the chatter at the kitchen table had stopped, and the other gals were staring at Abby Ruth, concern clear on their faces.

"—and he never said a thing to me. I'm not sure I can marry a man who thinks keeping secrets is the way to build a good marriage."

"Don't take my mistakes out on Teague."

"I'm confused."

"Of course you are," she soothed. "But you're not confused about how you feel about Teague."

"I need a few days to work things out. Desi is letting me stay with her." Jenny's sigh was tired and sad, which made Abby Ruth ache for her. If she could only go back and fix this situation, make it right. But making it right didn't mean she would've made a different decision in the beginning. Granted she could've told Jenny the truth right after they first ran into Red at the hospital in Atlanta.

Not only would it have ripped off the Band-Aid sooner, but Jenny might've been more forgiving of Abby Ruth's mistakes while she was still battling breast cancer.

At least Jenny wasn't getting on an airplane and taking off for Boston or some other place. She was staying right here in Summer Shoals, which meant they could all do their best to help her see reason.

"I'm more than happy for Grayson to come to Summer Haven for a few days. Bowzer too, if that'll help."

"It would. I'll ask Teague to drop them both by later today."

The other end of the line went dead, and Abby Ruth turned back to her best friends feeling as if someone had dropped a piano on her.

Maggie's eyes were as wide as a Houston freeway, and Lil was tearing a paper napkin to confetti. "What...what did she say?" Lil asked.

"The wedding is currently a no-go."

CHAPTER 20

After touching base with Teague to get his ETA at Summer Haven, Abby Ruth rounded up the rest of the gang, including Red. She, Lil, Maggie, and Red were already on the porch with tall glasses of Maggie's special tea when Teague drove up.

With his normal enthusiasm, Grayson bolted out of Teague's truck with the energy God had reserved for the young. Bowzer jumped out after him, and Ritter lifted his head in pseudo-interest.

Abby Ruth nudged the hound with her toe. "Go on. A little exercise wouldn't hurt you."

He gave her a droopy-eyed look that she suspected was actually a canine glare. But he lumbered to his feet and shuffled his way down the front steps toward Grayson and the puppy.

In contrast, when Teague stepped out of the truck, his normal healthy tan looked ashen, and his face was haggard, with dull eyes and grooves around his mouth.

"That is one miserable boy." Red slid a glance Abby Ruth's way. "I know how he feels. I felt the same way years ago when we had to break things off, Ru."

Abby Ruth couldn't think about all that right now. She had a wedding to fix.

Teague's footsteps were slow and heavy as he walked up to the porch. Maggie gestured to the rocker beside her and held out a glass. The fact that he slumped into the chair and just stared down into his glass told Abby Ruth everything she needed to know about his level of misery. Finally, his eyes met hers and he said, "I guess y'all know."

Lil patted his leg. "I'm so sorry, Teague."

He glanced over at Abby Ruth. "I really want to be pissed as all hell at you."

"You have every right to be angry."

"But you don't make your daughter's decisions for her." Teague's voice was steady. "She's the one choosing her reaction to learning about Red."

"I made it clear that I never told you about Red and me," Abby Ruth said.

Red grunted his displeasure. Abby Ruth couldn't win this one no matter what she did. She'd let everyone down.

"Her mind is whirling right now," Lil said. "You have to admit, this is all a great deal to process."

"We don't have a lot of time for her to whirl." Abby Ruth rocked and sipped. "The wedding is in nine days."

Maggie raised her hand like an elementary school student, waving it until finally Teague acknowledged her with a curt nod. "I hate to be the one to say something so potentially unpopular, but it's not like that's the only day the two of you can get married."

That was big coming from Maggie, because Abby Ruth knew how much she was looking forward to the wedding sting. And from the tightening of Teague's face, he didn't like Maggie's comment one bit.

His words reconfirmed it. "I've waited over ten years to

marry the woman I love. I'm a patient man, but I am not a saint. And in case no one around here has noticed it, she is pregnant with our baby." He shot a quick glance between Abby Ruth and Red. "And no offense, but I'd really prefer to have my last name on that baby's birth certificate."

The rocking chair arm bit into Abby Ruth's palm as she wrapped her fingers around it. Red reached over and carefully loosened her grip and lightly held her hand in his. He said to Teague, "We understand where you're coming from. Believe me, Abby Ruth and I are willing to do whatever we can to make things right, but Maggie has a point. Sometimes these things shouldn't be rushed."

Speaking of rushing, Grayson vaulted up onto the porch, Bowzer right behind him. Her grandson never slowed down, just went full speed toward Teague, who caught him around the waist and pulled him in for a big hug.

The love between those two was bright and clear and real. Teague might not be Grayson's biological dad, but he was the father of his heart. These two needed each other, and Jenny needed both of them. She knew it, but she needed to be reminded of it.

And Abby Ruth had an idea about how to change her frame of mind.

After a sleepless night and day spent curled up in Desi's guest room, Jenny dragged herself downstairs to the bakery. She shoved a bite of one of Desi's amazing éclairs into her mouth. Even the creamy filling and chocolate couldn't make her feel better. In fact, she was feeling sicker with each swallow.

Something caught her eye just out of view. Desi watched her from the doorway. She looked fresh and full of hope in her pink and black apron, and although she wore a smile, Jenny knew she'd hurt her friend's feelings.

"I should've insisted you make my wedding cake," Jenny told her. "I'm so sorry. I don't know what got into Mom." And now, there would be no cake because there would be no wedding.

"I'll admit that I was hurt at first, but it's your wedding day. I'm happy for you no matter if I make the cake or not." Desi leaned against the doorjamb. "But you have bigger issues than a cake."

Issues Jenny didn't want invading her head and heart right now. This situation was killing her. "You could've made me a wedding cake out of stacks of your éclairs, like those crème puff cakes. Do you know what I'm talking about?"

"A croquembouche. Cream puffs held together with caramel. Now that would be a wedding cake to remember." Desi softened her tone. "You can't just sit here eating baked goods day in and day out."

"The only thing right in my life is Grayson." She placed her hand low over her stomach. "And this baby. Every other part of my life is a mess. I even let *you* down."

"No, you didn't. We're friends no matter what."

"I'm so sorry I hurt you."

"Friends do that sometimes, and we forgive one another. Don't you think you should consider doing the same for the people you love?"

"You really think I should forgive all of them?"

"I do, but what really matters is what *you* think."

"I miss Teague. I need him more than ever, yet I pushed him away. And right now, I'm not sure if I'm ready to pull him close again. How could he have kept such an important secret from me?"

"Because it wasn't his place to speculate, Jenny. Think

about it from his point of view. What if he'd told you and he'd been wrong?"

"But he was right."

"He knew learning the truth would hurt you terribly. All he wants is for you to be happy." Desi's gaze went to the window for a few seconds before she turned it back to Jenny. "I take that back. Teague wants you to be happy with him. He's been so patient with you. He's going to be a great husband and father."

"It seems like everyone—Teague, Red, Mom—had a choice in this. Everyone but me."

"Trust me, I know how choices can mess up things in ways you never expected. I've made my share of bad ones."

Jenny knew Desi was referring to when her ex-husband had gone over the edge and taken her daughter. Thank goodness Teague and his team had defused that situation.

Jenny's own marriage to Grayson's dad hadn't been the best choice either. Sometimes things weren't as clear as they seemed when you made big life decisions. And when you made the wrong choices, righting them took time. Sometimes you just had to find a way to move on, even if someone was hurt in the process.

"You're welcome here as long as you want to stay, but you should go back home to Teague. You love each other, and that's the most important thing. Because loving one another means hanging on during the bad times, even when those bad times are your own making."

"I don't know if I'm ready to—"

"Maybe this'll help you sort it out." Desi ducked into the hall and came through the door carrying a large boot box.

"What's that?"

"It's from your mother." Desi placed the fancy box in front of Jenny. "She's trying. You have to give her credit for that."

Jenny stared at the box and pulled her hands to her chest to keep from reaching for it. "Does she think she can fix everything with a pair of boots?"

"Lord knows she's not perfect, but she's your mom. I don't know what's inside, but she stopped by earlier and asked me to give this to you."

Jenny pushed away the plate with the half-eaten éclair on it and pulled the box into her lap. Her mom had probably bought her boots for the wedding. Totally her style. She wasn't good at saying *I'm sorry* with words.

"Open it," Desi encouraged her.

Jenny gently lifted the top of the box. She blinked, momentarily confused by the contents. No boots. Instead, stacks of well-ordered newspaper clippings, certificates, and pictures lay inside.

"What is it?"

"Memorabilia, I think." Jenny remembered the day she'd found her baby book in her mom's trailer. She'd been so surprised that her mom had kept anything like that. Now this. She sifted through a stack of ticket stubs, postcards, and a couple of keys. Even flowers pressed inside a book. These were the memories of a romantic woman. She'd never seen this side of her mom.

Her heart ached for them both.

Desi lifted a small frame from the box. Two wallet-sized photos were framed side-by-side. "You?"

Jenny took the brass frame. "That's me," she said pointing to the one on the right. "I guess the other baby is my mom." She turned it over and slid the frame apart, removing the sepia-toned picture. On the back of the picture in ink it read *1945 James Thomas Jenson*. "It's my dad."

Desi leaned in closer to look at the picture again. "You two look just alike. If his name is James Thomas and he doesn't have red hair, why does everyone call him Red?"

"Guess you don't know much about pro baseball from the '80s."

"Don't know much about baseball at all."

"He got that nickname as a rookie when he hit three consecutive homers to the same seat on gold level in the Astrodome."

Desi laughed. "Makes perfect sense then."

"Sports nicknames are complicated," Jenny said. "The seat was the same one where Doug Rader hit the first gold-level home run in the Dome. And Rader's nickname was the Red Rooster."

"So gold level equals Red being called Red." With a slow shake of her head, Desi said, "In all my life, I would've never figured that one out."

"My mom used to tell me the story about how Red Jensen was the hottest rookie in the MLB back in the day." Jenny smiled, remembering. "Little did I know what she was talking about had nothing to do with his fastball. Can't believe I never put two and two together. I was named after him."

"Jennifer and Jensen. It's not that obvious," Desi said.

"I'm not a Jennifer. My name is Jensen Elaine Cady." Maybe Mom had wanted her to figure it out all along.

A stack of envelopes were rubber-banded together with an old press badge. She opened the last letter in the bunch. "It's a love letter." She glanced at the date. Seven months before she was born. She read each word, feeling the bond between them. "By splitting up, they were doing what they thought had to be done." She read silently and rubbed away the tears wetting her cheeks. "Red didn't want to leave her, and he didn't know anything about me." Red and her mom had had a deep love. Like hers with Teague.

Desi said, "Look. Ticket stubs to the Astros games. When were you born?"

"1982."

"These games would've been while your mom was pregnant with you. And here's an article she wrote about him way before you were born. There's one thing I can say about you Cady girls. Y'all know how to rock a love story."

CHAPTER 21

A part of Jenny's heart softened at Desi's words, and the rest of it went mushy at the sight of all the pieces of her mom's life—of her life—scattered in front of her.

"How about I leave you alone to think all this over?" Desi gave Jenny a quick hug, then disappeared into the back of the bakery.

Thank goodness Icing On The Cake was closed because Jenny didn't need the entire town seeing her ugly cry and chow down on éclairs.

The way things were going, this baby would either love chocolate and cream filling or never touch the stuff a day in her life. Jenny's own stomach had been protesting for a quarter-hour, but still she licked a smear of chocolate off her knuckle.

A tentative tap came at the bakery's front door, and Jenny looked around, hoping Desi would get rid of whoever it was, but she must not have heard that she had company. Besides, the bakery had closed an hour ago,

Jenny would shoo the person off herself. After all, her

red-rimmed eyes would scare away the boldest customer. But when she shuffled to the door, she saw Red on the other side. A part of her wanted to turn away, pretend she hadn't seen him and return to drowning her pain in pastries. But his smile was as hesitant as his knock had been.

She had a soft spot for men who knew they were in the doghouse. So she unlocked the glass door and opened it a crack.

"Can I come in?" he asked.

"Desi is closed."

"I didn't come here for cake."

Which meant he'd come here for her. A small part of her —the Abby Ruth Cady part—wanted to slam the door in his face. But honestly, she was too tired and sad to be mad anymore.

And she liked Red, really liked him. She'd believed her mom might've finally met the perfect man for her. She'd smiled over the idea of her mom and him together before she knew they'd already *been together*.

Now, she felt like a fool for not knowing about their past. Heck, she *was* their past.

She pushed the door open a few more inches and he didn't hesitate, pulling it wide and stepping inside quickly, probably afraid she'd change her mind. When she turned back to the little table she'd been occupying for a while, she realized flaky crumbs were strewn all over the place. Not only had she eaten éclairs, but she'd also massacred them beforehand.

No éclair deserved that.

As she sat, she gestured to the boot box sitting askew on the table. "I guess you know all about that?"

"No, but I'm betting it has something to do with your mother."

Jenny didn't know what to make of that. Maybe her mom and Red hadn't put their heads together. She slid the boot box off the table into a chair and held out a hand to invite Red to take the dainty pink-and-white chair across from her.

He didn't waste a second, just sat and stared at her. "Teague Castro is miserable," he announced. "And it's your fault."

A rebuttal fumed up inside her, but she stopped it before it passed her lips.

"He's my friend and I hate seeing him like that," he said.

She was miserable too, but she was an adult, and it was time she remembered that and stopped flailing around in her sadness. "It hurt me to find out that Teague didn't tell me he knew who you were."

"He didn't know. Only suspected. It hurt me to find out your mom had kept your entire existence from me for over thirty years," he said calmly, running his palm across a two-day growth of beard. "So if you want to play a game of Hurt Feelings, I'm pretty sure I'd beat you just as handily as the Astros pounded the Padres in the 1984 World Series."

After being around Red for the past few months, she'd known he was a pretty straight shooter. Heck, very few men could keep up with her mom, so it was obvious he had to be. Still, she rolled her lips in at his pronouncement because the Astros had swept that series four to zero. "I don't like to lose."

He smiled, and it was such a nice smile. White straight teeth and laugh lines at his eyes. Her dad was a handsome man and a charming one. "You came by that pretty honestly, Jenny. I mean, look at your parents."

"I lost out on you for years."

He reached across the table and took her hand in his, made a show of turning it over and running a thumb across her engagement ring, the one she hadn't had the heart to take off even after she'd pushed pause on the wedding. "We're human, which means we're our own centers of the universe. We look at everything from our own vantage point, because it's impossible to do otherwise. That's why it's important to consciously step back and consider other people's perspectives."

"Of course."

He released her hand, and Jenny ached for the feel of her hand inside the protective warmth of his again. "Then do it. I hate like hell that I missed out on so much with you. I was angry as all get-out at your mom when I realized what she'd done. But once I calmed down, I also realized why she'd done it. From her perspective, it was the right thing to do. Did she tell you about my wife?"

"A little, but I didn't really want to listen at the time." Later, she'd gotten online and devoured everything she could find about Red Jensen. "She had multiple sclerosis."

"Yes, and she took a real turn for the worse when your mom and I were..."

"Together?"

His eyes telegraphed his relief at her kindness, but he swallowed hard. "I'm an old man, and you're a grown woman, but I'm not sure that matters. It's hard to talk with your kid about sex."

That made her laugh. "Remember Grayson's question in the van the other day about how babies are made?"

"You looked like you'd swallowed an ostrich egg."

"Just saying I feel your pain."

"I wasn't a cheater. And even back then, that was pretty unusual in pro sports. My wife had been sick for a long time, but when I said for better or worse, I meant it. Nobody wants to think there'll be a lot more *worse* than *better*. But our marriage was overshadowed by her illness."

"Still, you didn't..."

"Not until your mom." He sat back in his chair and stared at the ceiling, clearly seeing something other than Desi's pink chandelier. "The first time I saw Abby Ruth, it was like being struck with a bolt of summer lightning. I'm pretty sure I stood there in that locker room with my mouth hanging open."

"She's been known to affect men that way."

"That would've been embarrassing enough, but then she gave me the once-over with those icy gray eyes of hers and said, "Forget your towel, Jensen?"

A choked laugh popped out of Jenny. "You were..."

"It was an Astros policy that all the players needed to be decent when a female reporter was in the locker room. There weren't a lot of them back then, but I'd never slipped up before. One look at your mom, and I'd forgotten that I was standing there butt naked."

That must've been a sight to see. "If it makes you feel any better, she must've been impressed."

"She's a hard woman to impress and an even harder woman to woo." His smile was wistful and slightly wicked. "We did that eye contact and look away thing for over a year before I could convince her to have a private dinner with me."

"She knew you were married."

"I can't tell you the number of times she turned me down. And when she said yes, she made it more than clear it was a dinner between friends."

"So you never went out in public together?"

"Only when she was interviewing me."

"I found a lot of archived articles where Mom interviewed you there for a couple of years." The attraction had obviously been more than mutual.

"She was amazing—strong, bold, beautiful. Some of the guys thought she was a ballbuster."

Suddenly, Jenny got a flash of insight. "Yet you were married to a woman who always needed you."

"I loved my wife when I married her, and I still cared for her."

"Which is the reason you didn't leave her for my mother."

"Your mom and I were in a no-win situation. We knew it, but we were in love and we didn't want to face it."

"Until you had no choice."

"And I didn't know at the time that she was pregnant with you."

Her mom had made a huge sacrifice for the man she loved. Right or wrong, she'd known she was strong enough to raise a child on her own and hadn't wanted to tear Red in half between her and his wife. Back then, that kind of a scandal could've irreparably hurt Red's career.

Jenny and Teague weren't faced with anything close to that. Yes, they'd missed too many years together, but it could've been worse. It could've been thirty years instead of ten.

And Jenny could raise a child on her own. She'd practically done that with Grayson because Daniel had been too busy trying to make a name for himself in Boston.

"It doesn't have to be that way for Teague and me." Certainty settled inside her. She had a man who loved her, and nothing was standing between them except for her hurt feelings and stubbornness.

"Jenny, the way he looks at you… Well, if I was a poetic man, I'd say it was magic. And it's obvious that he loves Grayson. We don't always get to choose our family, and we sure don't get to choose how they act. But you'd be a fool to let go of this with Teague."

"I know." And she did. She *was* going to marry the love of

her life. The rest would fall into place as she, Teague, Grayson, and this new baby began their lives together in Summer Shoals. She could see that life clearly, and she couldn't picture it without Red or her mom in it as well.

She eyed the last éclair sitting there in front of her, then pushed it across the table to her dad. "Maybe you'd like to share this with me."

The relief in his eyes and the mischief in his smile made her feel better than she had in days.

WITH A HEART HEAVY OVER JENNY CALLING OFF THE WEDDING, Lil flipped through the wedding magazines still stacked in the parlor. "I guess we'll have to contact all the vendors to cancel the wedding even though it was past the refund date. Abby Ruth would owe them the full fees regardless, but no sense in them preparing things that will never be used. Or maybe we could donate the food to Dogwood Ridge Assisted Living."

"And we need to let the guests know. I guess email will be the easiest way to do it. Do we have phone numbers for everyone?"

"I can post something in the paper stating a family emergency," Lil offered.

"Uh…that's pretty old school," Maggie said. "What about an update on Facebook?"

"That's so tacky!"

"No newspaper, no social media," Abby Ruth said, the hard edge in her voice irrefutable. "We're simply putting the wedding vendors on hold. Those two *will* be married. Sooner rather than later if I have anything to say about it."

Possibilities formed in Lil's mind, and she sat straight up in her chair. "Wait a minute. We've already passed the date to make changes now. Why not use it to our advantage? If the show doesn't go on, we won't be able to catch the wedding crook."

"She's right," Sera said. "All we need is a bride and groom."

"Don't you think people would be freaked out when they arrive for Jenny and Teague's wedding only to find some strangers?"

"Maybe it's not a stranger." Excitement bubbled inside Lil as an idea dawned on her and she turned toward Abby Ruth. "Maybe it's you."

"Me?" Abby Ruth backed up a step, almost tripping over her boots. "Not happening."

"Doesn't have to be a real wedding. We can have one of Sera's actor friends play the part of the preacher. You and Red are in love. You can't deny that."

"Can and will. I'm not walking down an aisle...fake or otherwise."

"We could let Bowzer and Ritter get married," Sera piped in. "I went to a dog wedding in California a few years back. Can you imagine how cute Ritter will be in a little bow tie and tuxedo tails?"

"Bowzer is not wearing a dress," Abby Ruth insisted. "That's the craziest thing I've ever heard. Let Maggie marry Bruce Shellenberger."

Maggie blushed. Lil had a feeling if Bruce ever did ask Maggie to marry him, she might be tempted to make that walk down the aisle. They sure had hit it off from the day they'd met while working the case at Dogwood Ridge Assisted Living. But playing with Maggie's heart with a fake wedding was out of the question.

Besides, this was Abby Ruth's mess to fix. If anyone's heart should be put on the line, it was hers. "Abby Ruth, I think you and Red owe this to Jenny and Teague. No one would be the wiser that it's a ruse to catch a criminal. After all, we do have to close this case."

A one-two, one-two-three-four rap came at the front door. Red's knock had become a regular part of their lives around here. Lil got up to let him in. "Perfect timing," she said with a grin. He stepped inside, and Lil hooked her arm through his and led him into the parlor. "Abby Ruth has something she wants to talk with you about."

Abby Ruth stood there staring at Red with wide eyes.

"Are you okay, Ru? What did you want to tell me?"

"I…ah…um…"

His brows pulled down over his nose, he turned to Lil. "What are you girls up to? She looks like she's seen a ghost."

Lil piped up. "We've decided we can't cancel the vendors or tell the guests that the wedding is off."

"Why not?"

Oh, dear. This was the tricky part. Red didn't really need to know about their side plans for the wedding.

"If it's about the deposits, I can cover—"

"It's not about the money. These three—" Abby Ruth swung an arm around, indicating Lil and the others, "—decided we need a stand-in couple."

"I don't understand. Do you think they'll change their minds between now and wedding time? I mean, I feel like I made some headway with Jenny, but I can't guarantee anything."

"Someone—" she speared Lil with a look as sharp as a rose thorn, "—thought it would be a good idea for you and me to get married so all those wedding expenses don't go to waste." Abby Ruth chuckled as though to laugh it off, but to Lil she sounded more like she had whooping cough.

"Abby Ruth Cady, are you asking me to marry you?" Was that a bead of sweat running down Red's brow?

Abby Ruth's pointed expression turned sour. "You could do worse."

"I didn't mean…that is…I…"

"Forget it," she said. "It was a joke and you had to be there."

"I didn't mean it like that." Red reached for her, but she sidestepped him.

"Not a word out of you," Abby Ruth warned. "I guess we have to make sure Jenny and Teague *do* get married."

CHAPTER 22

After leaving the bakery, Jenny went back to the house to savor a hot shower and get dressed—makeup and all. Sure, her jeans were a little tight around the middle, so she'd popped open the top button, but she was wearing a pair of cowboy boots with snip-toes, which made her feel like a million bucks.

On the short ride over to Teague's office, her stomach swirled. Her intense emotions the past few days had exhausted her, but not allowing Teague to be there for her through it all was a mistake she needed to remedy now.

She walked into the sheriff's department with shoulders squared and a big smile on her face. Jenny Cady might crater every once in a while, but nothing would ever keep her down for long.

She had too much to be thankful for and way too many good people in her life for that. Even if one of those good people drove her, and Teague, half-crazy most of the time.

She waved at Gloria. "Teague in his office?"

Worry shadowed the dispatcher's eyes. "Yes, but he hasn't wanted to see much of anyone. You ask me, he looked like he swallowed one of those Japanese balloon fish things."

Great, she'd made the man she loved look as if he'd eaten a big plate of poisonous blowfish. Shame on her. But she put an extra push in her smile for Gloria and strode down the hall like she owned the place. Just because she was in the wrong didn't mean she had to act like a whipped dog.

But when she opened the door to Teague's office, her resolve almost crumbled. He was sitting behind his desk, his eyes closed and shoulders hunched. He rubbed an absent hand across the bridge of his nose, and the shadows beneath his eyes made him look ten years older.

"Teague?" she said quietly. Her heart ached knowing she'd caused his pain.

He jerked straight so fast it sent his desk chair rocking wildly. "Jenny, I was… You look…"

"Like a rational human being?"

"I was going to say beautiful."

This man would never stop melting her heart. "Thanks." Feeling suddenly unsure, she said, "Do you have time to take a drive with me?"

If she'd thought his chair was out of control before, when he stood, it rotated like a supercharged carnival ride. "If you have bad news—like you've made a final decision bad news—I want you to just break it to me. Now."

She held out her hand, and he rounded his desk, one careful step at a time. How could she blame him for being cautious around her? She'd hurt him terribly, and it was time for her to make it right. With everyone. "Come with me to Summer Haven. I need to talk to Mom and pick up Grayson."

"Okay."

A few minutes later, they parked in front of the massive white house, and Jenny reached into the back seat to grab the wedding planner Lil had dropped off.

"What's that?" Teague asked.

"You'll see." She scrambled out of the vehicle, carrying the glossy white book in her arms.

They knocked on the front door, but no one answered. "Think it's breaking and entering if we go on in?" she asked Teague. "They have to be here. Mom's and Maggie's trucks are both here." Any other time she'd have knocked and just walked in, but after her recent behavior she'd rather receive the invite to come in.

"With these gals it's more like our civic duty to check to see what they're up to." He snorted. "Did I ever tell you about the time Lil and Maggie were up on the porch roof with chain saws?"

He was right. There was never any telling the type of trouble her mom and her friends might be up to. She knocked again, then went inside, but it was quiet.

"Mom?" Jenny called out.

The sound of the kitchen door slamming made her wonder if her mom had just made a hasty exit.

She and Teague walked down the hallway that bisected the first floor. Everyone, including Grayson and the two dogs, were streaming into the house from the backyard.

Thank goodness. "Hi. No one answered so I let myself in. I hope you don't mind," she said tentatively. "I wanted to talk to you." She looked toward Lil first, then bravely toward her mother. "To apologize."

"Welcome home, dear," Lil said with a nervous glance toward the others.

"What have y'all been up to?" Jenny asked. "You look guilty."

Surprised looks bloomed on the three women's faces, but Grayson gave out a whoop and ran her way. When he wrapped his arms around her middle, she grabbed on to him and held him tight. Bowzer danced around them, trying to find an opening to insert himself into the hug. Finally, Jenny released her son and gave Bowzer a good head scratch. "I've missed y'all."

"Us too," Grayson declared. "I like it here, but Mimi cooked something last night." He leaned in close to Jenny and stage-whispered, "I don't think it was supposed to be black *or* crunchy."

"Why don't you see if Miss Lillian and Miss Maggie would be willing to go upstairs to help you and Bowzer pack?"

Maggie and Lil immediately caught the hint and scurried to lead Grayson out of the room.

"Mom, can we talk?"

Teague placed a protective hand on her back, and it gave her strength.

Her mom's clothes were rumpled, and her hair was a mess. Her skin matched the color of the gray T-shirt she was wearing. The pinched expression on her face was so unlike her. It wasn't one of annoyance—those were fairly normal. This was an expression of fear and worry.

"Please?" Jenny motioned to the kitchen table.

Teague went into action, pulling out chairs for them both. He said, "I'll just head to the parlor and—"

Jenny grabbed his arm before he could leave. "No, this is about you too."

"Okay."

Jenny sat and swung the big white book onto the table with a thump, and Teague scooted in her chair. Did the same for her mom before he sat.

Mom eyed the thick wedding planner. "Guess you came to give that back to Lil."

"Nope," she said, "I came to give it back to you."

Abby Ruth held her hands in front of her like she was

warding off a voodoo spell. "I don't want it. I didn't want it in the first place."

"Are you sure?" Jenny asked. "Because it might be hard to pull off this wedding without all these notes and checklists."

Her mom's attention shot from the planner to Jenny's face, and her expression was a combination of caution and hope. "Are you saying the wedding is back on?"

"I am, and I think you're going to need this." She handed over the thick book. "That is, if you'll help me. Please?"

Abby Ruth snatched the book from Jenny's hands and hugged it to her chest. "I'm rehired as the wedding coordinator?"

"I'd love nothing more than you to help me with the most important day of my life. Do you want the job back?"

"Hell, yes!"

"Then it's all yours, Mom. I love you, and I want to put the past behind us and start fresh. All of us."

Jenny knew everything would be okay when her mom's mouth lifted into a broad smile. "I didn't think you'd ever forgive me."

"There's no changing the past. Didn't you always teach me that it doesn't matter what goes wrong but how you handle it when it does?"

"I'm so sorry I made such a mess of things, but I promise you it was with good intentions. At the time I really believed I was doing what was best."

"I know, Mom."

"And I know now that it wasn't for the best. It was unfair to you and to Red. To us all."

"No looking back," Jenny said. "Maybe we can tell Red together."

"He'll be so happy." Abby Ruth got up, carrying the wedding planner under one arm. "The girls will be happy too." She called out, "Lil! Maggie!"

Footsteps echoed from upstairs. Bowzer was the first to appear, sliding along the kitchen's slick wooden floors and thudding into a table leg.

Abby Ruth set the wedding planner on the table just as Grayson came bounding in with Maggie and Lil following behind him.

"Please tell me y'all haven't cancelled the wedding vendors yet," Abby Ruth said to Lil.

"Are you saying…?" Lil's eyes twinkled and her lips moved, but it was as if she was afraid to utter the words.

"The wedding is back on," Abby Ruth said, pumping her fists in the air.

"Does this mean we get to have the doves?" Grayson hollered.

"If you can find some, I'll release them," Abby Ruth said, and shouts of joy echoed throughout Summer Haven.

WITH ALL THE WEDDING PREP IN RECENT DAYS, LIL WAS taking a much-needed break in one of the front porch rockers when Maggie pulled up in front of the house. She emerged from the truck with boxes piled high in her arms, and she bumped the truck door closed with her butt.

"What in blazes is all that?" Lil called out.

The boxes teetered, and Maggie executed a nimble shuffle-ball-change to steady them. "I've been shopping."

"I can see that." Lil jumped from her chair and met Maggie at the steps. "Let me take a couple of those before you kill your fool self."

Maggie rebalanced the remaining items. "There's more in the back of the truck."

Lil cocked her head, reading the label on the side of one of the boxes. "Stuffed animal hidden cameras?"

"Bruce found all this stuff for us on Craigslist. And it's not costing us a cent."

"I never trust free," Lil said with a sniff and set aside her load.

"He paid for it, and I'm helping him fix his garage door and put up some shelves. Easy as pie, but you know he's not all that handy, so it's a win-win."

"No man is handy in comparison to you," Lil said.

"I'll take that as a compliment." Maggie carefully lowered the boxes onto the front porch decking.

"As you should," Lil said. "Now what the heck are we doing with boxes of hidden cameras?"

"With these, we'll have this place totally covered for the wedding. Everything is wireless, and Bruce will be able to watch live footage and record too. He's so amazing."

"You're so smitten."

Maggie beamed. "He's great. I love spending time with him, and we're having fun working on this plan."

"I'm happy for you, Mags." Lil poked inside a box and pulled out something fuzzy that she couldn't quite identify. "Where's the camera?"

"Behind the eyes."

That was a tad creepy. "Will we have to dissect the animals to remove the cameras so we can use them at the wedding?"

"Well…not exactly. Bruce said the way they're made, the transmission devices are wired in the threading. We need to keep them intact."

"And how do you expect to spy on people with dozens of stuffed animals?"

"We'll use them as table centerpieces."

Lil's burst of laughter caused Ritter to howl and come running to the front door. "You don't think that will be the least bit suspicious?"

"Stop laughing. This will work. And if you want to talk about suspicious, let's chat about Ritter. Why is he in the house?"

"Don't change the subject. We're discussing this surveillance scheme of yours."

"I'll make it work." Clearly hurt, Maggie gathered up her boxes and hugged them in her arms. As she scrambled to get inside the house with her bargains, Ritter lumbered out while the door was still open.

"Thanks a lot, you traitor. I told you this was just between us," Lil said to the mutt. He pushed his nose under her hand, and she gave him a scratch. "You're a good boy." She walked out into the yard. "Come on, Ritter."

He made a poor attempt to hop down the front steps, ears flopping, then trotted alongside her to the backyard. She put him inside the garage. "Don't look at me like that with those eyes. I'm on to you."

She never thought a dog could capture her heart like this. She reached into her pants pocket and tossed a cookie into the air. Ritter snapped it mid-fall, and it was gone in one gulp. "What did I tell you about chewing your food?"

Ritter sat and let out a woof.

"Who's training who here?" she scolded him but reached into her pocket and tossed another cookie. Ritter caught this one and gave two good chomps before licking his lips. "That's a good boy."

Maggie came out the back door. "Are you out here talking to the dog?"

"Of course not. Just putting the stinky mutt back where he belongs." Ritter plopped down with a whimper, and she tried not to make eye contact with him. That dog seemed to understand everything she said.

"Okay, well, Bruce is on his way over to help me hook everything up, but I want to install the two cameras on the roof before he comes. I hate to make him feel bad, but there's no way he can get up on that roof. As uncoordinated as he is, he'd fall and hurt himself for sure."

"Wouldn't do much for his ego to see you up there either," Lil said.

"Exactly. Can you help me with the big ladder?"

"Sure." Lil followed Maggie into the garage, avoiding Ritter's baleful stare the entire time. Together they eased the ladder onto their shoulders and carried it out to the front of the house without much problem.

"Thanks, Lil. If you can steady the ladder, I'll grab the cameras and install these two quickly." Maggie clipped a hot pink carabiner to her belt and slipped on two teddy bears by the ribbons around their necks. With the bears dangling from her belt like drunken pandas, she climbed the ladder with the ease of a seasoned firefighter.

Pride swelled in Lil's chest. Maggie never stopped amazing her. In her seventies, this woman could still do most things younger women would struggle with. Lil pressed her weight against the ladder to ensure Maggie's safety.

A horn honked twice from the driveway. Turning in expectation of Bruce Shellenberger's arrival, Lil was surprised to see Teague getting out of his sheriff's cruiser.

"What are you two up to now?" He asked, his tone tight.

"Hey, Teague." Lil wiggled her fingers. That man had the most impeccable timing. This wasn't the first time she and Maggie had been caught on the roof. Of course, last time they'd done it on purpose to trick him into trimming the trees for them. That was before Lil had realized how self-sufficient she and her friends were as a team.

Maggie clomped around on the porch roof muttering and hopefully coming up with a story Teague would believe.

"Please tell me you don't have a chain saw up there again," Teague called up to her, taking off his hat and tossing it on the ground beside the ladder. Then he put his foot on the first rung.

"What are you doing?" Lil asked him. "We have this under control."

He didn't slow down for a nanosecond, and soon he was on the porch roof. "And what exactly *is* it you're doing up here? Wait. Are those stuffed animals on your belt?"

Lil backed away from the house far enough to get a look at a stunned Maggie and an accusatory sheriff.

"I'm putting in a security system," Maggie said matter-of-factly. "Can't be too careful these days."

"You think those fuzzy bears on the roof will scare people off?"

"Doesn't seem to be working on you, but then you're one of the good guys."

"Thanks," he said. "I think."

Maggie smiled and went about the business of positioning teddy bears strategically at the roof corners.

Lil shielded her eyes to check Maggie's work. From here the nanny cams didn't look like more than clumps of leaves or small squirrels. No one would even notice.

CHAPTER 23

For three solid days since Jenny had announced the wedding was back on, Abby Ruth and the girls had been pretending to consult with Honey and marking off tasks in that gigantic wedding planner at a pace that would have impressed even Elisabeth with an *S*.

They'd had to work quickly, but Abby Ruth and Jenny had taken time to go to Red's house together and let him know the wedding was back on. He'd been so touched that he'd pulled them both into a hug that went on for nearly a minute. Abby Ruth's breath caught remembering the look on Red's face when Jenny asked if the two of them, together, could give her away at the wedding.

In that one moment it was as if all the years they'd been apart had disappeared. And Red had sure stepped up to the plate to help out with all the wedding prep that needed to get done. He'd become chief runner and fetcher.

With his help, they'd made up lost ground and added some touches, like the lavender sachets Lil wanted but Abby Ruth had vetoed before. It took him trips to four stores to gather enough light blue tulle circles for the wedding, but he'd taken the task as seriously as the World Series.

They'd even conjured up some white doves. Only six, but that would have to do. A promise was a promise, and Abby Ruth had no intention of ever letting Grayson down.

They'd just finished working on the menu for the rehearsal dinner when Sera walked into Summer Haven with a huge box.

"UPS just showed up." Sera hugged the package to her chest. "I thought this would be all for nothing when the wedding was cancelled, but now it's just in time."

"Something for the wedding?" Abby Ruth asked.

"Kind of." Sera handed it to Abby Ruth. "It's for you."

"What is it?"

"Open the box and see."

Maggie grabbed the scissors from the knife block on the counter and handed them to Abby Ruth. "Here you go."

Abby Ruth sliced through the tape and opened the flaps. "Is this a garment bag? Sera, Jenny already has a dress."

"It's not for Jenny. It's a mother-of-the-bride dress."

Hell's bells, she hated to hurt Sera's feelings, but there was no way she was wearing a dress.

"I know what you're thinking, but take a look at it first. You're in for a surprise." She pressed her fingers together like she was praying. "Please. Just trust me."

The zipper released with the ease of melting butter, and inside the bag was a long, slim dress in a western cut, covered with bugle beads the color of bluebonnets. "What in the world?"

"You can wear your favorite boots with this dress," Sera told her. "Pull it out of the bag and turn it around."

"Wow." No other word could describe the back of the elegant dress. It had a cutout the shape of the Texas star. Unique and sexy and so her. "I have to admit, it's pretty." A grin spread wide on her face as she held it up to her body. This was a dress she could see herself wearing. "My black boots *would* look nice."

"That dress will look great on you. Go try it on."

"Where in the world did you find something like that?" Lil asked Sera.

"Do you remember the year Jessie Wyatt was up for an Academy Award?" Sera asked.

Maggie's jaw dropped. She looked at Sera, then back at the dress. "Of course! I knew I'd seen something like that before. This was the dress she wore."

"Seriously?" Abby Ruth tried to shove it back into Sera's hands. "No way. A dress once worn by a famous actress has to be worth a fortune."

"I didn't know it at the time of Jessie's funeral, but when Marcus and I returned to California, I was contacted by her attorney. Jessie left me all her clothes."

"Goodness." Maggie blinked. "Will you have to rent a storage unit to hold them all?"

Sera chuckled. "Marcus is having a room added to our house. I might set up a museum for Jesse out at the Gypsy Cotton Gallery. Could be good for tourism around here. I don't know, but I do know that dress is perfect for this occasion. Consider it yours, Abby Ruth."

Abby Ruth couldn't imagine living like that. Adding on a room for more clothes seemed cuckoo. Her horse trailer had served her just fine before she'd landed in Summer Shoals. Sometimes Summer Haven felt too big.

Which made her think of Red living in Teague's small house. It was snug, with enough room for two. Maybe Red's choice made more sense than she'd realized, because small and cozy was her style too. What would it feel like to live there with him, to wake up beside him every day? Not that he'd ever asked.

Abby Ruth quickly tabled that thought for later consideration. "Thank you, Sera. But I'll be giving this back right after the wedding."

"Whatever makes you happy," Sera said.

"I'll tell you what makes me happy," Lil said. "That Jenny and Teague worked all this out."

She would never tell a soul, but Abby Ruth was slightly disappointed that she and Red wouldn't have to playact at being the bride and groom. Still, right now she was the happiest a mother could be. Her daughter was finally marrying the man Abby Ruth had always considered family, and more importantly, he made Jenny happy. And Jenny's happiness was all Abby Ruth had ever wanted.

"Perfect," Maggie said. "Because we may need you to run down these cons. That might be a little harder if you and he were playing wedding couple."

"Uh-uh," Abby Ruth said, pouring on the stern tone she'd used with men in the sports industry her entire career. "If the real wedding is back on, then the sting is off."

"Wow," Sera said. "Never thought I'd hear you say something like that."

"Things are entirely too dicey for me to risk upsetting Jenny again so soon after our complete family meltdown."

"Have you forgotten that one of those swindlers took Lil's rings?" Maggie asked, her hands going to her hips. "We can't let someone get away with that."

"You know as well as I do those things have probably already been pawned." Abby Ruth caught Lil's wince. "Sorry about that, but you know it's true."

"Abby Ruth is right. My rings are probably long gone. Not just my rings, but Virginia's jewels too. The only way to prevent anything from going wrong during this wedding is to cancel every vendor. There's no time for that."

Maggie squared off with Abby Ruth. "Don't you want justice for the women you claim to care about?"

"Whoa, what has you so riled up today?"

Maggie's feisty posture relaxed. "It's just that we worked so hard to get Lil's rings back when we took down our very first bad guy. Not only do those rings represent Lil's marriage, but they're a symbol of the G Team. Our unity. It's part of where all this began."

"She has a point." Sera wrapped her arm around Abby Ruth. "And we already have a plan. In fact, you don't have to be involved at all, Abby Ruth. You just forget all about the case and enjoy your moment as mother of the bride."

CHAPTER 24

On June fifteenth, the sun was shining brightly, and Georgia had finally received a bit of a break from the recent heat wave. The perfect day for a wedding.

Abby Ruth headed to the carriage house to see if Maggie had heard from the florist yet. Time was ticking, and not one arrangement had arrived. And as if that weren't bad enough, Winnie hadn't brought the bride's bouquet yet. Wasn't like her daughter could carry flowers plucked out of the garden.

"Mags? Are you out here?"

"Over here."

Abby Ruth spun toward Maggie's voice, where she saw just the top of her dark-haired head poking up like a gopher in a pea patch. But instead of a pea patch there were flowers galore.

"So this is where the flowers are. That's why I was looking for you. I was getting worried."

Bruce waved. "Hi, Abby Ruth. We have it all under control."

"Why is it the more y'all tell me that, the more I worry?" She rounded the end of the table and looked at the beautiful arrangement of flowers. Something glossy seemed to look back at her. She stepped closer to the arrangement and poked at it, disturbing the greenery. "What the heck is that thing?"

"They're cameras." Maggie rushed over and rearranged a couple of glossy leaves, which camouflaged the beady eyes that had been staring at Abby Ruth.

"Like a nanny cam?" Abby Ruth picked up the arrangement and eyed the furry thing with a ringed tail. "Is that a lemur?"

"Yep. We have stuffed monkeys, bears, and all kinds of stuff."

"What kid wants a lemur staring out at him? You ask me, there's something shifty about them."

"Bruce got us a heckuva deal on these nanny cams, so I couldn't be picky. Most important thing is we'll have everything under surveillance. Every table. Every angle."

"You don't think people will notice? Jenny will kill me."

Maggie tucked the leaves into place, using a piece of green camo duct tape to secure them to the stuffed animal housing the camera. Only one shiny black eye was left unconcealed. "It's fine. Trust me. We had to get creative, but we could guarantee the safety of the Hope Diamond with all the security I have in place today."

Bruce cleared his throat.

"With Bruce's help." Maggie gave Bruce an ooey-gooey grin.

Bruce beamed. "I'll take these out to the tables."

"Thanks, Bruce," Maggie said.

He grabbed two arrangements and hurried out.

"You two are adorable together," Abby Ruth said. "Bruce and Maggie sitting in a tree—"

"Oh, stop it." Maggie swatted her hand. "Like you have

much room to talk with the way you flutter your eyelashes at Red."

Ignoring the potential truth of that statement, Abby Ruth strolled over to a white box sitting on another table. She traced her fingers across the intricate scrolling that had the look of leather tooling. "Did you make this?"

"I did. Don't go trying to change the subject."

Abby Ruth turned to hide the flush on her cheeks.

Maggie swatted at her arm. "You'd better scoot, or you'll be wearing jeans to this wedding…and you know Sera and Lil would have a fit if that happened."

"I'm just feeling a little nervous."

"I understand, but don't be."

Bruce came back in and dragged a lawn chair out and set it in front of Maggie's workbench. With the touch of a button, the dusty old television flickered to life, then a grid of images filled the screen.

"Yes!" Bruce fist-pumped then turned to Maggie for a high-five.

"It works!" Maggie gave him a hug.

Abby Ruth's heart filled at seeing those two enjoying this project together. Dang it, this wedding stuff had her as emotional as one of those women who cried during Hallmark movies. She sniffled to gather herself. Maggie was right. Probably best if she went and got ready.

"Thanks for working on this with us, Bruce." Abby Ruth waved as she turned to leave. Maybe a nice brisk walk around the grounds would give her enough time to get her head on right.

She'd made an awful lot of memories here at Summer Haven since Teague coerced her into spying on Lil and Maggie. Who would've thunk she'd still be here, and as thick as thieves with them. The grass had finally grown in over the swampy septic tank fiasco, and right there in the curve of the driveway was where Red had beaned that baddie with a fastball as impressive as any he'd thrown in the pros.

Summer Haven really was a beautiful place for a wedding. The gazebo had been beautifully restored, even Maggie couldn't argue that. Today it was draped with twinkle lights and white tulle flecked with glitter. Girly, yes. But Jenny deserved a fairytale today.

Assuming a greedy ogre didn't mess up the whole thing.

Put on your suit of optimism today, Abby Ruth.

She would not let a single thing ruin this day.

Inside the gazebo, a handsome young man was setting up the cake. When they'd said a six-layer cake she'd thought it sounded like it would be too large for the small wedding, but it was what Hannah and Brandon had ordered. No one had mentioned that the bottom layer was a good twenty-four-inches wide—from here it looked more like a kitten condo than a cake. They'd be eating cake for a year.

Good thing she was a fan of the stuff.

She spotted Teague—handsome in his tux—standing near the crazy fountain at the front of the property. Probably wishing he was already on his honeymoon, if she knew him.

The fountain was made from ornate mosaic designs, twelve in all, and had the reputation for granting wishes. One of Lil's ancestors had taken the once understated and lovely architecture and decorated it with ornate mosaics that told stories. Some of them rather risqué.

"Well, Tadpole, this is it," Abby Ruth said as she strolled up to him.

He turned, hands shoved in his pockets, wearing a lopsided grin. "Been waiting for it long enough."

"That you have. You look like a groom model in the glossy bride's magazines." She gave a long, low wolf whistle.

"Okay, that's a little weird," Teague said.

"Oh come on, sugar. I'm so happy you and Jenny are

finally together. This is a special day." She reached up and tugged on his bow tie. "You clean up nice, too. I'm proud to have you as my son-in-law."

"I was just thinking about when you first moved here."

"Feels like a million years ago now, doesn't it?"

"It does." He pointed toward the fountain. "I can't tell you how many coins I've tossed into that fountain wishing for Jenny and me to finally be together forever."

"Never hurts to hedge your bets." Abby Ruth wondered if she should toss a coin or two in that fountain and wish for love too. Butterflies tickled inside her at the thought of a second-chance romance with Red. "But your dreams are coming true today, and nothing's gonna ruin that."

Teague glanced at his watch. "I have to go check on some of our guests and make sure everything is covered with my deputies."

"It's time for me to get dressed too." She reached up and gave Teague a hug. "I'm so glad we'll officially be family now."

Once inside the house, Abby Ruth dressed and admired herself in the full-length mirror in the Sweet Vidalia Room. Jessie Wyatt's dress couldn't have fit better if it had been made for her. Funny, since Jessie was a good six inches shorter than Abby Ruth, but the skirt hit at tea length, which showed off her favorite boots, and that was okay by her. Besides, that meant she could tuck her Glock in her boot and no one would be the wiser.

Cars had been filing into Summer Haven's grounds for the past twenty minutes. A special day. And what made it even more special would be Red and her, side-by-side, giving away the bride. The thought overwhelmed her, making her hands unsteady. There'd been a time when she'd dreamed of a day like this for herself. But she'd come to terms with Red being out of her life forever. *Never say never* echoed in her mind.

All the craziness that had cast a dark cloud over them lately had seemed to lift. She went downstairs and knocked on Lil's bedroom door before entering.

When she poked her head inside, Jenny smiled. "Hi, Mom."

Sera tucked a bobby pin into Jenny's up-do, which left her neck bare. "Isn't her hair perfect?"

A wave of emotion rolled over Abby Ruth as she took in the sight of her only daughter in the wedding gown she'd picked out for her. She held her hands to her nose, which tickled at the threat of tears. "You look beautiful."

Jenny stood and walked over, her flowing skirt swishing with every step and the beads on her dress sparkling and flashing.

A piece of lint on Jenny's gorgeous dress caught Abby Ruth's attention, and she reached out to flick it off. But the darn thing was stubborn and clung to the lace. She used her short nails to pick it out and realized another half dozen pieces of "lint" were clinging to Jenny's bodice.

"What is it?" Jenny asked.

Abby Ruth peered closer. "Where has this dress been?"

"Right here in Lil's room. Sera pulled it out of the bag twenty minutes ago."

Abby Ruth turned in a circle, checking each corner of the room. Why in the world would Jenny's dress have Ritter's fur embroidered into it?

"Where is he?"

"Who?" Sera asked.

"Hollis Dooley's dog."

"Don't you mean your dog?" Jenny asked dryly.

"I have a sneaking suspicion that ol' hound dog's been unfaithful." Then she spotted it, a corner of something that looked like a red pillow sticking out from under the dust ruffle around Lil's bed. She stalked over and yanked it out. Sure enough, it was a velvet dog bed big enough for a mastodon. And wouldn't you know it, tiny pieces of lint matching the ones on Jenny's dress were scattered all over it. "Sera, did you know Lil was letting that dog sleep in here?"

Both Jenny's and Sera's eyes widened. "I…uh…well…"

A tap came at the bedroom door. "It's time," Maggie said from the doorway.

Sera picked up the bridal bouquet, a cascade of long-stemmed white roses bundled with satin ribbons that Winnie had made for Jenny. It was gorgeous, Abby Ruth had to admit. And should be for the moolah she'd shelled out for it.

Jenny took the flowers from Sera with a smile, then her brows drew together. "Is that a polar bear in my bouquet?"

Maggie ran to her side, tweaking the flowers to camouflage the stuffed animal nanny cam. Easy to hide in a pile of toys, a little harder in a bouquet. "It's an old Irish good luck symbol. Just keep it tucked inside."

Jenny shrugged. "Okay."

"Umm, and you might not want to toss that bouquet. I have a smaller one for you to throw when the time comes."

"You really have thought of everything."

Jenny was none the wiser to all that was going on right under her and Teague's noses.

Abby Ruth handed Jenny a long, thin blue box. "Sugar, I know your dress is new, and the something borrowed and blue can be my dress, but I wanted you to have this for the old."

"The borrowed and blue is for me, not you, but don't worry, I have that covered." She did a booty shake that probably meant she'd bought some undies that would later make Teague's eyeballs pop out. "What's in the box, Mom?"

"Open it." Abby Ruth bit her bottom lip.

Jenny opened the small velvety box. She lifted the shimmery bracelet out of the box. "It's beautiful."

"It was your great-grandmother's. My mom's mom. She left it to me, and I want you to have it now."

She draped the delicate row of pearls nestled into the center of filigree flowers across her wrist. "Are you sure?"

"Positive." Abby Ruth took the bracelet and unhooked the latch. "Let me help you." She fastened the bracelet around Jenny's wrist.

"It's so pretty."

"Your great-grandfather gave this to her on their wedding day. She always said it was what brought them so many good years together. They'd been married sixty-three years when she passed away."

"Thank you."

Maggie placed a hand on each of their shoulders. "It's time to get things rolling, girls."

"Are you ready?" Abby Ruth took Jenny's hand.

"So ready."

They walked out into the hallway, and Maggie leaned forward, peering past them into Lil's bedroom. "Where's Grayson?"

"I thought he was with you," Jenny said. "Grayson?" She hurried down the hall, looking in the empty rooms.

Maggie ran up the stairs, with Abby Ruth and Jenny right behind her.

"Grayson, where are you?" Jenny called.

Abby Ruth turned to Maggie to keep Jenny from hearing. "Where is Honey?" So help her, if that girl had anything to do with Grayson being out of pocket, she would pay.

"She called earlier saying she'd blown a tire on the way down from Atlanta and wouldn't arrive until right before the ceremony."

Relief whooshed through Abby Ruth. "Y'all wait here, and I'll go look for him."

Jenny nodded.

"I'll check the whole house," Maggie said.

Abby Ruth strode across the front porch and into the yard.

Daisies in jewel tones had transformed Summer Haven's lawn into a fun yet elegant wedding venue. The flowers Hannah Huckleberry had ordered made everything look so bright and cheerful, but Abby Ruth was a long way from cheerful with her grandson currently MIA.

The processional music began. Everyone turned expecting the ceremony to start, but rather than the ring bearer coming down the aisle, Abby Ruth stalked between the rows of folding chairs to the gazebo stairs.

She gave a polite wave and homed in on Teague, who was talking to Red.

As she approached, she watched Teague's expression go from happy to worried. She was certain he thought Jenny had called things off. Again. "Don't worry, Tadpole. It's not what you think."

"Then what?"

"Come with me." She hooked a finger and headed back toward the house, stopping only to ask the justice of the peace to make an announcement that they needed ten minutes.

"What's going on?" Teague asked when they were out of earshot of their guests.

"Grayson got off to somewhere. We just need a minute or two to track him down."

He tucked his fingers into his collar and pulled it away from his neck. "I told him to stay put."

"He's ten. Give him a break." Hell, she was over fifty years older than he, and she could barely sit still all morning.

The guests were beginning to talk amongst themselves, and the volume of chatter was on the rise. "I'll find him," Abby Ruth assured them.

"And I'll help," Red said.

"People are getting antsy," Teague said. "And my nerves are pulled tight too."

"Don't worry. We're on it," she said.

"That's what worries me the most." Teague followed her through the yard to the house. When they walked inside, Jenny was descending the stairs.

"Jenny?" Teague spun around, putting his back to her. "I don't think I'm supposed to see you in your dress."

"Seeing my dress won't jinx this wedding after everything we've been through, but we do need to find Grayson," she said. "He's not up here. We can't get married without him."

Teague met her at the bottom of the stairs and placed his hands on either side of her arms. "You're right. Nothing can jinx us. And I don't want to wait any longer to marry you because I love you."

"I know." Jenny kissed his cheek. "I feel the same way."

"Then let's get this show on the road. I bet Grayson's sneaking some playtime in the garage. Why don't you check there? I'll go back and explain to the guests."

Abby Ruth said, "I'll head out to the creek and look for him there."

Everyone chimed in with a location where they would look, then scattered.

Abby Ruth heard Teague make his announcement out front. "Stay in your seats," he said. "We have a missing ring bearer. Nothing to worry about. Thank you for your patience."

A loud gasp made Abby Ruth turn toward the gazebo. Wet up to his forearms with a nose full of mud, Bowzer bounded up to Teague. The pup then proceeded to shake, sending Georgia clay slinging in a ten-foot radius.

Women and men dressed to the nines jumped up from their chairs.

Abby Ruth ran in Teague's direction.

"What the…" Teague brushed at his suit. "I told Grayson to not let Bowzer out of his sight. I knew having a dog in the wedding was a bad idea." As he went to grab the dog's collar, he paused, hand out. Bowzer's collar was missing. "Great. He's lost the rings too?"

If the rings were gone, this situation was more serious than Grayson becoming impatient with all the wedding day hoopla. Abby Ruth bellowed, "Lil, get the girls over here!"

Lil and Maggie hurried to her side, and she glared at them. "Jenny's rings are missing, which means your plan went kaput. I thought y'all said you had this under control. Where's Honey?"

"Who the heck is Honey?" Teague asked.

"She still wasn't here last time I checked," Lil said.

"If she took the rings…" Maggie covered her mouth.

Lil grabbed Maggie's arm. "Oh, no. Do you think she did something to Grayson?"

"I better go check with Bruce to see if he caught anything on one of the cameras." Maggie swung around, already chattering to her beau through their Secret Service earpieces and mics as she hurried out of the room.

Abby Ruth felt a hand on her shoulder. Teague's head was cocked to one side, and he wasn't smiling. "I'm not going to like this, am I?"

Lil gulped. "Don't jump to conclusions. This is probably totally unrelated. A coincidence. Grayson has to be here somewhere."

A loud howl came from the distance, and chairs toppled as people stood to see what was going on. Three barks and a loud bay echoed across Summer Haven's grounds as Ritter ran like a retired greyhound between the rows of chairs, headed straight for Bowzer.

Bowzer crouched, tail wagging then turned and raced up the gazebo's steps with Ritter on his heels. The dogs sideswiped the justice of the peace, who was a man of equal height and width. He tottered, trying to keep his balance, but gravity prevailed.

CHAPTER 25

Teague caught the man before he hit the ground, but as if in slow motion, the dogs careened into the cake table.

"No!" Teague hollered at the dogs.

Bowzer ran underneath, catching the black tablecloth. But the cake barely moved as he came out on the other side and crashed right through the gazebo's latticework.

"That wouldn't have happened if I had fixed the gazebo," Maggie said, her voice full of self-righteous indignation.

An audible sigh of relief came from the guests, but Abby Ruth watched as the scene continued to play out like a bad reality show. Big clumsy Ritter wasn't quite as lucky as Bowzer. He hit the table, and the fancy cake swayed.

When Ritter emerged, the cake followed his momentum and toppled in a slide of buttercream and decorations. On his back, the white frosting and purple flowers lay like some type of sugary saddle. He lumbered through the hole Bowzer had created, knocking aside more latticework.

With all the hullabaloo, Ritter sideswiped the cage holding the white doves Grayson had so desperately wanted.

The door came loose, and the birds went airborne. Bowzer did a quick U-turn and barked at the birds, sending them into a bigger panic. They dive-bombed Ritter, sending feathers and frosting spiraling into the air.

When Grayson's pup realized Ritter was wearing the cake, he homed in on his friend and went to town licking the sweet confection from his fur and covering himself in the process.

Sera hurried over and grabbed Bowzer by the scruff, urging him back to the house.

Abby Ruth could only imagine the words that went with Jenny's expression as she stepped out onto the porch to see Sera and that dog covered with frosting.

After all those professional repairs, the gazebo railing had given way so easily. Maggie was right. If she'd made the repairs, that never would've happened.

Red raced to Abby Ruth's side. "What can I do?"

"Get Ritter. Quick!"

Red grabbed the dog, but he continued to bay like a hound on a deer's trail. Ritter tugged so hard that he was dragging Red through the yard. "If you ask me, Ritter is trying to tell us something. It's like a Lassie moment." Red pulled his handkerchief from his pocket and shoved it under the dog's nose. He'd given a matching one to Grayson this morning. "Find Grayson," he said to Ritter.

Ritter pushed his nose into the handkerchief. Then that bloodhound took off through the yard. Red finally lost his grip on the dog's collar and trotted along behind him.

Abby Ruth spotted Honey crossing the yard. Oh, that woman. She definitely had something to do with all this craziness. "Teague. Hurry! Go ask that woman about Grayson!"

Abby Ruth ran to catch up with Red, who was still following Ritter. "Stupid dog is heading to the garage where I keep his food. This isn't a Lassie moment. He's just hungry. Come on, we'll lock him up in there, then find Grayson."

Red grabbed Ritter's collar again. "Good plan."

But as they trotted closer to the garage, a pounding sound came from inside.

"Is that corn hole board holding the door closed?"

"It looks like it." Abby Ruth's breath caught. Something was most definitely wrong. Red must've read the look on her face because he broke out into a full-scale run.

Abby Ruth sprinted after him. The closer she got, she realized she was hearing Grayson's voice amid the pounding coming from inside the garage.

Red yanked the corn hole board out from under the door handle and sent it sailing off into the yard.

Abby Ruth swung the door open. "Grayson?"

Sweaty and red-faced, her grandson rushed through the door and into her arms. "Those guys took mom's wedding rings, then locked me in here!"

"Are you okay?" She hugged him tight. If anything had happened to him, she never could've forgiven herself. "Guys? What about a pretty blond-haired lady? Did she lock you in here?"

"No, two men. I'm sorry, Mimi." He pulled out of her hug, a scowl on his little face and his hands in fists. "I only left Bowzer for a minute, and when I came back, those men were stealing the wedding rings off his collar. Teague's gonna be so mad. I promised I'd be careful, and he trusted me. "

"It's okay, buddy." Two men? Abby Ruth's heart pounded. She and the gals had missed a clue somewhere along the line. "What did they look like?"

"I jumped on the guy in the blue shirt, but they picked me up and locked me in here."

"Oh, Grayson." Abby Ruth struggled to keep her composure. When she got her hands on those men, they would be sorry they ever messed with her family. "What did they look like? What was the other guy wearing?"

"They were tall." Poor kid hung his head, but she saw the tears welling up in his eyes. "I'm going to be in so much trouble. Teague made me promise not to lose those rings."

Sera jogged toward them. "You found him! Thank goodness. Jenny's about to hyperventilate."

"He's okay." Abby Ruth rubbed Grayson's shoulder. "It's okay, sport. Just tell me what the other guy was wearing."

"He had on a suit."

"Look!" Red pointed toward the carriage house. Two men matching Grayson's description, one in a blue shirt and the other in a suit, were hustling around the small white structure.

"Running like that? They look guilty to me," Abby Ruth said. She took off in that direction, with Sera right behind her. "You two wait here," Abby Ruth called over her shoulder to Red and Grayson.

Sera broke into a sprint, but her dress was skimming the ground. She untied her frosting covered wrap-around skirt and let go of it, sending her dress sailing like a parachute behind her. "Stop!" she yelled as she kicked out of her high heels.

The two men turned and caught sight of the women pursuing them. They cut left and took off running toward the creek.

Sera was gaining on those baddies, with Abby Ruth on her six, until they drew closer to the trees where prickly sweet gum balls littered the ground. Then Sera slowed, hopping through the sharp obstacles in her bare feet and nothing but a pink thong.

Darn it all, the kidnappers were now splashing through the creek, trying to get to the other side. Still wearing her dress and boots, Abby Ruth zoomed past Sera.

"Don't you mess up that dress. It's irreplaceable!"

Abby Ruth couldn't give two hoots about a dress, but she did care about Sera. She unzipped as she ran, pausing long enough to step out of the fancy gown and hang it from a crepe myrtle branch. She took off again, chasing those guys in her bra and panties. She felt like a Dallas Cowboy cheerleader running around in half nothing and tall boots.

She pulled the Glock from her boot before plunging into the waist-deep water. "Stop or I'll shoot."

She fired a shot in the men's direction, a foot over their heads. "I know you hear me. Don't make me shoot you in the ass to make you stop." But the two men kept wade-running and bolted out of the creek, water streaming off them.

A woman's raised voice suddenly cut across the rolling landscape. "John Erik! Kenny Ray! What are you doing?"

Wait a minute, those names sure sound familiar.

Wide-eyed, the men stopped and turned.

Abby Ruth tromped out of the water and pointed her gun at the two men. "Where are my daughter's wedding rings?"

But they weren't looking at her. They were staring back across the creek. She angled her body where she could keep an eye on these two numbskulls and get a gander at what had them so spooked.

Across the water, Maggie and Lil had their arms full of Sera's and Abby Ruth's clothes, but that wasn't what had captured the men's attention. They were looking at the woman standing, hands on her hips, beside Teague.

Honey.

Teague started pulling off his boots as if to wade into the water with Abby Ruth.

"I've got this," she said. "No sense in us all getting wet." But she knew he wouldn't listen.

She waved her gun at the two men again to motion them back across the water, then heard something behind her.

"What is that ruckus? Get up out of that brush or I'll start shooting."

A man with red hair and beady eyes rose from the bushes and raised his hands over his heads. Ah, so this must be possum boy. She waved him over to his co-conspirators and said, "March."

Which was when she recognized the one in the suit as the young guy who'd avoided her and Lil at the cake and gift shop place. "John Erik? Don't you make enough at that fancy place you work?"

"It was all for a good cause, I promise," he mumbled.

She prodded the three men through the water, and they met Teague halfway. He said, "You will explain all this."

Of that, she had no doubt.

When she, Teague, and the idiots stepped on high ground, she frisked them before Teague could get to them. She was so hopping mad that she barely registered they were nicely built men. Nicely built, but rotten to the core. She patted across something hard in John Erik's jacket. With a slap to his chest, she demanded, "What's this?"

She yanked open his jacket, not giving a fig that the buttons popped this way and that. Inside the interior pocket, she discovered not Jenny's rings, but Lil's. She tucked them inside her boot then snapped her fingers in front of the next guy's nose. "Which one of you has my daughter's wedding ring? Give it up. Right now."

Once Kenny Ray, who she now recognized as the florist delivery driver, reluctantly handed over Jenny's rings, Abby Ruth turned to the guests standing six deep in a half circle at the shore's edge. "No charge for the entertainment. Y'all get on back to your chairs because we have a couple that finally needs to get married."

CHAPTER 26

Abby Ruth was not only madder than a wet cat, she also was wetter than one after forging the creek.

Thank goodness she'd insisted on wearing that weird bra Sera had said was necessary under Jessie Wyatt's dress. Seemed like a jog bra to her, but then dresses and fancy undergarments had never been high on her list.

Bad enough that she was standing here beside Teague facing down these snake-bellied sneaks in her underwear and boots, but if she'd been forced to pursue them with her boobs bouncing wild and free, she was afraid her future son-in-law wouldn't have had a chance to haul their butts off to jail.

She'd have been the one carted away because she would've murdered them.

"Face down." She prodded one man in the back with her gun, forcing him to the ground. The others had at least a little sense because they followed his lead. She yanked at Possum Boy's collar, and sure enough, he had a tattoo on his neck. It only took a shove at Kenny Ray's sleeve for her to confirm the smudge of dirt she'd seen beneath his watch was, in fact, a tattoo with the same swirly design. She had no doubt John Erik had one to match on his biceps.

Teague and one of his deputies stepped in and took control of the three suspects.

The sound of splashing water came from the creek, and Abby Ruth turned to see Honey stomping her way through the water's edge in front of the crowd.

"Kenny Ray? John Erik? What in tarnation do you think you're doing?" She waved toward where Lil and Maggie were waiting. "These women grabbed me and accused me of being a thief or leading some kind of theft ring. Next thing I know everyone is barreling their way down here, and the three of you are making tracks into the woods."

A woman's drawl carried out over the crowd that had yet to disperse from the shoreline. "Hi there, Tuck."

Abby Ruth spun around and caught a look at the body attached to that voice. Virginia. And all her wedding crasher friends. They were beautifully dressed, and Stella held a familiar gift box. But was Virginia seriously flirting with the bad guy? The same one who had taken her jewelry?

Honey marched right up to the guys Teague and his deputies now had in cuffs.

"Who are you, ma'am?" Teague asked.

"Honey. Honey Tucker."

"I'm going to have to ask you to back up, Miss Tucker."

"I'm sorry, Honey. You gotta understand," one of the numbskulls said. "We just wanted you to have a nice wedding because you deserve it. It ain't cheap. Bubbles, balloons, birdseed, buffets." He shook his head, still mumbling a list.

Honey stilled. "What're you saying? I thought the whole reason y'all were taking on extra jobs with the wedding vendors was to put money aside to help with the wedding, and for the discounts. We had a plan. This was not it."

"That's how it started, but..."

"I cannot believe this." Honey's eyes filled with tears. "Y'all know better."

"If you're not responsible for all this," Abby Ruth asked, still not convinced Honey wasn't somehow in on the game and just trying to save her own pretty skin, "then who are these guys?"

"My idiotic brothers." The tears in the young woman's eyes when she turned toward Abby Ruth were real. Abby Ruth knew enough about pulling someone's leg to be able to tell the difference between crocodile tears and these.

Wait a minute... Honey Tucker and Virginia's Tuck. Now things were coming together. And Honey wasn't in on it after all. That kinda put a different light on the whole thing, but unfortunately, the legal system didn't really care why the law was broken. Good intentions didn't right wrongs.

"How much?" Honey demanded, pointing at one of the guys. "How much did you steal from people?"

"You're not defending them?"

"No, because we used to run some of these same scams when we were teenagers. Momma and Daddy weren't always around, which meant the fridge and cabinets were bare a lot of the time."

One of the brothers spoke up, "They passed on when John Erik was eighteen, and we had to do something so we could all stay together."

"So you stole," Teague said.

"Nothing folks couldn't stand to lose," one of the guys defended.

"We all worked too, when we could after school. But it's expensive feeding teenage boys," Honey told Teague.

"Y'all can tell all that to the judge at the bail hearings." Teague motioned to his deputies to pull the men to their feet. "Hate to ask this of you since it was your day off, but if you could escort these gentlemen in for booking, I'd appreciate it. I have a very special lady who I'd like to make my bride today."

As everyone paraded back to Summer Haven's gazebo, all Lil could think was that this wedding had certainly turned into the mess that Abby Ruth had been so worried about. She deserved an apology.

Lil walked over to where Red and Sera were busy trying to help Abby Ruth shimmy back into that gorgeous dress. "I need to apologize to you."

"For what?" Abby Ruth's voice was muffled because she was half in and half out of the dress.

"We all pushed you to let us corner the thieves at this wedding. That was downright selfish. Today should've been a time for family and friends and celebration, but we made it about justice."

Sera tugged on the dress's hem, and Abby Ruth's head popped out the top, her hair like a citron-crested cockatiel that had made a hard flight south for the winter. Her grin was as fierce a one as Lil had ever seen. "Come here," she said to Lil.

Oh, dear. She knew the woman had a gun on her, but still Lil stepped closer.

Abby Ruth leaned down and nudged Lil's arm. "Here. I thought you might not want this to be taken as evidence."

And into Lil's palm dropped two pieces of cool metal. Her rings. "How did you—"

"Those good ol' boys aren't the only ones with pickpocket skills." With a hip shake and hair fluff, Abby Ruth said, "Now, I think it's time for this wedding to finally take place."

"That's if we can get the justice of the peace back on his feet," Maggie said.

"Who knew Ritter had it in him?" Abby Ruth marveled. "Never saw that old dog move that fast before. He really did send the JOP on an extreme flight, didn't he?"

Red took Abby Ruth's hand as they all headed up the hill toward the lawn. "You know what this means, don't you?" He looked right at Lil. "Ritter is a hero."

"He's right, Lil." Abby Ruth gave an apologetic shrug. "We really can't make a hero sleep outside. That wouldn't be right."

Lordy goodness. At least now she'd have an excuse to bring him into the house without admitting to her friends that she'd fallen in love with the dog. But something told her Abby Ruth might be on to her and Ritter.

"Fine, but if he can't get that flatulence problem under control, I'll expect you to administer Bean-o." It wouldn't do for Lil to give in too easily or Abby Ruth would suspect something for sure.

"Maybe Ritter could spend more time at my house," Red said to Abby Ruth. "I wouldn't mind you spending more time with me too. You know I plan to be in Summer Shoals for the long haul. Or as long as you're here, right?"

The smile on Abby Ruth's face made Lil's heart soften toward the tough-as-nails woman.

"I feel like we're getting a second chance, Red," Abby Ruth said softly. "Maybe not another first down with our own daughter, but as grandparents to Jenny's children."

"I like the sound of that," Red said. "I love you, Ru."

"I...ditto."

Lil had never heard Abby Ruth sound so vulnerable or look so happy, but she took a breath and pulled her shoulders back. "Enough of this mushy stuff. We have a wedding to finish today." With a wide swing of her arm, she motioned everyone back toward the gazebo.

When they made it back to the lawn, Red and Abby Ruth

split off to join Jenny. Lil, Maggie, and Sera continued on toward the gazebo, where most of the guests had taken their seats although the chatter was still loud. The justice of the peace was steady enough on his feet to announce, "If everyone will please take your seats, we can resume these nuptials."

They turned to head back to their seats, but Teague stopped them when he said, "Ladies, I sure would love it if y'all would stand up for me."

It wasn't traditional for a trio of over-fifty women to act as groomsmen, but then again there wasn't much traditional going on around Summer Haven these days. It was hard to stand on ceremony when life was so much more fun when it was full of surprises.

The prelude music began. The sound of the organ and violins filled the air, and the crowd watched Grayson walk down the aisle, Bowzer on his left and Ritter plodding along on his right, all three of them streaked with Georgia red clay and frosting. When Grayson and the dogs joined Teague, they turned toward the guests, grins on all their faces.

The "Wedding March" gave Lil that warm feeling in her chest as it always did, and the crowd came to its feet. If she'd thought Grayson's smile was huge, it had nothing on Jenny's expression.

Or those of her mom and dad walking on either side of her. They stopped at the end of the aisle, and the sheer love Jenny and Teague were beaming at one another would've lit up Summer Shoals for the next ten years. Lil's gaze shifted to Abby Ruth, only to catch her and Red looking at each other the same way.

Maybe this wasn't the last wedding Summer Haven would host. That filled Lil's heart with such joy, she was all but bursting with it.

The justice of the peace asked, "Who gives this bride?"

Abby Ruth said, "Her mother—"

"And father," Red said, in sync, with an obvious squeeze to Abby Ruth's hand.

Jenny stepped out from between them and toward Teague. Toward the rest of her life.

He gave her a quick grin and said, "You have to admit this is perfect. I'm barefoot and you're pregnant."

Thanks bunches for reading *Wedding Mints and Witnesses*!
What's next?

Discover how Teague and Jenny's reunion story starts in
CHRISTMAS COOKIES AND A CONFESSION.

Sheriff Teague Castro made a mistake ten years ago that cost him the love of his life. But Jenny Northcutt has always been the woman for him, and he's ready to do whatever it takes to get a second chance at love.

Jenny is a divorced mother, and she has zero time or energy for romance. But her own mother's recent move to Teague's small town is forcing Jenny to come face-to-face with him, the man who destroyed her belief in happily ever after. Now, Jenny can't deny the spark is still alive, but this time more than her heart is at risk.

Teague cooks up a plan to woo Jenny, but a local theft could ruin both the Christmas holiday and his odds of winning her over. Now, with a mysterious crime to solve, Teague must once again keep a secret from Jenny.

Will their painful past repeat itself, or will they get the gift of a second chance at love?

Read the first chapter of CHRISTMAS COOKIES AND A CONFESSION at the end of this book.

RECIPES

WEDDING MINTS

Easy, creamy and sweet mints that are ready (and oh so easy!) to eat right after you make them. But if you can control yourself and don't plan to sample them right away, refrigerate or freeze them. You can flavor these with peppermint, spearmint, vanilla, almond, or pretty much anything your little heart desires. Need them to be extra pretty? A little food coloring will do the trick. For special occasions, like a wedding or an investigation, purchase rubber molds and press the mints into shape.

INGREDIENTS

- 1 - 8-ounce package cream cheese, softened at room temperature
- 1 - 2-pound bag of confectioner's sugar
- Food flavoring or extract of your choice

- Food coloring if desired
- Granulated sugar, for coating mints

DIRECTIONS

1. Place cream cheese in a large mixing bowl. Using an electric mixer, start adding powdered sugar until you reach the consistency of play dough. IMPORTANT INFO: You will NOT use the whole bag. If the dough is sticky at all, keep adding powdered sugar.
2. Place equal portions of the dough into separate bowls for each color and/or flavor you want to make.
3. Add a drop or two of flavoring and mix to incorporate. Taste and add more flavoring until you get the taste you're looking for.
4. Add desired food coloring and mix well.
5. To make mints, take a marble-sized portion of dough, roll it in granulated sugar, and press into a mint mold. Remove mint by inverting the mint mold. The mint should pop right out. Repeat with remaining dough.
6. Store in the fridge until ready to serve. Or make ahead and freeze.

LILLIAN'S SAND TARTS

Bake a batch of these beauties up, and you might just be tempted to hide them away for yourself. Try to be like Lil and share with your closest friends!

INGREDIENTS

- 1 cup softened butter
- 1 cup confectioner's sugar
- 1 teaspoon vanilla or almond extract
- 1 3/4 cups all-purpose flour (and a little for your hands)
- 1 cup finely chopped pecans

DIRECTIONS

1. Preheat oven to 270° F.
2. At low speed with your electric mixer, cream the butter and ½ cup of confectioner's sugar until smooth. Then beat in the extract.
3. At low speed, gradually add the flour, scraping sides as you go until well combined, but don't over mix.
4. With a spatula, mix in the finely chopped pecans into the bowl.
5. Flour up your hands to make shaping the sticky mixture easier.
6. Take out about 1 tablespoon of dough and shape it into a crescent.
7. Place the cookies 1-inch apart on the prepared cookie sheets. (Super-duper baking tip: Line your cookie sheets with parchment paper to keep cookies from sticking an over browning. Parchment paper is honestly a gift from heaven!)
8. Re-flour hands as needed.
9. Bake for 40 minutes.

10. Dust generously with additional confectioner's sugar while still warm.
11. Move to wire rack to cool completely. Store in airtight containers and sprinkle a little more confectioner's sugar over them.

MAGGIE'S SPECIAL ICED TEA

When Maggie and the gals have a hard day (or a celebration), they turn to Maggie's special iced tea recipe. It's sweet taste with a kick tends to soothe any troubles or make a good day just that much better. Oh, and if you're tempted to leave the "special" outta this tea, then please note that it'll still taste pretty darn good, but it won't be Maggie's tea!

Maggie recommends a glass jug for this recipe, but heck, use what'cha got, people!

INGREDIENTS

- 3 family-sized tea bags (or 10 regular-sized tea bags)
- Water
- 1½ cups sugar
- A bit of "special" - either bourbon or Irish whiskey. Maggie's been known to enjoy some Crown Royal, but Abby Ruth is solidly in the Jameson camp.

DIRECTIONS

1. Place the tea bags into a gallon-size glass jug (or whatever you have on hand).

2. Boil up your water (a tad less than a gallon because you'll be adding in some sugar and some "special").
3. Once the water has come to a full rolling boil, gently pour it over the tea bags in your jug.
4. Let the whole shebang steep for about 3-5 minutes, depending on how strong you like your tea. Maggie prefers it strong, so she goes the whole 5 minutes.
5. Stir it up a bit and then remove the tea bags. Use a slotted spoon, or a wooden spoon if you want to wrap the tea bag strings around it and squeeze all the liquid out.
6. Toss in about a cup and a half of sugar and stir until dissolved.
7. Chill the tea in the fridge for as long as you can stand it. Once the tea is cool, add the "special" one jigger at a time until you're satisfied with the taste and strength.
8. Pour that deliciousness over a tall glass of ice, take it to the front porch, and sip your worries away!

AUTHORS' NOTE

Dear Reader,

As any good fiction authors do, we've taken a few liberties here and there within this story. If you're a baseball aficionado, you probably already know that the Houston Astros did not win the 1984 World Series. In fact, they didn't even play in the series! That year, the Detroit Tigers faced off against the San Diego Padres, with Detroit winning the series. As of this writing, the Astros (bless their little hearts) have only played in a single World Series. In 2005, they went up against the Chicago White Sox, getting walloped when the Sox swept the series (meaning Chicago won four and Houston a big ol' none). Red also came by his nickname from hitting home runs. However, major league pitchers aren't normally on the batting roster. What can we say? Red is a superstar. And we wanted him to have an illustrious career as a pro player, so we gave the Astros and him a little fictional boost, knowing our readers wouldn't mind.

Big hugs and home runs,
Kelsey & Nancy

BOOKS IN THE SERIES

IN FOR A PENNY

COLLARD GREENS AND CATFISHING

DEVILED EGGS AND DECEPTION

FRIED PICKLES AND A FUNERAL

WEDDING MINTS AND WITNESSES

Jenny & Teague Novellas

CHRISTMAS COOKIES AND A CONFESSION

SWEET TEA AND SECOND CHANCES

ACKNOWLEDGMENTS

Once again, we want to thank the amazing folks who help us bring these fun mysteries to you.

HUGE thanks to our bang-up editing team: Deb Nemeth and Tom Justice. Without you, the grannies would never shine so brightly.

A special thanks to Heather Machel, who keeps Kelsey in line on a daily basis and also does some of the best research in the countryside. If she can't find the answer, it doesn't exist.

To Kelsey's Sass Kicker fan group: thank you for celebrating and supporting every book release!

And to those who help us daily behind the scenes: Miss Bettie, Andrew, Tech Guy, and Smarty Boy - we couldn't give our fans the books they love without *your* love and support. Thanks for understanding when dinner duty is on you because we're in Grannyland!

AND TO ALL OF YOU READING THIS ~ THANK YOU!

ABOUT KELSEY BROWNING

USA Today bestselling author **Kelsey Browning** writes contemporary romance, romantic suspense, and cozy mystery. Her Georgia-set, co-authored Seasoned Southern Sleuths mystery series is described by readers as "The Golden Girls meet Dirty Harry." Her single title romances garner reviews that call her writing funny, sassy, and full of sizzling chemistry. Originally from a Texas town smaller than the ones she writes about, Kelsey has also lived in the Middle East and Los Angeles, proving she's either adventurous or downright nuts. These days, she makes her home in northeast Georgia with her tech-savvy husband, her smart-talking son, and a (fingers crossed) future therapy pup. Find Kelsey online at KelseyBrowning.com.

For info on her upcoming releases, subscribe to her Sass Kickin' News.

facebook.com/kelseybrowning
instagram.com/kelseybrowningauthor
amazon.com/author/kelseybrowning
bookbub.com/authors/kelsey-browning
goodreads.com/kelseybrowning

ABOUT NANCY NAIGLE

USA Today bestselling author **Nancy Naigle** whips up small-town love stories with a dash of suspense and a whole lot of heart. She began her popular contemporary romance series, Adams Grove, while juggling a successful career in finance and life on a seventy-six-acre farm. Two of Nancy's novels, Christmas Joy and Hope at Christmas, premiered on Hallmark Countdown to Christmas in 2018. Now happily retired, she devotes her time to writing, antiquing, and the occasional spa day with friends. A native of Virginia Beach, she currently calls North Carolina home. Join Nancy on Facebook and sign up for her newsletter at www.NancyNaigle.com.

facebook.com/NancyNaigleAuthor
instagram.com/nancynaigle
amazon.com/author/nancynaigle
bookbub.com/authors/nancy-naigle
goodreads.com/nancy_naigle

ALSO BY KELSEY BROWNING

PROPHECY OF LOVE SERIES

Sexy contemporary romance

Stay With Me

Hard to Love

TEXAS NIGHTS SERIES

Sexy contemporary romance

Personal Assets

Running the Red Light

Problems in Paradise

Designed for Love

SEASONED SOUTHERN SLEUTHS
MYSTERY SERIES w/NANCY NAIGLE

Southern cozy mysteries

In For a Penny

Collard Greens and Catfishing

Deviled Eggs and Deception

Fried Pickles and a Funeral

Wedding Mints and Witnesses

JENNY & TEAGUE NOVELLAS

Contemporary romance with a dab of mystery

Christmas Cookies and a Confession

Sweet Tea and Second Chances

STEELE RIDGE SERIES

Romantic suspense collaboration with Tracey Devlyn & Adrienne Giordano

The BEGINNING

Going HARD

Living FAST

Loving DEEP

Breaking FREE

Roaming WILD

Stripping BARE

Enduring LOVE

Vowing LOVE

STEELE RIDGE: THE KINGSTONS

Romantic suspense collaboration with Tracey Devlyn & Adrienne Giordano

Craving HEAT

Tasting FIRE

Searing NEED

Striking EDGE

Burning ACHE

NOVELLAS

Sexy contemporary romance

Amazed by You

Love So Sweet

ALSO BY NANCY NAIGLE

The Adams Grove Series

Book 1:: Sweet Tea and Secrets

Book 2:: Wedding Cake and Big Mistakes

Book 3:: Out of Focus

Book 4:: Pecan Pie and Deadly Lies

Book 5:: Mint Juleps and Justice

Book 6:: Barbecue and Bad News

Boot Creek Series

Book 1:: Life After Perfect

Book 2:: Every Yesterday

Book 3:: Until Tomorrow

Single Titles

Sand Dollar Cove

Christmas Joy

Hope at Christmas

Christmas in Evergreen

Dear Santa

The Secret Ingredient

Christmas in Evergreen: Letters to Santa

Recipe For Romance

Christmas Angels

inkBLOT – co-written with Phyllis Johnson

Read on for a fun excerpt from CHRISTMAS COOKIES AND A CONFESSION, A JENNY & TEAGUE NOVELLA.

Chapter One

For half a second, Teague Castro took his eye off his target to glance at the woman in the firing lane on his right. Eye and ear protection snug against her face, Abby Ruth was intent on the outline of the zombie fifty-odd yards away. With a sound like a giant rubber band being popped, she emptied her Glock, hitting the walking dead in the heart with every shot.

If Teague could get his deputies to shoot half as well, he'd be a happy man. But Abby Ruth Cady was one of a kind. How many men could say their future mother-in-law could shoot a tick off a hound's ass without disturbing a strand of fur? Very few.

Then again, she wasn't truly his future mother-in-law. Yet. He still had to win Jenny back. Hard to do when the woman wouldn't even answer his calls.

His grip suddenly unsteady, he released the magazine on his own 9mm and removed the remaining ammo. He sure had no business handling a firearm when he was shaking like a drunk coming off a five-day bender. Thinking about Jenny did that to him.

Abby Ruth reloaded, adjusted her long-legged stance, and proceeded to give the target a hole in the chest the size of a big man's fist. With her trademark white shirt and slim jeans tucked into a pair of eye-blinding turquoise boots, she was lean and fit at sixty-one. Since she'd moved to Summer Shoals, Georgia a few months ago, the older men had sniffed around. In normal Aunt Bibi style, she'd tossed back a few beers with them at Earlene's Drinkery, but that was the extent of it.

Finally, Abby Ruth pulled out her ear plugs and shoved her protective glasses to the top of her head, making her short gray hair stand up as though she'd been shocked by a wave of electricity. "I swear to Jesus, boy. If you thought any louder over there, I'd need better ear protection." She released her clip, double-checked for any remaining bullets before wiping down her gun. "Your brain waves are so damned powerful, I'm pretty sure they sent my last shot off target."

"That'll be the day." Teague chuckled and leaned over to press the switch to bring Abby Ruth's target forward. Sure enough, one shot was about a millionth of a centimeter outside the main hole. "Yeah, I can see you were distracted."

"That little bit can be the difference between the upper hand and the lower rung. You know that as well as I do." Her eyebrows hit her hairline. "Now, why don't you buy me something to drink and tell me why you invited me out to shoot today? I have a feeling it wasn't because you wanted to remind yourself this old gal can outshoot you when she's drunk, blindfolded and down in the back."

As a former journalist, she was no one's fool, that was for damn sure. Teague slung an arm around her shoulders and led her outside to an empty picnic table. The December day was bright and cool, but they'd both worked up a sweat shooting. "Orange soda?"

"I do love a man who remembers my preferences."

His front pockets produced enough change for two drinks. The coins jingled into the chamber of the old style drink machine. The whole shooting range might be outdated with the if-it-ain't-broke-don't-replace-it mentality, but it was still functional. The cans rumbled to the opening one by one. He carried the cold drinks back to the table, popping the top of Abby Ruth's before handing it to her. They sat and sipped in companionable silence for several minutes.

His win-back-Jenny agenda was stalled, but enlisting Abby Ruth's help felt reckless right now. She was smart. She was shrewd. And she had a way of taking over a situation.

And that was something he couldn't allow. But after seeing Jenny again a few weeks ago, he knew more than ever he wanted her in his life, here in Summer Shoals. How the heck he would convince her it was a good idea was a whole other story.

Abby Ruth set down her drink with a *thunk.* "Spill it, kiddo."

"She won't return my calls."

Abby Ruth swung her legs up on the bench to face him and sighed, proving he didn't need to specify who *she* was. "I could make excuses for her behavior. She's always had a stubborn streak."

"No idea where she got that," he muttered, coaxing a laugh from Abby Ruth.

"She's not real good at admitting when she's made a mistake."

"You sure she wasn't adopted?" he teased.

She pointed a finger at him pistol-style. Good thing it was just her finger because the paper lying on the table between them proved he'd be stone cold dead otherwise. "I can admit when I'm wrong. Rarely happens is all. If you think you can win over a woman by insulting her, it's no wonder she ran off without a word."

He winced at the memory of Jenny and her son's visit to Summer Shoals. What had started out as a nice birthday party for Abby Ruth had turned into a belly-ripper for him when he blurted out his feelings for Jenny, then kissed her. He'd hoped for fireworks. The explosive kind that resulted in professions of undying love.

But the fireworks had been more like a backfire. Before he knew what was happening, Jenny had taken off to Boston.

And he damned well knew it wasn't because that kiss had been lame. He hadn't kissed Jenny in over a decade, not since he screwed up so royally and she married that over-polished bag of ties in Boston not long after. But he still remembered what she felt like, tasted like. Like a Black Cat firecracker—hot, combustible, unpredictable. And like one of those red pepper suckers sold down at the drug store—sweet, spicy, addictive.

That candy always made Teague sweat, but he couldn't resist it.

No more than he could resist Jenny.

"Look," he said. "She's divorced and I want her back. I let her go once because I was careless and stupid."

"You were a boy. Y'all all start out that way."

"Well, I'm not a boy now." He leaned forward on the old picnic table. "Have you talked to her since she went back to Boston?"

"Yeah," Abby Ruth admitted. "But you know us. We're the five minutes on-and-off types. I Skype with Grayson a couple of times a week though."

Jenny's eight-year-old son was a disconcerting combination of Jenny's dark-haired vibrating energy and her ex's slick polish. Kid could probably put himself on the ballot for Summer Shoals' mayor and win the race.

Teague tried like hell to ignore the ache in his chest insisting that Grayson should be *his* son. That he and Jenny should've figured things out long ago and made a family together. The time they'd wasted. It would make him sick, except that was just another waste of time.

"And if you're wondering if she's mentioned you since my birthday party," Abby Ruth said, "the answer is no."

Well, that was a rusty knife to the gut.

"But she's never been one to kiss and tell," Abby Ruth said. "So why haven't you hauled your sorry butt up to Boston and knocked on her door?"

"Because I've been giving her some cooling-off space and trying to figure out how the hell to make Summer Shoals—" and himself, "—more attractive to her."

"Yeah, you went off halfcocked when she was here, which isn't like you. You got a plan this time?"

"Does she still take pictures like she used to?"

"No," Abby Ruth said. "Being a single parent keeps her busy. Most of the shots she takes these days are of Grayson. But Lord knows, that girl has an eye. When Grayson was a toddler, she had him look through a paper towel roll and took his picture. Sounds kinda creepy, but those photos of his eye and part of his chubby little face are my favorites. Who else but Jenny would've thought to do that?"

"Not sure if you've heard, but Angelina Broussard is heading up a holiday art competition starting this week."

Abby Ruth's mouth turned down as if she taken a slug of three-month-old milk. "Is there anything in Summer Shoals that woman doesn't have her bony little fingers in?"

He wasn't touching that. No need to stir the pot of animosity always simmering between Abby Ruth and Angelina. It was no secret that Angelina wanted to be

Summer Shoals' queen bee, and there was nothing Abby Ruth liked better than to take a flyswatter after someone she thought was getting above her raising. "If Jenny were to enter and win, it could be good for all of us. The winner gets several thousand dollars in prize money and a yearlong stint as artist-in-residence at the high school."

"You don't say." She tapped her chin with her soda can. "So why haven't you called her to tell her about it?"

"Because, after my..."

"Colossal screwup, you're too chickenshit to risk it?"

He laughed and shook his head. This woman. She was stubborn and outrageous and painfully honest. But neither she nor her daughter would ever be boring. And as much as Teague enjoyed living in a town where the excitement consisted of a new blue plate special at the Atlanta Highway Diner, he damn sure didn't want to be bored for the rest of his life. "That about sums it up. But no risk, no reward. I'm planning to call her and break the ice by encouraging her to enter the art competition."

"You may need to do more than encourage." In an unusual show of affection, Abby Ruth grabbed Teague's hand and squeezed. "Takes a strong man to keep up with the Cady women. And that pansy-ass Daniel Northcutt sure couldn't make that cut. I don't know what knocked you and Jenny sideways years ago, but I can tell you it hurt my heart then. And not a day has passed since that I haven't wished things could've been different. But as wrong as I think Jenny's marriage to old pasty-face was, without it I wouldn't have Grayson. And you know he's a pistol and a half."

"Think she'd ever take him out of Boston?" That was the kicker.

A slow, sly smile crept across Abby Ruth's face. "Well, she hasn't said as much. But honestly, what's keeping her tied up north now? If Grayson were to have a positive male role model down here, there's nothing saying he couldn't visit his daddy a few holidays and a couple weeks in the summer instead of every other weekend."

That made the guilt roiling in Teague's gut simmer down a little. "Okay, then it's time for me to stop letting her call the shots." He wrestled his cell phone from his pocket. "Bet I can get a flight from Atlanta to Boston today. I have to talk her into this art show fast, though, because there's only one spot left and the entry deadline is tomorrow."

"Sounds like the faster Angelina gets Jenny's pictures, the better." Abby Ruth put her hand on his phone. "I have plenty of her pictures to choose from. Maybe we enter them for her. Then she can't refuse to come."

Teague liked the idea. And hated it. Secrets were the reason he and Jenny were no longer a couple. "I don't know—"

"Tell you what, I'll claim it was all my idea. The better to keep you out of Jenny's crosshairs if she pitches a hissy fit." She pushed off the bench and tossed her drink into a recycling bin. "You go sweet-talk Angelina, and I'll meet you there with some of Jenny's work."

Teague prayed like hell this didn't backfire.

A half-hour later, Abby Ruth met him in front of Angelina's cotton-candy painted house, with a big envelope under her arm. "Well, what did she say?"

"She wants to see the pictures before she'll agree to take the entry form I filled out for Jenny."

Abby Ruth snatched the paperwork out of his hand and marched up to Angelina's door. "I'll take it from here. The less this whole thing has your fingerprints on it, the better."

The fifteen minutes he stood in Angelina's yard felt like the retreat of an Ice Age. Finally, Abby Ruth sauntered outside. He watched her face for a sign she'd been successful, but there was no tell. That woman had one hell of a poker face. He waited, his gut like a daiquiri in a blender.

"We're in," Abby Ruth hiked one boot up onto his front bumper. "I knew these pictures would win her over. She was like putty in my hands."

He sincerely doubted that, but his relief was so huge that he wasn't about to call Abby Ruth on it.

She pulled out her phone and handed it to him. "She's more likely to answer the phone if she sees it's me calling. Let's see if we can't convince her to do this art show."

Made in the USA
Coppell, TX
24 August 2020

34692297R00166